Seeing the Wires

All his life, Patrick Thompson has been inspired by the rolling landscape of tarmac, low-rise concrete slabs and bread queues that is Dudley. He has written for as long as he can remember. *Seeing the Wires* is his first published novel.

Seeing the Wires

PATRICK THOMPSON

HarperCollins*Publishers*

HarperCollins*Publishers*
77-85 Fulham Palace Road,
Hammersmith, London W6 8JB

www.fireandwater.com

A Paperback Original 2002
1 3 5 7 9 8 6 4 2

A catalogue record for this book
is available from the British Library

ISBN 0 00 710520 7

Set in Sabon by Palimpsest Book Production Limited,
Polmont, Stirlingshire

Printed and bound in Great Britain by
Clays Ltd, St Ives plc

Thanks to: Annette Green, my agent; Jim Rickards, Chris Smith and Sarah Hodgson, who got landed with editing this thing and had to take it in turns; and of course thanks to Dudley, my inspiration.

For Em

Even in Dudley, ritual murder is frowned upon.

PART ONE

Sam, aged thirty

Chapter One

I

When I was a student, I used to have a job on the building sites. Nowadays, I steer clear of building sites. It was a different story then, though, because of this loan that the country had been good enough to arrange for me. I had known for some time that at some point the country or, to be more specific, the Bastard And Shitwit Building Society (I've changed the names, for legal reasons) would want their money back.

I'd spent it. I'd spent some of it on useful work-related things like books and pens and paper and all of that. I'd spent far more of it on having a nice time, and from the way the professionally unemotional creatures at the B&S Building Society behaved, I wasn't sure they'd understand about having a nice time. They certainly wouldn't understand about me paying for it with their money. I suppose it was their money, really. Technically. Then again, they'd given it to me, and anyone could have told them I was unreliable. If they'd asked Jack – my best friend, who we'll get to presently – he'd have told them flat out: do *not* lend this man any money. Jack never did. Jack knew me well. Until I went to university, we got on tremendously. After that, I didn't see much of him until I stopped being a student. He didn't like students. He preferred groups like Psychic TV, and filling himself with metal odds and ends. He'd been spending a lot of time with Eddie Finch, who worked on one of the local papers. I'll tell you about them later on.

To be honest, I didn't go to university because I had a great career planned. I went because things were uncomfortable at home. There were family troubles.

I'll tell you about those later on, too.

The building society and I exchanged letters – theirs frank and to the point, mine circumspect. They agreed that I could pay back all of the money I owed them at thirty pounds a week for the rest of my life, with the clear hint that if I didn't keep up, they'd find a far worse arrangement.

'You've had a lucky escape,' the manager, Mr Fallow, advised me.

I had, I thought. I might have been forced to work *there* until the debt was cleared. I told him how grateful I was, shook his hand, and left him straightening his tie.

I had a degree – a second in Historic Peculiarities, which we'll get to presently – and I was more or less able-bodied. How difficult would it be to get the sort of job where I wouldn't even notice the loss of thirty pounds a week?

As it turned out, very difficult indeed. The only office jobs going were for people inputting data, and they paid low wages. I was not qualified to be a team leader or supervisor. I knew this, because during the course of what felt like several hundred interviews several hundred people told me so. The building society became concerned, and started writing to me with helpful suggestions. To give me that extra bit of impetus, they charged me for each letter. When I asked why, they explained that it was to cover their administrative costs. They charged me for that letter too. I doubted this. I had seen their adverts in the job pages and they paid around three pounds a day. They were charging me fifteen pounds a letter. It surely didn't take one person five days (or five people a day each) to write a letter three lines long with my name misspelt at the top of it.

I wrote to them, including these calculations, and asked them to take into consideration the administrative costs incurred in the writing of my own letter. If they would pay thirty pounds into my account, that should cover it.

They paid the money in. Mr Fallow was nothing if not fair. Then they sent me fifteen letters explaining that they had done so, charging me fifteen pounds per letter. I could no longer afford food or rent. I explained this to my landlord, Mr Jellicoe, who said, 'Don't have food then.'

At least he didn't charge me for the advice.

I spread my job-searching net a little wider. I ruled in some areas I had ruled out. I considered more physical jobs. Eventually, I got a job on a building site on the bleak outskirts of Dudley, helping to dig the foundations of what turned out to be the ugliest factory in existence.

It was easy enough work.

I would rise at seven, get washed and dressed, and be at the bus stop by eight. Some time later, a white Bedford van would pull up, and I'd hop in. I had to use the van. I could have walked to the site – I live in Dudley, and it was less than a mile away – but collection by van was a condition of the job.

'That's what it's there for,' the foreman – Mr Link, who we'll get to presently – told me.

I would get into the back of the van and spend a short, uncomfortable journey bouncing about on a stack of shovels, picks, and hefty sacks of gravel and sand. The van was driven by Darren, a short youth with a good-sized collection of foul language and a full head of very black hair, which looked dyed. The van was co-piloted by Spin, a black man who never spoke at all. They would pull into the bus stop and I would clamber into the back and settle myself in among the implements, and as I closed the rear doors someone at the bus stop would say something disparaging.

I don't know what it's like in the rest of the world, but in Dudley the bus stops are where old people gather when they aren't gathered at the post office. They like bus stops. They don't like people jumping the queue. I wasn't in the queue, strictly speaking, but they didn't like me getting into a van at the bus stop before they had a chance to get on a bus and go to town and complain about how much everything cost and how many worrying new vegetables there were nowadays. I wouldn't have minded one or two of the less obviously incontinent ones getting in the van and having a lift but we only went to the building site and there were no queues there for them to stand in.

There were trenches. I helped to dig them. I thought that building sites used mechanical diggers for the foundations. I asked Mr Link about it.

'Well, we could,' he said. 'But you cost a lot less and the last JCB we had got stolen.'

'Stolen?'

'Joyriders. I can't see what joy there is in a JCB, myself. I'd rather have a Jag.'

He did. It was part of being a foreman, Darren explained.

The foreman had a Jag and everyone else shared a van and did all the work. That was the building trade according to Darren. It seemed simple enough.

Mr Link had – as well as the Jag – thinning black hair containing thick black grease, presumably placed there deliberately. He had sideburns several years after they were last fashionable and several years before they were next fashionable. He had watery eyes and looked uncomfortable in the hard hat he had to wear because of regulations. The main purpose of hard hats, Darren told me, was not to protect the heads of workmen. The main purpose of hard hats was to make visiting dignitaries look twats.

'Office people,' said Darren, 'never get the hang of hats.'

Spin nodded, silently.

'There you go, Spin agrees.'

Spin nodded again.

'Thing is,' said Darren, dragging on his cigarette, 'the thing is, some people are hat people and others are foremen and managers. That's what it is.'

He smoked on. Working on a building site apparently consisted of a lot of smoke breaks interrupted by short periods of digging. I was able to keep up with this and the wages were higher than I would have expected. I saw a light at the end of the overdraft. I paid Mr Jellicoe some of the rent he thought he was due and began to reimburse the building society. Things were, I thought, on an even keel.

II

One day – it was summer, and the sky was clear and blue, but because we were in Dudley the temperature was cheerlessly low – I was digging foundations when I turned up an old coin. It was nothing special – a shilling, slightly dented and much corroded – but Darren had a look.

'We find things sometimes,' he said. 'Digging. You turn things up.'

Spin nodded, silently.

'Once found a bone,' said Darren, 'off of a dog we reckon. Well, Spin thought it was a dog, anyway. He knows his bones, does Spin. Used to do archaeology at the Poly.'

'What, Spin was a student?'

Spin nodded, silently.

'We all were,' said Darren. Looking at him, I doubted it. He must have caught my expression.

'I done Social Anthropology,' he explained, 'at Cambridge. Bloody freezing and flat, Cambridge. Course, I finish the course and get ready for one of those graduate jobs, thirty grand a year and more holiday than workdays. That's when I realized Social Anthropology might not have been the course to go for. Same with Spin. There's no call for archaeologists. At least he gets to do digging, keeps his hand in. Only person on the site hasn't got a degree is Mr Link.'

'What?'

'Left school at fifteen, self-made man, blah blah. Don't get him started on it. What did you do then?'

'When?'

'When you was a student. I mean, the rest of us was students but don't look it. You *look* like a student. Only poorer.'

'I did Historic Peculiarities.'

'You did *what*?' Darren dropped his shovel. It seemed like

a strong reaction. Most people just said it was a waste of taxpayers' money.

'Historic Peculiarities.'

Darren and Spin exchanged a look.

'Is that one of those new courses?'

'It was. There were only three of us doing it. I don't think they run it any more.'

'Well,' said Darren, picking up his shovel so he'd have something to lean on. 'Well. So, what was that all about then? Historic Peculiarities?'

III

Historic Peculiarities, explained Janet Blake – senior lecturer in Historic Peculiarities – was the study of missing bits of history. We knew what had happened at time x, and time y, but did not know what had happened between them. Historic Peculiarities attempted to find the links between apparently disparate events. In practise, this involved a lot of creative writing and very little analysis.

The typical Historic Peculiarities exam question would be along the lines of: 'The Spanish Armada – The Fire of London. Connect.' There was no typical answer. The best way to answer a Historic Peculiarities question was to write as much as possible in the time allowed without ever committing yourself to a point of view.

I took the subject because I was interested in history and peculiar things, interests I shared with my best friend Jack. He didn't go to university, he got a job in a printing company on the outskirts of Oldbury. While I was spending money I didn't have on having a good time, he was spending his time earning money so he could spend it on his hobby, which was body piercing.

We'll get to that later.

I did a three-year course in Historic Peculiarities. There was the option to do a fourth and perhaps continue as far as a doctorate, but the building society weren't keen. I was still interested in history and peculiar things. The building society was still interested in regaining its money. So I gave up Historic Peculiarities and became, for several months, a digger of foundations.

IV

'Got you,' said Darren. 'It was one of those complete bollocks courses. Thought I'd picked a bad one. Bloody hell. So, how much do you owe the bank then?'

'Building society,' I said. 'A couple of hundred, now.'

'Lucky sod,' said Darren. 'I still owe them me first born, and Spin's had to sell one of his kidneys.'

They both smiled. Darren pocketed the grubby shilling that had sparked off the conversation.

'Tell you something,' said Darren. 'You know the castle?'

Of course I knew the castle. Dudley Castle is hard to miss, in Dudley. It isn't as though there's a lot else to distract your attention.

'There were some historic peculiarities up there,' said Darren, 'so Spin was saying. Witches, warlocks, comets, Templars and all sorts of stuff. You could have done a thesis on that. You might have got a first then, like Spin.'

Spin nodded, silently.

'What sort of things?' I asked. I'd lived there for twenty-five years, and it was the first I'd heard about it.

Before Darren could tell me, Mr Link turned up, a hard hat sitting uncomfortably on his head.

'Darren, Spin,' he said. He looked at me. 'I can never remember your name,' he told me.

'Sam.'

'Oh yes,' he said. 'Historic Peculiarities. And these two are Archaeology and Anthropology. Once upon a time, we used to get actual workers. Now they've all done City and Guilds and set themselves up as limited companies and all I get is students paying back their overdrafts, drinking me out of teabags and chatting about social awareness. Which is all well and good in its place, but it doesn't get trenches dug, does it?'

We shook our heads.

'Well,' he said, 'and there it is. Now. How are you at heights?'

'I'm okay with heights,' said Darren. Spin made a gesture indicating the same. It was a complicated gesture, and it went on for a little while. He raised his hands above his head and looked up at them, and nodded. He drew his hands down past his face, looked left and right, and shrugged. He held out his arms and mimed balancing, while nodding. He looked down and held out both hands, thumbs up. He clapped. Mr Link nodded at several points during the gesture, and then the ending caught him by surprise and he forgot to nod in the right place.

'I don't like heights,' I said.

'Don't like them, or won't do them?' asked Mr Link.

'I don't like them. I get dizzy and then I freeze.'

'Vertigo. Fair enough. You can stick with trenches. You don't have to go up, to do trenches. Down is preferable, I always think. But not too far down, because then it gets claustrophobic. A strange thing: all the students we hire want to do the digging. Never the walls or the scaffolding. Personally, I think it's to do with Dudley. There's old stuff all over the place. The castle, the mines, the railways. If you ask me, they should bulldoze the bloody lot of it and start again with a few decent roads and a car park and maybe a pub, but that's just me.'

'What will we be doing?' asked Darren.

'Scaffolding,' said Mr Link, in a tone of voice that suggested he'd already told them once.

Spin went into another series of hand movements.

'What?' asked Mr Link.

'He's dubious as to scaffolding,' explained Darren, acting as an interpreter.

'Dubious?'

'He believes that it acts as a receiver or transmitter of messages from elsewhere, being as it is a matrix of regular angles constructed in tubiform metal. That's when it's up, obviously. When it's not, it's just a pile of tubes in the back of the truck.'

'Tubiform matrix?' asked Mr Link. 'What, and you got all of that from him waving his hand about?'

Darren nodded.

'Hell's bells,' said Mr Link.

Darren and Spin stood patiently.

'Well?' asked Mr Link. He switched to jovial mode. 'Either of you up to working on my tubiform matrix? Only it'd be nice if you'd get on with it, because we're expecting a message from Arcturus and we need the scaffolding up before it gets dark. Besides, we might be able to make use of it when we put the top beams on this thing.'

He indicated the framework of red metal struts: six large ones to a side and a network of smaller ones connecting them. Trenches ran around the outer limit of the structure. I had helped to put them there.

'What's it going to be?' Darren asked.

'Factory,' said Mr Link.

'What sort?'

'Finished, if we get the scaffolding up. Come on.'

Mr Link led Darren and Spin to the pile of metal tubes and hefty brackets. The brackets looked like something that might have come from a medieval dungeon, and that made me think about Jack, because Jack is a body piercing aficionado and he looks like the sort of thing medieval dungeons might have used in their adverts if they'd had newspapers to place them in.

'While we're erecting Luke Skywalker's radio set, would it be okay if you carried on with the trenches? Only I seem to remember that we had this agreement where I paid you and you did work. You seem to be interpreting it slightly differently, in that I pay you and you stare vacantly into space.' He sighed. 'Students.'

'Ex-students,' I said.

'Even worse,' he said. 'Feel like digging?'

'Oh yes,' I lied.

'Good, because it would trouble my conscience greatly if I had to sack you because you were useless.'

He often gave us these pep talks. I think it was something to do with morale.

V

Other than Mr Link and the physical problems – blisters, aches, herpes – working on building sites was fun. It was like playtime. At school the only time you were allowed to mess around in mud was at lunch break, unless you were in remedial class. You weren't allowed to handle tools.

On building sites mud and tools were only the beginning. After that there were mechanical things, scaffolding, swearing, and tea.

There were pranks, too. I had to go to Supplies and get a left-handed screwdriver. Darren sent me to get a spirit level with a slower bubble. Spin asked me to get something but I didn't know what he meant. It was something that rotated, but I wasn't tuned in to his gestures and Darren was out getting some dents knocked out of the scaffolding. I was the new boy, so I was the stooge for all of the pranks. I didn't mind, as it passed the time and I wasn't often injured.

After a while I noticed that I was still the new boy.

'We're a good team,' explained Darren. 'Mr Link likes to stick with people he knows.'

Spin nodded.

'It saves training people up. You're the best we've had, so far.'

I was pleased. I hadn't been told I was the best at anything by anyone before. Except for Jack, who said I was the world's best wanker.

'Well, you're the only one, really,' said Darren. 'No one wants to do trenches these days. Most of them go into burgers until they get something in an office.'

Spin mimed frying burgers with one hand, and picked
his nose with the other. I hoped that was part of the gesture.

'I don't mind trenches,' I said. 'I like digging.'

'You're still the new boy, though. Can't be much fun. Get
all the jokes played on you. Haven't you had any offers yet?
Office jobs?'

'Not yet,' I admitted. I hadn't applied for many. I worried
about that, but not enough to do anything about it.

'We'll have to do better jokes then, won't we? Can't keep
sending you to Supplies for things that don't exist. Don't
worry, me and Spin'll think of something new while we do
the roof.'

They went up the scaffolding. All that afternoon I watched
them, wondering what they were up to. I couldn't hear
anything Darren was saying, and Spin's gestures were difficult
to follow. I was a bit worried, to tell the truth. They buried
one of my boots once, filled the replacement with hot tar and
I scalded my toe. They were boisterous, as my mother used to
say of schoolyard psychopaths.

So I had an idea. I would strike first. I couldn't get them
to fetch something from Supplies, because they always
made me do that. I couldn't fill their boots with anything.
It had to be something mild, just enough to make them
think twice. And it would have to be Darren. I had no
idea what Spin would find funny, other than me with
hot toes.

I thought about Darren's hair. It had looked dyed the first
time I saw it. After working with him for a few weeks I was
sure that it was dyed. From time to time it would start to
look less black, and thinner, and then he'd go off to fetch

something and come back with a head of glossy jet hair and inky fingers. I was suspicious.

A weak spot, I decided. That night I popped into a pharmacist's and bought a quantity of Grecian 2000. I took it home, wrapped it in brown paper and addressed the parcel to Darren. I wrote on the back:

'If not delivered, return to Building Standards Office.'

The next day I left it next to the kettle in the Portakabin that was our headquarters, after Darren and Spin had made their way up the scaffolding. I left it leaning against a packet of Hobnobs and then got on with digging. The foundations were widespread, and it was difficult to keep close to the Portakabin. I didn't want to miss anything. Darren and Spin didn't seem to want to come down. Most days they were down every few minutes, for tea or cigarettes. That day they were happy in the scaffolding, thirty feet up, basking in the drizzle. I tried not to look as though I was hanging around. I noticed I'd dug the foundations much deeper than usual that day. If I wasn't careful we'd end up with a leaning warehouse. I didn't think Mr Link would like that. I kept going off and digging, trying to leave myself with a clear view of the Portakabin at all times. I angled around, turned back on myself, dug where I'd already dug. I thought about putting the kettle on and attracting them down with tea, but then they'd know I was up to something. I never made the tea. I knew how, but it didn't interest me.

It was lunchtime before they came down. Darren made for the Portakabin, patting his pockets and frowning.

'No fags,' he said. 'Here Spin, do us a tea. I'll pop down the shops and get some. Want anything?'

Spin indicated his preference and Darren made his way off

the site. Spin entered the Portakabin. A moment later he emerged and looked about. He held the parcel. He shook it. Hearing an engine, I thought that it would be Darren returning with his cigarettes and whatever it was that Spin wanted. A tongue, perhaps. Then I remembered that Darren had walked to the shops. It was Mr Link. He pulled up close to Spin and got out.

'What's this?' he asked. Spin handed over the parcel and gestured at length.

'By the kettle?' asked Mr Link. 'I don't think so. Post comes to the office, not out here. Let's have a look at it then.'

He opened the parcel and inspected the contents. His face grew bleaker. He was never exactly a bundle of joy, but this was as grim as I'd seen him.

'I think we'll be having a word with our student friend. Mr Haines, could I trouble you to pop out of that deep pit you've dug for yourself?'

I considered hiding.

'There's no point hiding down there, the foundations are square and we can find you. Come on.'

I dragged myself up to ground level and squished over to them. Mr Link raised the Grecian 2000 and looked at it.

'Getting old isn't funny,' he said. 'You'll find that out one day.'

He looked at Spin. Spin gestured at length, and then held his sides.

'Ah,' said Mr Link. 'I see. So this was a prank, then? This waste of company time? Bit of a laugh? I have nothing against a bit of a laugh.'

Spin raised his eyebrows.

'Is this your idea of a joke?' Mr Link asked me. I nodded.

'Fair enough. Jokes happen on building sites. But I think we'll have no more. And we'll say no more about it,' he said, surprising me. I'd expected to get the sack. Perhaps I really was the best temp they'd had. Anyway, it did the trick. It must have done. They only played one more joke on me.

VI

To cut things short, I used to work on the building sites. After we finished that factory, we moved to the other side of town and put up a warehouse and then we did some office buildings in the classical warehouse style. My overdraft became smaller despite the best efforts of Mr Fallow and his staff. I worked on sites as far away as Wolverhampton and Tipton, despite the language barrier.

The buildings were always the same. I mean, they had different functions – this one was a hospital, this one an office, this one a luxury hotel with many and varied facilities – but they all looked like warehouses.

'That,' Mr Link would say, surveying whatever we had just finished bundling together, 'is what a building is meant to look like. Square, straight, flat on the top and no fancy business.'

Darren and I had decided that Mr Link genuinely believed this. Strange beliefs and superstitions were common on building sites. Spin believed that scaffolding formed matrices that could tune in to otherworldly broadcasts. Darren believed that if he dug far enough down, his trench would connect with the mines that ran under Dudley and he'd be able to tunnel under the off-licence and get all his drinks for free. Mr Link believed that all buildings should be cuboid and without decoration or, ideally, doors and windows. I believed that I was at the beginning of my life and things would turn out okay without me putting much effort into it.

'Square and straight,' Mr Link would say. The rest of us would look at each other and try to get away. 'Nothing fancy. Gargoyles and curlicues and all of that are all well and good for cathedrals, but the modern building is regular. Solid. No weaknesses in the structure.'

This was clearly untrue. In high winds the warehouses we put up fell apart, great sheets of prefab spinning off into the night like a giant conjuror's playing cards. The structures were riddled with weaknesses, apart from the foundations. Those were solid.

'Some of them fall down,' Darren said.

Mr Link gave him a poisonous look. 'That,' he said slowly, 'is because there are weak spots. Windows! Doors! How can we make a solid structure when there are parts of it that *open*?'

'It's sort of fashionable to have doors and windows,' said Darren.

Spin explained, by use of gestures, that it was traditional to have doors set into buildings so that people could enter and leave them.

'That's the thing,' explained Mr Link. 'If it was a decent building, they wouldn't *want* to leave.'

Spin explained, by use of gestures, that he had thought of something else he could be doing. Darren and I went with him, leaving Mr Link looking at our latest construction – a theme pub on the main road between Stourbridge and Wolverley – and thinking how nice it would look without the windows spoiling the purity of the architectural line.

One morning, the building society sent me a letter including a monthly balance. There was a note of congratulation enclosed, signed by Mr Fallow. My account had become positive for several days. It had since become negative again, of course.

They charged me £15 for the congratulatory note.

The next month, there were more positive days. My account went from red to black, like an infected wound. I no longer needed to work on building sites to pay off my overdraft. I was able, instead, to look for a less well-paying graduate job.

I said a farewell to Mr Link and the gang on a Friday at the end of a bright and cold February. We went to the pub.

'I knew you'd be going,' said Mr Link. 'You've been even less use than usual these last couple of months.'

I waited for him to say something good about my trench-digging abilities. He sipped his stout instead. Then he looked up.

'I'm always sorry to see a good worker go,' he said, 'and I'm seeing one go now.'

I was startled and grateful. He caught my expression.

'Bloody hell, not you,' he said. 'Our Spin here is leaving today. Got a job with local radio.'

Seemed about right, I thought. Spin had always had this thing about receiving signals.

VII

I left the building trade and got a job with the local council. I can't say which one, because they'll sue. I worked in the banking section. This made me think of heavily defended vaults and leather-topped desks, for reasons known only to my subconscious. The reality was less impressive. In a large open-plan office – much like the interior of one of the buildings I used to dig foundations for – rows of desks were set regular distances apart. The distances had been chosen to minimize what the team leaders had learned to call Unauthorized Human Interaction, which is to say chatting. There was a lunch hour which it was mandatory to take but which, it was hinted, might better be used for working in. There was an agreeable overtime rate for which no one qualified. A shift system meant that you always had to get up too early and always got home too late. At Christmas a certain amount of jollity would be tolerated: a few strands of sparse tinsel stapled to the ceiling tiles for twelve days.

I would get in at 7.30 AM, regardless of which shift I was on, because I couldn't afford a car and the bus service was unreliable. I would switch on my computer so that the people in IT would know I was there.

IT was housed on the top floor in a chaotic office full of dangling wires and tangled cables and parts of things that had become dislodged. IT was not subject to the same rules as other departments. IT had a different timescale. They would say, I'll be there in five minutes. They would arrive in anything up to a month. Everyone wanted to work in IT but there was no way to get there without having arcane and detailed knowledge of Babylon 5.

After logging in, I would look out of a window until nine when a few other people would start to trickle in. I would open up a spreadsheet or two and mess about with figures.

I would do that for eight hours. Then I would go home.

I once asked the man at the next desk to mine – a breach of council policy but I was in a daredevil sort of a mood – what happened to all of the figures we put into spreadsheets.

'Well,' he said, pushing his spectacles onto his nose, 'when we finish each sheet they are amalgamated into another spreadsheet and ratified against a third spreadsheet held at head office. If they match, they are themselves amalgamated into another spreadsheet. Each of these transactions is logged on a fifth spreadsheet. This fifth spreadsheet is checked against the performance timetable laid down in the spreadsheet kept at area headquarters, and then the results of all of these cross-checks are entered into a spreadsheet.'

'And then?'

'Then they bin it and we start all over again.'

'Why?'

He looked at me. His spectacles – the perennially unfash-ionable type with a heavy black frame – began their descent to the end of his nose.

'What?' he asked, confused.

'Why? Why do we do all of this work just to have it thrown away?'

He looked at me some more.

'Because they pay us to,' he said, and never spoke to me again.

VIII

I still work there. I've moved up, or rather across. Diagonally, really. I've moved diagonally. I now lead a team of six people. I know the names of four of them. I meet with other team leaders and we discuss our teams as though we were talking about badly behaved pets. I have been on courses designed to encourage bonding between staff, and I have not been in any way encouraged to bond with staff.

I'm like everyone else out there in the world of meaningless office jobs. It's what I do in the daytime to pay for the rest of my life. It's what I do to pay for what I *do*.

The rest of my life is far more interesting. For example, there's my best friend, Jack who can't go through those metal detectors in airports without bells going off and guns being drawn.

Chapter Two

I

After working on building sites I was glad to have a job in an office. I wanted a job in an office. I also *didn't* want one. I wanted to be unconventional, but I didn't have the money for it. An office job would provide the money to be unconventional, but an office job was all about being conventional. I had to fit in to make enough money not to fit in.

Having an office job meant being unconventional in less exciting ways. I would put paper clips in the drawing pin box. I coloured in red sections of the year planner that should have been coloured yellow. This wasn't the sort of anarchy I'd imagined when I listened to the Sex Pistols all those years ago. So an office job was conventional, I was right about that. I was only wrong about the money.

I must have got something wrong somewhere. I had less money than when I was a student earning nothing. In those days there had been more money to spend. Working on building sites the money turned up in envelopes and there was no mention of tax. Working in an office, the money didn't turn up. Once a month I got a piece of paper explaining where most of my wages had gone and how much of them I could keep. Then the B&S Building Society kept the rest. I began to want to work on the building sites again, getting fat little envelopes at weekly intervals and telling B&S nothing about it.

I had outgoings. I had to pay the rent and buy groceries and bus passes and other non-frivolous items, like cigarettes. Cigarettes aren't frivolous; the health warnings prove it. I don't like smoking, but not being able to afford to smoke makes me want to smoke. It wasn't as though I had money to burn. I didn't even have money for firelighters. My wages belonged to everyone but me. Leaving little for entertainments. Once a week I'd go for a drink with Jack and get mildly confused. We usually went to the Messy Duck, a quiet pub which was situated down the road from the zoo, standing alone next to an area of ground designated unsuitable for buildings. I would look over the ground with my practised trench-digger's eyes, spotting the greasy pools of rainbow-topped water, the cracks leading down to the mineshafts, the thrown bricks and the broken glass, the condoms.

I couldn't understand that. There must have been better places. Even in Dudley.

The Messy Duck was a quiet pub. I'd been in louder monasteries. You often got the impression that you were keeping the landlord up. He was a thin man with sad eyes and an off-putting manner. At around ten he'd switch off the jukebox and unplug the fruit machine. Between ten and half past he'd yawn pointedly. After that he'd just turn off the lights and stand by the door, holding it open. I would feel uncomfortable and intrusive, but it didn't bother Jack. He seemed to like being in uncomfortable situations. That helped to explain his hobby, I suppose. He would *have* to enjoy being uncomfortable. How else could you explain his piercings? They were all about discomfort. If they didn't bother him, they bothered the people around him.

Jack was coloured and studded. I didn't know the full extent of it – I didn't want to know, there were parts of him I wouldn't want to see in any condition, with or without rivets – but I knew that it was extensive. I imagined bolts and studs connected by chains. I imagined nails driven into areas of unnatural colour. I didn't know what sort of tattoos he had. I doubted whether he went for the old-fashioned tigers and hearts with daggers. He'd prefer something more modern, like Celtic twiddles and spirals, or perhaps barcodes.

I could have been wrong. For all I knew he had a portrait of Britney across his pectorals and Made In England etched across his scalp. I found out what he actually had much later, under distressing circumstances.

We'll get to that later.

'Why?' I once asked him. 'Why go through all the pain and risk? All those stories you hear about people getting tattoos at little shops then going down with leprosy and melting into their cornflakes. Why not stick with jigsaws?'

'It's not that painful mate,' he said. 'Not as bad as going to the dentist.'

'I thought you enjoyed going to the dentist.'

'I do,' he said, surprised. 'Except the noise of the drill.'

'So you like being hurt? It's a masochism thing?'

'No. It hurts, but that's not all of it. That's the start. You break your arm, you've got a bond with any other bloke with a broken arm. Start a conversation like that.' He clicked his fingers without making a noise. He'd never got the hang of it. 'Everyone pierced is with you. Everyone else is waiting to come in. It's a ritual thing isn't it? I don't know, mate. You're the fucking graduate. Why do you think I do it?'

'Because you're unstable.'

'Could be that, granted.'

He had a mouthful of beer and looked thoughtful. At that time the eyebrow ring was new, and he was swollen and intrusively red. I couldn't look him in the eye. I had to look at the wound.

'You do it for attention,' I thought out loud.

'Course I don't. What about all the stuff you can't see? How's that attracting attention? Take away the stuff in my face and I'm normal.'

'I wouldn't say you were normal.'

'I wouldn't say *you* were.'

'At least I don't set alarms off at airports.'

'You don't go to airports. You don't go anywhere. That's what this is. That's why you don't get it. I've gone somewhere else. I've become someone else. I've taken my body and changed it.'

I wasn't sure about that. The more I knew about body modification, the more I thought it was all to do with filling in blanks. If you weren't complete, if your identity wasn't fully drawn, then you coloured yourself in or nailed a new identity to yourself. It was all about superheroes. Outwardly, they were normal, but under the clothes someone else, run through with metalwork, extravagantly tinted.

'I set off alarms,' he said, 'because I transmit. I have wires and connections. I'm a radio. I pick up traffic reports. I pick up messages people like you don't get. I send out signals.'

'You're sending some out now,' I said. I'd known Jack

for many years but I wasn't one hundred per cent sure that he wouldn't produce a knife and lay waste to the local population. Which, at the moment, was me. I looked for help. There was the landlord. He would be useless. It was down to me to deal with Jack's insanity. I'd always thought he might have a screw loose. Possibly an actual screw, somewhere around his genitals. So I did what I had to do. I let Jack carry on, and I nodded from time to time. I can't help it. I'm British.

'Different signals,' Jack was saying. I'd missed something.

'Oh yes,' I said, 'very true.'

'I've become a matrix,' he said.

'Spin used to say there were matrices at building sites,' I said.

'The scaffolding?'

I nodded.

'I wouldn't know about that,' said Jack.

That had been a month ago, in the same pub, at about the same time of night. Since then Jack had had the bodywork touched up in a few new places. He turned up late, halfway through my second pint. I knew he'd had something new pierced, because he was walking as though he had a porcupine between his thighs. He was wearing a jumper that had been washed on the incorrect cycle. The sleeves ended inches before his hands began. His wrists were covered in bright swirls and healing scabs. He bought us a pint each and sat, wincing.

'Oof,' he said, reaching under the table and tugging at something.

'Do you mind?'

'Not really,' he said. 'Ow. *Ow*. I don't think that's where *you* belong, is it?'

He fidgeted and fiddled and finally settled, nicely uncomfortable.

'What's it this time?' I asked. I had to know, even though I didn't really want to. It was like watching operations on television. I'd want to switch channels or put my hands over my eyes. Instead I'd sit and watch, horrified. He shuffled carefully. When he winced, his eyebrow ring stood straight out from his brow.

'Perineum ring,' he said.

'What?'

'Perineum. It's the hairy bit at the back of your bollocks.'

'I know *what* it is. I meant, "*What?*"'

'I hadn't had it done yet.' As if that explained it. 'These stools are a bit hard, aren't they?' He adjusted himself indecorously.

'Not really, no. Perhaps having your perineum pierced has made you sensitive.'

'I won't be riding my bike for a couple of weeks, that's fucking certain.'

'So it's the bus, is it?'

'It will be this week. Perhaps I'll catch you on your way home. Everything nice at the office, is it? No sudden shortages of pens or anything?'

Jack often baited me like this. He was saying my life was mundane. I knew that. I was the one living it. I sometimes had an urge to hide a powerful magnet somewhere near Jack, just to see what happened. He settled at an angle, as though preparing to fart. The landlord eyed him sleepily.

'You should try piercing,' Jack said.

'I don't want to try it, but if I'm ever taken captive by the

Spanish Inquisition I'll put them on to you. You'd get on like a castle on fire.'

'What's that? History jokes from the history student? Three years taking drugs care of Johnny taxpayer and you think you know everything. Seeing as I kept you in beer all that time, while I was working for a living, I'll let you get the next round in.'

I got the next round in.

'Is he the full shilling?' the landlord asked me, nodding at Jack.

'He's missing some loose change. Actually, he's all loose change.'

'Looks like he's wearing it in his ears. My daughter goes in for all that. Face like a cheesegrater. I tell her she'll end up no good, attracting some pervert into kitchenware.' He subsided and looked miserably at the crisp boxes.

'It'll just be a phase,' I said. He gave me a gloomy look.

'They said that about bloody disco music.' He returned to his inspection of the crisps and I returned to Jack.

'Cheers,' said Jack, taking his pint. His mouth was pierced but he didn't have any liprings in. They interfered with drinking. He had a small barbell through his nasal septum, his eyebrow ring, and a cluster of rings and studs in each ear. It was all low-key. I saw worse at the bus stop. But it gave me an iceberg feeling; his most dangerous features were out of sight. Under his clothes there would be all sorts of awful things, tintacks and fishhooks, staples and cutlery. He didn't have many in his face because of his job. He worked at a printers outside Oldbury and the management didn't allow facial jewellery. They feared that some dangling item might get caught in the machinery, leading to death or litigation. At the least, that day's print run would be ruined. It wasn't a big company. They did special supplements for the local papers, posters for local rock groups, one-off histories of the local area, that sort of thing. Sometimes they'd bring out limited runs of the latest book by one of the local authors. These were sold in local shops to nobody I ever met. Jack had joined as an apprentice and had worked his way up to foreman.

I hadn't been to the printers. I imagined it to be a huge dark building, enormously lengthy and tall, with remote thin windows. It would be full of complicated machinery, wheezing and huffing; wetly-printed papers would be shuffled all over the place by conveyor belts, carried to the ceiling and thrown into loops and vertical drops like screaming people at a theme park. Apprentices in inky overalls would pull tall levers and operate sprockets; from time to time, with a thin shriek, one of them would be gathered by the machinery and whirled around the room.

Jack emptied his glass.

'That'll be your round,' he said. He'd lost count. It wasn't worth arguing about. That was all I seemed to do with Jack, hang about on the outskirts of an argument we never actually visited. I couldn't remember how we'd been at school. Perhaps we'd been exactly the same. I got another two pints. When I took them back to the table, Jack was fiddling with a beermat. I was relieved to see that he'd stopped adjusting his metalwork. It was embarrassing, even though there was only the landlord there and he was more interested in his crisps. He held up the beermat and studied it.

'We did a run of these,' he said, 'with jokes on. For a beer festival in Humberside. We all had to bring a joke in. They didn't use mine.'

I didn't ask Jack what the joke was. His jokes were the sort
Bernard Manning would have turned down as too offensive.
'So how is the printing trade? Any interesting gossip from our
local reporters?'

'Someone's filling the mines with stuff. Banned toxic stuff
so horrible you couldn't even offload it in fucking Guatemala,
and someone's lobbing it under Dudley. The hospital's sinking
into the ground. Teenage literacy is down, teenage pregnan-
cies are up, and teenagers should be seen and not fucking
heard.'

'The usual, then,' I said. Jack nodded his head in agreement.

'I saw Eddie Finch the other week,' he said.

'Oh?'

'Said he'd be in for a drink later. If nothing came up. He
has to man the phones in case a story breaks. Pensioner loses
cat, cat loses sense of direction, man paying by cheque is killed
by everyone else in the supermarket. It must be all fucking go,
working on the *Herald*.'

Eddie Finch worked on the *Pensnett Herald*, which covered
the events in Pensnett. Pensnett was a stretch of road outside
Dudley with three shops and a bad reputation. I'd never
been there myself, but I knew someone who'd stopped for a
newspaper and escaped with stitches and a persistent nervous
twitch and was told he was lucky. There was a fun run there
once a year, which was like the London Marathon only you
ran a lot faster. The *Herald* was always full of crime reports
and obituaries. Like the notices in the local shop windows, it
suffered from displaced apostrophes. Eddie covered some of
the reporting, most of the horoscopes and all of the frequent
letters from 'Angry of Kingswinford'. He was a minor reporter

on a minuscule newspaper. He drank, however, as though he
was auditioning for a place in Fleet Street before Fleet Street
moved out of Fleet Street. From time to time he'd join us for
a drink. Though I didn't often drink much, if Eddie joined us,
I would drink more. More than I could cope with, usually.
Then I'd wake up dizzy and lost with a glutinous headache
and vague memories of appalling things that, it would turn
out, I had done.

'He said he'd be in by nine,' said Jack, checking his watch.

'Is he?'

'Not unless this is bolloxed. Probably just as well if he
doesn't come in. Lisa doesn't like him much.'

'Because he drinks?'

'Because he's a journalist. She doesn't trust them. She says
everything you tell them goes in the papers.'

'I've told him lots of things and he hasn't put any of them
in the paper.'

'You don't have anything worth printing. Not these days.
I think we could have kept him in material when we were
young.'

'I don't know. Anyway, Lisa's right. I don't trust Eddie.
Not when he's drunk.'

'He's *always* fucking drunk.'

'There you are then.'

I wasn't sure where I was. The conversation kept heading
off somewhere, then turning back before it got there. Jack
was on his way to another subject. Perhaps he wanted to talk
about Lisa. He usually did. She was his girlfriend. They had
met at some sort of convention for body-piercing aficionados.
It had been held at Stourbridge town hall. The two of them
had noticed each other across a room full of pinned flesh.

Chromed instruments curved out of the crowd; by the light of surgical lamps they started to chat, and snapped together like a ring binder. They had met again a day or two later and one thing had led to one more thing. One more thing had gone on for a month, and then Lisa moved in with Jack and Jack decorated several rooms.

It all sounded serious to me. I fell head over heels all the time, but I'd never done any decorating. I watched decorating on the television while I was waiting for a real programme to come on. Decorating happened at a stage of a relationship that I had either missed or never reached. I thought that it would probably be the latter. I could start relationships, but I wasn't very good at them. It was like starting fights after a few drinks. It made sense at the time, but you ended up with a headache and no money and all of your mates wishing you'd shut up about it.

I hadn't met Lisa. Jack said she was wonderful, but I wasn't going to take his word for anything. He was hardly going to say she was an old boiler with a bosom full of rivets. That's not the sort of thing you say in the first couple of months. If you get through the first six months you can say anything you like. I think. I've never got past four.

I must have been picking the wrong girls.

Jack was happy with Lisa. I knew this because he kept telling me so. He told me so more often than I wanted him to, and after he'd had a few more drinks he'd tell me about it non-stop.

He had a few more drinks.

'She's lovely,' he said, 'she's a peach. You hear that? She's a peach.'

'Round and hairy?' I asked.

'None of yours,' he said, 'as it happens. None of your business. She's wonderful. I don't know what she's doing with me.'

'Perhaps she got one of her rings caught in one of yours. What are you going to do? Is there room between the tattoos to fit her name in? Or is it just going to be her initials?'

Jack went several shades darker. 'That's you, isn't it? Always having a go. You've never got this far. Know why? Because you'd rather be out there taking the piss. Have you ever *been* in love?'

'Yes,' I said, truthfully. I was forever falling in love. It was easy; like falling off a bike. I was in love right then. I was going steady with a girl, as it happened.

I'll tell you about her later.

'Well then,' he said, 'well then. This is real. Lisa is different. This is different.'

'They're all different. You said that Jo Branigan and Andrea Horton were different. You thought both of them were different at the same time, for a week. Then you decided they were actually the same.'

'Lisa is different differently.'

He looked at me helplessly, drunk and infatuated.

'It's the same,' I said, not knowing why I was pushing him. It was instinctive. It was easier than falling off a bike.

'This is different,' he insisted.

'Oh yes, you work in a printers so naturally you know more about anything than I do, I'm just the one who went to university.'

'What do you know about? Books. You wouldn't know the real world if it smacked you in the face.'

'If I smacked you in the face you'd know about it.'

I wasn't sure how the conversation had turned nasty. Beer, probably.

'How about if you murdered me?' asked Jack, leaning into the conversation. 'You're the history man. You know why? Because you don't want to remember your own history. You want to go back before that. You want other people's memories. I remember everything.' He rolled back his sleeve; swirls and spirals ran up his arm, between swellings and scabs. 'Look at this,' he said, 'I'm receptive. You with me? I'm *receptive*.'

'Receptive to hepatitis B, septicaemia, traffic reports . . .'

That calmed him down. 'Have it your way then,' he said. 'How's the niece?'

'Haven't seen her since I went to university.'

'Typical student. How old is she now then? Three, four?'

'Four.'

'You know she's never met her Uncle Jack?'

I did know that. I liked it that way.

'I'll tell you what, I'm not doing anything Saturday. We'll pop round and see her. And your brother, we don't see him much now.'

'We fell out. Family things.'

'Oh yes. Right. So I'll pick you up about eleven then, and we'll go and see what they're up to these days.'

Wonderful, I thought. That'd be a smashing day out.

II

The next day I waited for my hangover to leave and Jack to arrive. My money was on Jack getting there first. Eddie Finch had turned up eventually, and he was better at drinking than I was. Reporters are like that because they don't have to get up and go to work in the mornings. Although I knew I couldn't out-drink him, it had seemed important to keep up. It was my competitive edge.

I fed the hangover coffee and Nurofen until it calmed down. Jack turned up late, driving his van. He'd had it for years, since we were seventeen. It had been his first car. It looked like it might have been his grandfather's first car. The last time I'd seen it, it had been blue. He'd sprayed it white.

'A white van gives you the freedom of the road,' he explained on the way to my brother's house. 'People see a white van, they know it's going to go all over the shop. White vans have their own rules. Cut people up, park on lawns, run over dogs and children. It's accepted . . . What the fuck is *she* doing?'

'The speed limit?'

'Not in this baby, baby,' he said in what he thought was an American accent.

'Hasn't your sister got a baby?'

'Little boy,' Jack admitted. 'Called it Liam.'

'Nice,' I said.

'No it fucking isn't. Hold on, I can skirt round this lot.'

After a short and frightening trip, he pulled up on the pavement outside my brother's house. My brother is older than me, and married, and has a child. For those and other reasons he thinks he's more grown up than I am. He may be right. I never fancied growing up. There didn't seem to be an alternative, though, unless you killed yourself young.

The last time I'd seen my brother we'd argued. It's what brothers are for. When we were young we used to quarrel over anything – what colour the curtains were, how high the sky was, anything at all. Ten minutes later it'd be forgotten. We always got over them.

Jack rang the doorbell. I looked at the front garden. Tidy, with children's toys. A plastic tractor, a deflated ball, a duck on a stick. A wooden one. The door opened and Tony, my brother, stood looking at us, confused.

'What?' he asked.

'Visiting,' said Jack. 'Thought I hadn't seen you for a while. Nor your Caroline. She in, then? And I've never even *met* the sprog. What is she now, two?'

'Going on five,' said Tony, giving me a grim look. Perhaps he hadn't got over our last argument after all. Caroline appeared behind him, carrying a tea towel and a small child endowed with her mother's blonde hair and her father's brown eyes.

'Whassit?' asked the child, giving us a look. She didn't seem shy. She looked at Jack.

'Whassit in his face? Why's pins in it?' She reached out a small hand. Jack leaned closer.

'All right there kiddo,' he said. 'I'm your uncle Jack, and this is your uncle Sam, but we won't worry about him.'

'Jack!' cried the child.

'Sam,' said her mother, with considerably less enthusiasm. 'Been a while. Didn't get your letters. Suppose the post office must have lost them.'

'Too busy with keeping out of the way,' said Tony. His expression was easing. 'Come in then, the house prices'll drop if you stay outside. Is that your van?'

'Mine,' admitted Jack.

'Good. It'll piss them right off. They're all scutters down the road.'

He led us to a small, comfortable lounge. There were fewer chairs than people. To make room Jack sat on the floor, wincing on the way down. At once the little girl toddled over to him and poked at him with a podgy finger.

'Look!' she said, tugging at one of his facial rings.

'Is she okay doing that?' asked Caroline.

'Sure,' said Jack, 'she could do it for England. Here hold on, trouble, let's pop one out and you can have a look at it. What's this one's name, then?'

'Samantha,' her mother said.

'Named her after your brother-in-law? Lovely gesture.'

'You must be joking,' said Tony, brightening. 'Fine start in life that'd be, named after the ugly one in the family. Named her after someone I used to know, as a matter of fact.'

Caroline gave him a hard little look, which he pretended not to see. The house smelt like a laundry, I noticed. There were drying clothes on all the radiators. Jack unsnapped an eyebrow ring and gave it to Samantha who examined it intensely.

'Jack!' she exclaimed, handing it back to him. 'Another!'

'I haven't got that many I can do in polite company, sweetheart,' he told her. I always felt awkward around children, as though they might vomit on me or ask me something appalling. Jack seemed suited to it. I suppose he was colourful.

Tony disappeared into the kitchen and returned with tea in sad mugs. Mine had faded Muppets on it. I took a sip. It tasted strange. I thought about the pranks on the building sites. Some of those had involved tea with added ingredients.

'Milk powder,' explained Caroline. 'The little monster gets all the real milk.'

'Not a monster!' explained Samantha. 'Jack's got fings in his face.'

'Things,' Tony corrected her. 'Not fings. And we don't talk about people.'

'Do,' said Samantha. 'Do too.' She looked at Jack. 'Mummy and Daddy talk about Sam,' she said. 'Not me. A bad one. Is she here?'

'I think she might be,' Jack said, looking at me. I could see him storing that one up for later use.

'Here, I'll put the television on,' said Tony. 'We like the television, don't we?'

'Jack!' said Samantha, and then forgot she was standing and fell over. 'Bump,' she said, 'ouch.'

Tony and Caroline exchanged a look. It was the sort of look you only get to exchange once you're a parent. I like children, although I don't think they fit in with my lifestyle. Being single makes having children difficult, especially for men. Caroline hoisted Samantha up and aimed her at Jack, and Tony ferreted the remote control from under a cushion and turned on the television. It crackled.

'Growly,' explained Samantha. 'Jack? Whassit in the nose?'

Jack began to reach to his face, before being distracted by the television. I looked to see what had caught his interest. It looked like Dudley Castle.

'Dudley Castle,' the narrative informed us, 'has not survived intact.'

'What's this?' asked Tony. 'Can't be Time Team, that's Sundays. And I can't see anyone in a woolly jumper.'

'They have a lot of woolly jumpers,' said Caroline.

'Only one each,' said Tony. 'Woolly jumpers and a small piece of pottery that they find every week because they take it with them. What's this?'

'Views of Dudley,' said Jack, scanning the TV guide. 'A documentary. Five sites of interest in Dudley.'

'Five?' asked Tony.

'Well, it doesn't specify who'd be interested,' I said. 'If it's sites of interest to traffic light fans they could do it.'

'Charity shops,' suggested Jack. Samantha was still looking at him, entranced. I felt a pang of jealousy. She was my niece. Jack had a nephew of his own, and I didn't see why my niece had to like him. I wasn't even sure why I did.

The view on the television changed, passing from the view of the town to what looked like a dull row of houses.

'And this is of interest, is it?' asked Tony. Caroline shrugged.

'Turn it over,' said Samantha. 'Tweenies.'

'Hold on,' said Jack, paying more attention to the screen than it seemed to merit. 'Just a minute there, I want to watch this.'

'Why?'

'It's interesting, you know? This is where we live.' He tuned the rest of us out. Samantha whiled away the time by pulling at his piercings. The documentary spent a while dawdling around the row of dull houses, and then took in some other equally dull views, the old railway tracks down by Dudley Port, a set of new houses on the Russells Hall Estate, a grubby factory on Pear Tree Lane, the collapsed priory that lay in pieces behind the college. One or two other houses featured, but they could have been anywhere. Jack sat entranced.

'Boring,' said Samantha. 'Boring on the telly. Tweenies.

Tweenies.' For the last word she used a register only available to small children and military experiments into sonic weapons, a sharp squeal that punctured your head like a frozen skewer.

'Sorry, kiddo,' said Jack, 'I've been hogging the box.' He turned over and we tuned in to the Tweenies, and very bright they were. Jack didn't seem to be watching it, though. I was watching him. Tony was watching me, and so was Caroline. They were both watching me but in different ways and I didn't want to catch their eyes. Jack was looking at the set, and absently fending off Samantha, but he wasn't really with us. He'd gone into himself, I thought. In fact he'd gone much, much further.

Before long, we'd all be going there with him.

Chapter Three

I

I've had more girlfriends than you might think likely. But they don't stick around for long. They're like summer colds: they turn up, send you light-headed for a couple of days, then two weeks of headaches and it's all over. There have been quite a few of them and all but one of them have gone their own ways. There have been several, but in terms of time spent together they don't add up to a single long-term relationship. That's total time together. I'm not adjusting for moods and tantrums.

I don't want to sound ungrateful here. It could be worse. Some people are surprised I've had a girlfriend at all, let alone one you could take outdoors in daylight. And they've been convenient. They haven't overlapped. I've had friends with overlapping girlfriends and it always ends up with shouting. There are reprisals and cars have to be resprayed. It's all too much trouble. I've stuck with girlfriends who don't overlap, but they haven't stuck with me.

I was in town getting a new bus pass, thinking about girlfriends. It was summer in Dudley: the time of year when the sky goes a brighter shade of grey. There seemed to be more young people than the year before, but there always seemed to be more young people than the year before. It was me, getting older. It couldn't be many more years before I'd go out in the middle of summer in thirty cardigans and a flock of coats. I watched pretty girls teetering on the edge of adulthood, poised on the brink of stretchmarks and hoovering.

The travel centre is next to the bus stop, and it's got a queue in it. The queue has been there since the travel centre opened, and it hasn't got any shorter. The travel centre was moved to the bus depot five years ago. Before that, people had to queue in the town centre, where the travel centre used to be before it was knocked down so that the council could build some new public toilets by the market before the smell from the old public toilets led to an epidemic.

The queue isn't there because the people working in the travel centre are slow. They're not slow, they're friendly and efficient. I'm biased about this, but take it from me, considering the sort of things they have to deal with they're bright and lively. There are two young women in very crisp blouses with well-ordered haircuts. Straight fringes. Behind them is a door, and behind that you can see part of an office. An older woman sits in there and sometimes comes out and looks at everyone in the long queue the way you'd look at an unexpected boil on your scrotum. She has hair that's been forced into a state beyond tidiness. It's pulled away from her face, not without good reason. For many years I thought that no one knew what she did, but I now have insider information.

The two girls sit on low stools behind small windows in a Perspex screen with fingermarks all over it. There are fingermarks next to the ceiling. Someone must have stood on the counter to do it. In front of one window is an old woman trying to get a bus to a village that fell into the sea sixty years ago. In about half an hour, she'll try to pay with a money-off voucher for shampoo. In front of the other window is a woman trying to buy a student pass for her son, who isn't with her. She'll be going through all the possible variants.

'Well, he could go to Birmingham by bus, then get the train to Cardiff, and then get the local line to his digs. How can we do that?'

It turns out that we can do that by filling in eighteen ninety-page documents, while everyone else waits and the old woman by the other window gets older. After filling out the documents and handing them over, it turns out that the woman can't have any passes or tickets because her son has to sign everything, twice. Besides, he might be better off with a super saver plus for part of his journey but he'll need to go to Cardiff to see about that.

The old woman remembers the name of the village she wants to go to, and it isn't the one she'd been talking about after all. That was something she saw on television.

The mother decides to leave it, she'll pop back later and bring her son along. He'll need a passport photograph, but he won't be able to get one at the travel centre because the photo booth is broken. There are two obnoxious children in it, surreptitiously pinching one another under the sign asking parents not to let their children play in the photo booth. No one claims the children. Everyone ignores them, secretly hoping that they'll do themselves some severe harm.

The mother's place at the window is taken by another woman with a son who also needs a student pass or a free ticket to somewhere. This time the student is with her, looking bored and mumbling. The old woman gets her return ticket to Barmouth, which hasn't fallen into the sea and is where she wanted to go all along, and discovers that she has to pay for it. This hadn't occurred to her. She's about a hundred and fifty but she hasn't got the hang of shops. She produces a purse and begins taking very small coins from it, one by one. Her ticket will cost her eighteen pounds something, and she's prepared to count small change until she gets there.

The son won't tell the girl behind the counter where he wants to go. He mumbles embarrassedly. He can see the bright white shape of the girl's bra through her crisp white blouse. He tries to look away, but it's difficult. He is hunched over the form because he has an erection. He's seventeen and his mother is with him. He puts together a series of unlikely fantasies involving himself and the two girls and many of the other people in the travel centre, including the old woman with the endless supply of sixpences and, of course, his own mother.

Everyone else has the right money, and they have it ready, and they know what they want. One of the two children in the photo booth swears meaninglessly. No one pays any attention.

I know all about the travel centre, because I get my bus pass from it. Once a month my bus pass needs renewing and the travel centre is where I have to go to renew it. I stand in the queue and, in the fullness of time, I get to the front and get another month's travel on the randomly driven and unevenly scheduled buses.

For months I noticed one of the girls serving there. She was attractive, I thought. I noticed her eyes. I also noticed that she was at the other window, whichever window I got to.

As I only went there once a month the chances of getting to her window were low. At twenty-eight day intervals I would look sideways at her while someone else sorted out my bus pass. She had a name badge on, but I couldn't read it at that angle. Once, while I was trying to make out her name I caught the girl who was serving me eyeing me the way you'd eye a cockroach in the butter dish. From her point of view, I was glancing sidelong at her colleague's chest. I looked at her chest instead but it didn't cheer her up.

I began to consider getting a different type of bus pass, so that I could go in at fortnightly intervals.

I don't know what it was that I found attractive about her. I find strange things attractive. This has been a bonus, considering some of the things I've been through. She had neat hair and tidy features. She had angular cheekbones and a straight nose. It looked as though someone had gone over her face with a geometry set, sorting it all out and getting it symmetrical. She had dark eyes. I couldn't say what colour they were because I was always off to one side of her and never less than three yards away. I wanted to know. She was thin, and I liked that. She had wrists like a sparrow's ankles. She didn't have any rings on her fingers. This was good on two counts. Firstly, it meant that she wasn't married or engaged. Or that she was, but she was embarrassed about it. Secondly, it might mean that she didn't like jewellery, which was a good thing. I couldn't afford to buy jewellery.

I was planning birthday presents for a girl I had never spoken to. Things were getting serious before they'd had a chance to be frivolous. The next month I arrived at the front of the queue and found that I was yet again at the wrong window. I went to the back of the queue again. I had a feeling that I needed to move the relationship forward. Speaking to her, for example. When I got to the front of the queue, I thought, I'd ask her out.

I waited for what felt a ridiculously long time, moving forward in slow shuffles, hoping she wouldn't go to lunch or die of old age before I reached her. Over the dandruff-strewn shoulders of grubby Midlanders I watched her dark eyes. She called the main office to ask about timetables. She advised people where to get off. She gave bank cards to the third woman, who came out of her small office blinking and sullen to check them. A person away from her, one transaction away, I lost my nerve and went home.

I had to find change for a month's worth of bus travel. I got most of it from down the back of my sofa.

A month later I went through the same procedure, but this time I kept my nerve and asked her out.

Her name was Judy, which wasn't surprising. She said she'd go out with me, which was. Her eyes were a very dark blue. If they'd been a shade of paint, they'd have been called something like Midnight Shades. Her fringe was so straight it looked like it'd cut you if you touched it. She either had a local accent or a cold. I was so stunned when she said that she'd go out with me that I forgot to get my bus pass.

I had to find change for a month's worth of bus travel. There was nothing left down the back of the sofa. I had to buy things that only cost four pence so that I'd have the ninety-six pence fare in change. Even in Dudley there isn't much that only costs four pence. Some of the buildings, perhaps, or the freedom of the city.

Even without a bus pass I had to travel to meet Judy. We met at pubs and at the cinema, where I tried to find out what she wanted to see while looking as though I was deciding. There's a ten-screen cinema close to Dudley; nine of the screens show the latest blockbusters, and the other one is closed for cleaning. We saw the latest blockbusters, and I bought us four pence worth of assorted sweets from the pick'n'mix booth.

If you're ever in the position of having to spend very little money on confectionery that's paid for by weight, go with marshmallows. They don't weigh much at all and they're bulky.

With our bag of two marshmallows we'd sit and watch Arnie save the day, listening to stray parts of the soundtracks of other films. As the lights went down Judy's eyes would get darker. I had trouble not looking at them. I had trouble not looking at Judy.

We passed the two-week mark, moving into what was, for me, new territory.

She kept on going out with me. What was wrong with her? I kept buying her small quantities of cheap marshmallows and meeting her when the travel was cheapest. She seemed to like it.

One thing led to another, and that led to itself, repeatedly.

The time came to introduce her to my friends. I didn't know where Darren and Spin had got to, and I didn't have friends at the office. It'd have to be Jack. If she wasn't put off by Dudley pubs, and sweets with the consistency of sandy snot, then she might just be able to take Jack.

I asked her if she'd like to meet him, and she said yes. He said he'd like to meet anyone who'd go out with me for more than a month, as it would constitute a once-in-a-lifetime experience. I arranged a date and we got together.

II

Jack got on with Judy. Sometimes I didn't like how well they got on together. I was jealous in two directions. I didn't want to be jealous at all. I wanted happiness and joy. I wanted enough money to pay back the building society all of their correspondence-producing costs before they went bankrupt. I wanted more money than that, really. I wanted enough money to buy an island, hollow it out, and live under an imitation volcano with a swivel chair and a cat and a stack of underlings in boiler suits. I had to keep things in perspective, however. On my wages I wouldn't be able to buy an island for several hundred years, and that wasn't allowing for island inflation.

I could always lower my sights and sponsor a traffic island. That can't cost much. Companies do it, at least in the West Midlands. You're in the traffic, beside the latest traffic island, and there next to the discarded shoe and the McWrapper is a sign saying:

This traffic island is sponsored by Keegan's Home for the Bewildered.

That can't cost much. The only time people see the things is when they're stuck in traffic, wondering whether there's a reason for the traffic jam and hoping it's a juicy accident. So the name of the company becomes subconsciously linked with stress and waiting and death and no one uses the company ever again, and the managing director in his Portakabin somewhere outside Tipton waits by the dormant telephone until the receivers come and shut him down. Still, at least it's something to look at while you wait for an accident you can get to before the emergency services arrive and hide all the body parts.

This could just be me.

I told Judy about my days at the office and she told me about her days at the travel centre. I had always known it was a bad queue to be in. Many strange people stood in it. Dandruff was rife, coughing was likely, gaudy skin diseases drew the attention and there was the smell of people who misunderstood the use of soap. There would be strange men in combat gear and huge women with foul tattoos and hairstyles copied from '70s footballers. There would be someone in a faded Queen concert T-shirt. There would be a young woman with the sort of eyes you normally saw on a dead fish.

I thought the queue was bad and I only saw it from the back for one hour each month. Imagine, Judy said, seeing them face-on for eight hours a day, six days a week, shuffling towards you to ask you for tickets on the space shuttle. She'd spotted me months ago, among the living dead. I was always going to the other window, and she thought I fancied Lynn, her partner. I did fancy Lynn but I didn't mention it. You can only push your luck so far before it falls to the floor and shatters. I asked what happened in the office at the back.

Maureen happened there. Maureen was a supervisor and was in an age range starting at sixty. There was no upper limit. She spent the day in the back office. She had a chair and a desk and a packet of Rich Tea biscuits. She had a calendar with pictures of pigs on it. She had a few framed photographs of children. Judy thought they were her grandchildren. Lynn thought they were her victims. No one thought they were pretty. Maureen had a kettle and a sink and she could check bank cards. She liked checking them. She enjoyed it more if they turned out to be invalid. She had twenty/twenty vision and all her own teeth. She had a medical complaint which was never specified but which meant that she was unable to take incoming calls. Lynn had to take them.

Lynn was a blonde midget, full of energy from the tips of her toes all the short way up to her uncontrollable frizzy hair. She fidgeted in her chair all day. I was careful not to call her perky while Judy was in earshot. Since I didn't know how far Judy's hearing range extended, I never called her perky at all. Not out loud. She was, though. She had a perky bosom. I had often tried not to notice it. Of course, I had once stared blatantly at it, so as to divert attention away from the amount of attention I had been paying to Judy. Lynn remembered me looking at her chest. She thought I was a pervert, but gradually mellowed. One night, Judy and Lynn came out with me and Jack. The idea was that Jack and Lynn would hit it off, so that we could go out as two couples instead of one couple and a straggler.

Jack refused to hit it off.

'She's a midget,' he said. 'What am I, Billy fucking Smart?'

'Billy fucking Stupid,' I told him. We were in the men's toilet in the Curdled Milk, a Dudley theme pub. The theme seemed to be bad taste and watery beer, but I might have been missing something. Jack was missing something. He was missing the urinal, completely. I wasn't looking at his dick – well, you don't, do you? – but there was a glint of metal from its vicinity. Perhaps that accounted for the spray he was producing. I moved to stand some distance behind him but I still didn't feel safe.

'She's not a midget,' I said. 'She's compact.'

'Compact? She needs to sit on a cushion to reach the table.

That's a fucking dwarf, chief. If I showed her this she'd run a mile.'

'If you showed *anyone* that they'd run a mile.'

'Shows how much you know. I showed it to your girl-friend and now I can't get her off the phone. On all day and night she is. Out-fucking-rageous. Can't get enough of it.'

'I didn't know she was into scrap metal.'

'Ha ha. At least she isn't a fucking midget.'

'She might be. Film stars are all midgets. It's well known.'

'What about Robert De Niro?'

'Midget. All done with camera angles. He can't reach the top shelf in the newsagent.'

'Robert De Niro doesn't go to newsagents, he has people to do it for him. He's seven feet tall in his socks. He's a wiseguy.'

'He's an actor. And he only ever plays the same role, so it's hardly difficult.'

'Oh?' Jack looked round, doing up his zip. 'And what role's that?'

'He always plays Robert De Niro. Every film he's in, he's himself.'

Jack was affronted. He was a fan of Robert De Niro. I had been, but it was something I was trying to grow out of. You can't be impressed with New York gangsters when you leave puberty. It has to go the way of Clark's Commandos and Action Man.

'You talking to me?' asked Jack. 'There's nobody else here.'

'Too true,' I said, leaving him to it.

Chapter Four

I

Eddie Finch met Judy at a party thrown by a friend of someone Jack knew. The party looked as though it had been thrown with some force, if not much accuracy. It was held in all of the open areas of a three-storey town house on the more expensive side of Stourbridge. There was a spiky record playing somewhere, and someone said that someone who'd once been one of Pop Will Eat Itself was being the DJ for the night. Judy talked to me but I couldn't hear her. I could only hear the record. I was trying to identify it.

I do that with music. I can't help it. Instead of listening to whoever I'm with, I try to work out what the song is. It isn't deliberate. It's my ears. They prioritize. Music over conversation. That may be something to do with the conversations I usually get caught in at parties.

Judy sidestepped a slug of red wine that fell to the carpet with a thud. She looked at me and said something. I laughed, hopefully appropriately. A thin white man with thick dreadlocks gave me a stare that might have cleared the student union bar. It didn't work in Stourbridge, even on the more expensive side. I gave him a look of my own.

Judy tugged me between people who felt as though they were made of elbows and broomsticks, my can of Supa Brew Ice Special brimming over with high-alcohol, low-taste lager. I saw what she'd seen; Jack, reeling down the stairs, carrying a glass that might have been full before he'd tipped it over a quantity of guests.

Although he'd invited us, Jack wasn't sure whose party it was. He was fairly sure, he'd said in the Frog's Sister earlier that evening, that his friend Craig knew someone at the party. It would all be okay. They'd be happy to see us. We could get some drinks from the off-licence on Nail Street and drop in. I wanted to stay in the Frog's Sister. It was quiz night, and they had easy quizzes if you knew your Black Sabbath albums. When Jack went to the bar to get another round in for himself – 'You've got loads there mate, you don't need another one' – I asked Judy whether she'd like to go to the party. I tried to make it sound unappealing.

'It'll just be like a student party,' I said. 'Lots of people in a house, someone crying on the stairs, someone being sick in the bedroom, lots of people we don't know. You know.'

'I don't know,' said Judy. 'I haven't *been* a student. I don't *go around* with students. I don't know enough about student parties to know whether I want to go to one or not. It's just as well you're here to help me with it, otherwise I might go out and have some fun or something.'

I don't pretend to know everything about women. I know they like to go in clothes shops for hours picking up things they don't like and saying how horrible they are. I once asked Spin about it and he shrugged.

'That's a shrug, chief,' Darren said. 'Easy one. No one understands women, not even women.'

I didn't understand them. I understood Historic Peculiarities well enough to pass exams. If there had been an exam
for understanding women my paper would have been returned
with a cutting comment on it and I'd have been forced to
retake it the following September. I knew that Judy was in
a mood without needing to know anything else. There were
clues. She kept putting things down forcefully. She answered
questions with sharper questions. She'd mentioned not being
a student. That helped. She thought that I was patronizing
her by telling her what the party would be like. Add that to
her bad mood – and I was usually careful not to add anything
to her bad moods, they seemed to get along well enough by
themselves – and that was enough.

'We could go,' I said. 'If Jack's going. I mean, it's Friday
night. It's not as if we have to get up tomorrow.'

'Yeah well, if it's no trouble for you. I'd hate to put
you out.'

Just then I wanted to put her out of the window of a moving
train, but these tender moments are what makes a relationship
special.

'I'd love to go with you. When I was a student I didn't go
out with anyone like you.'

'What, female?'

No, beset by inexplicable mood swings. I mean, come on. If
I was stuck with a twenty-eight day cycle that sent me insane
one week in four – I'm not a biologist, so I might have got
some of the details wrong on this – and it started in early
adolescence, then by the time I was twenty I think I might
just have got the hang of it. I might think, hold on, he hasn't
stopped loving me after all. I might think, I know, I'll just *tell*
him what the problem is and that'll be that. I might think,

hold on, it's three weeks since last time this happened, it'll be menstruation, just like it was last month and the month before that and every other bloody month, and there's nothing wrong.

Jack returned from the bar with drinks for himself. He'd got a pint and a short. I wanted a pint and a short, and I had half a pint. Judy was drinking gin and tonic.

That's another thing. If I was female and heading towards the ovary-popping time of the month, I'd steer clear of gin.

Then again, I've had plenty of bad times on whisky, and I'll still drink that if there's any going.

'You coming?' Jack asked, downing his pint. 'You'll get in with me. You stick with me,' he said, arranging himself around Judy and talking into her face from close range, 'and we'll be fine. I don't know about this miserable git though. We might have to dump him somewhere.'

'Yeah,' said Judy. 'What's *wrong* with you tonight?'

She drained her gin and tonic and stood up. I followed her to the party, via the off-licence.

II

We got in with no trouble. The man who opened the door didn't recognize us, but he didn't live there and he didn't give a fuck. I know this because he told me so. He told all three of us, one by one and then all together. He took my shoulder in his hand and told me from very close range.

I don't know what he'd been drinking, but it wasn't mouthwash.

I shrugged him onto Jack and went into the hall. Everyone

was drunk and talking too loudly. A girl was crying on the stairs and another girl was comforting her by pointing out the pitfalls of all male humans. I seemed to be in a themed evening. Then, looking at the male humans in the immediate area, I saw that she had a point. Girls grow up and become women, boys become men but the growing up part gets left out. Some boys were dancing. Some were singing. Some were involved in competitions involving drinking. No one was winning.

'They're not worth it,' said the girl on the stairs who wasn't crying. The other one gathered herself and looked around. From where she was, halfway up the stairs, it must have seemed like Dandruff Central. I had thought that the long-haired look had died out with the end of grebo, that short-lived Midland sound that sounded exactly like the Midlands – industrial and stupid. I had been wrong. The hall was packed with leather jackets and straggling unwashed manes, ripped jeans and split boots. It was as though Marilyn Manson had been decanted into a kaleidoscope. From the horde came the smells of cider and patchouli. I didn't see many tattoos. They weren't well enough off to have tattoos.

Tattoos arrived, in the form of Jack.

'Stone me,' he said, 'what's this, fucking Donnington? What's that fucking *music*?'

He went in search of it.

'Are we going to have a drink?' Judy asked me. I nodded. I had four cans of Supa Brew Ice Special and a bottle of the cheapest red wine. You have to take a bottle of the cheapest red wine to parties. Everyone does. It doesn't matter whether it's six hundred bikers in a clapped-out semi or a dinner party with minor royalty, it's only polite.

I gave Judy a can of Supa and opened one myself. It tasted

terrible. If it hadn't had the alcoholic content of Dean Martin, it would have been undrinkable. It tasted so bad that you could forget what it was doing to your body. Supa comes in packs of four and costs less than either embrocation or lighter fluid, which come in packs of one. It isn't advertised. It's gained popularity through word of mouth. Which is strange, because once you've had a can or two, you can't speak.

I'm not very good at drinking. I can drink as much as the next man, but I'll fall over a long time before he does. I know my limits.

But I can't stick to them. I recognize them as I see them receding into the distance far behind me. I've had one too many, I'll think. Better have one or two more.

Then I start on the shorts.

We didn't have any shorts with us, so once the cans were gone I unscrewed the wine bottle and swigged from that. Judy began to move in and out of my field of vision. So did everything else. The red wine stains became more widespread. I had them on my clothes. I had them on everyone else's clothes. I found myself in the bathroom, with my forehead against the tiles above the bath. Someone had been sick in the bath. It wasn't me. I had been sick in the sink. Remembering that, I was sick down the wall I was leaning against. I rested on the floor and listened to people knocking on the door. There was some very bad language. I was sick in the bath.

A chunk of the evening vanished.

I was on the stairs. There were more stairs than I remembered. I trod on a stair that wasn't there and had a rest at the foot of the stairs for a while. A pair of men looking like the bastard offspring of a terrible union between Lemmy and himself helped me to my feet and spoke to me. I couldn't understand anything they said. They sounded like warthogs. They looked like warthogs. The man who had once been in Pop Will Eat Itself walked past us. He looked like a better-known warthog.

Another chunk of the evening vanished.

I was outside, sitting on the drive. It was uncomfortable. Someone had been sick on it. It wasn't me, I was sick on the lawn and on a cat that had been up to no good in the shrubbery. Legs were next to me. I looked up them. Standing over me were Eddie Finch, Jack, and Judy.

'Eddie!' I said. 'I didn't know you were here tonight.'

They exchanged looks.

'He's always like this,' said Judy. 'He's too wussy for this sort of thing.'

'Always was,' said Jack. 'Used to throw up if he had Woodpecker, and that's pop.'

'How much has he had?' Eddie asked.

'Half a pint,' said Judy.

'As much as that?' said Jack. 'He's getting to be one of the big lads.'

'Wine,' Judy added. 'Two cans of Brew and half a pint of wine.'

'Well most of the wine's on the garden,' said Eddie.

'Two cans of Brew? Call a fucking ambulance,' said Jack.

'You're an ambulance,' I said. I knew I'd got the joke wrong, but they were all drunk and I thought I'd get away with it

'There, he says he wants an ambulance. He knows he's overdone it. Stick to the Vimto, mate.'

I noticed that Eddie had put his arm around Judy, and that Judy didn't seem to mind. I told them both what I thought about that. I tried to tell them, anyway. The words came out overlapping and stretched.

'Yeah mate,' said Jack. 'You've had a bit too much tonight. See Eddie? He's going to take Judy home. Put her to bed, mate. What you'd be doing if you weren't on the drive of this charming residence. I'll take you to mine, you sleep on the floor. Throw up on the floor and I'll murder you. Fair play? Fair play. Eddie's got his car here. Haven't you?'

Eddie nodded.

'Shame you're nobody special,' said Eddie. 'Good story if you're famous, drunk in Stourbridge. Good story if you do criminal damage on the way home.'

'Useless bloody story if it's just Sam on the pop,' said Jack. Judy leaned down to kiss me. She came in too quickly and I flinched. Jack and Eddie picked me up.

'Now the walking thing,' said Jack. 'We need to do the walking thing.'

We were in the park, close to the lake. Another chunk of the evening had gone. It was like having your life edited by the British Board of Film Classification. All of the scenes ended in odd places and some things were missing altogether. A duck quacked a series of little quacks. It sounded like it was laughing. I was sick in the duck pond.

'That's the vomiting thing,' said Jack. 'We've done that. We've done a lot of that. We don't need to do it again. It's not helpful. You don't like it, I don't like it, and I'm fucking sure the ducks aren't happy about it. The walking thing. This is Mary Stevens Park, and I don't live here. I live at my house and we have to get there in time to go to bed. Now do a straight line. Not into the lake. Leave the cat alone, Sam.'

I was in Jack's kitchen. There were noises from upstairs.

'Lisa's up,' said Jack. 'Because of what you did to the cat.'

I was sitting on a chair that seemed to slope in all directions at once. Jack was sitting opposite me. He slumped his elbows on the table then put his face close to mine. His nostrils twitched and he moved a little further away.

'I never got to tell you, did I?' he asked. 'Eddie got in the way. Must have known there was a story coming. I was going to say, do you remember when we were twenty? When we killed those five people?'

I threw away a chunk of the evening.

I was in bed. It was a hard bed, and the room was doing acrobatics. It did flips and cartwheels and somersaults. I could smell vomit. Perhaps it was the cat from four or five memories ago. The smell surrounded me and I fell asleep in it, just like Jimi Hendrix. Except that I woke up the next day.

III

In the morning anything could have happened. I wouldn't have known about it. I didn't wake up until the afternoon. By that time the smell of vomit had become the smell of dried vomit.

Someone had been sick on me in the night.

Jack gave me a cup of coffee and some helpful advice about drinking, and then I went home. I remembered Judy leaving with Eddie. Eddie didn't strike me as reliable. What was Jack thinking of, letting Judy go off with Eddie Finch? Eddie Finch would have sold his grandmother's kidneys for an exclusive. Come to that, Eddie Finch would have sold his grandmother's kidneys just for a laugh. I didn't know what he might have done to Judy for a laugh. I'd be sure to count her kidneys the next time I saw her.

She was at my house, waiting for me. She made me a cup of tea and made me have a shower. After the shower she sniffed me and told me to take my clothes outside and burn them.

'Don't bother getting out of them either, you drunken bastard,' she said.

I had a feeling she was upset about something.

'I'm sorry I was drunk,' I said.

'Drunk? I can cope with drunk boyfriends. They're easier than sober ones. At least they're honest. But there's drunk and there's paralytic. How did you get home?'

I didn't know. That had fallen out of my head.

'I knew it,' she said, scrunching her face. A scrunchy face on the girlfriend means, Sam's in trouble.

'We went to the park,' I remembered. 'There were ducks.'

'Lovely. You and Jack went for a stroll in the park. I was driven home by Eddie Finch, who has always wanted to be a rally driver. How do I know this? Because he drove me home at seventy miles an hour, going sideways for a lot of the time. He has fog lamps and bumper stickers and roll bars. There's you, puking all over the wonders of nature, and there's me, being driven home so fast I got there before I went out. Of course, I had to sleep with him. He'd driven me home, it was the least I could do.'

'You're joking?'

'I may be. We'll have to see.'

'How many kidneys do you have?'

'What?' Judy went to the living room and came back with a cigarette. She had started smoking after going out with me for a few weeks. I'd tried to give up but it hadn't worked. She hadn't tried to give up. She claimed she didn't smoke much. If she didn't, either my cigarettes were evaporating or we had some woodlice in the wainscoting that were going to have chest problems when they got older.

I didn't know what wainscoting was. I thought it was something low in the house, around the level of skirting boards. Or was it on the roof? I wasn't sure. I did know that I shared the house with woodlice. I presumed they were busy eating the floorboards from under me. If you went into a dark room and switched on the light, there would be one or two woodlice in the middle of the room, heading for nowhere in particular.

Woodlice have an interesting life cycle. As I understand it, based on personal observation, there are four stages in the life of a woodlouse. Firstly there is the not-existing stage. You don't see baby woodlice, perhaps because they're the size of molecules. You do see them when they get to the second stage, which is pretty small woodlice. Then they become pretty big woodlice, and then they become unmoving woodlice that turn out, on closer inspection, to be empty shells. If you turn them over, all of the workings have gone. They're empty. No legs, no feelers, just shell. How do they get to the middle of the floor when they're empty? Why do they go to the middle of my living room floor to die? Where do their insides go?

All of these questions. Woodlice made less sense than women. Silverfish were also peculiar. Every now and then one would turn up in the kitchen sink, zipping about and looking at the leftovers in the plughole. You can't catch silverfish. I've tried. They're too fast, and if you do catch one, you open your hand and there's no silverfish. There's a little patch of silver powder. Woodlice turn into empty shells when they die, but silverfish go one better. They turn into glitter dust. I've been plagued by strange insects ever since I moved into the house. Perhaps I was cruel to them in a former life.

'Are you listening to me?' Judy asked.

I knew this question. It didn't have a right answer. If I told the truth – that I had no idea what she'd been talking about because I'd been thinking about woodlice and silverfish – I'd be in trouble. If I lied, she'd ask me what she'd been talking about and I'd be in trouble when I didn't know. There are a couple of wildcards for this – decorating the kitchen, say, or buying some new curtains for one of the rooms upstairs – but you can't rely on them.

'I think I'm going deaf,' I said, trying a new approach.

'Going bloody mad, more like,' said Judy. 'Why don't you *listen* to me?'

'I have a headache.'

I did an expression of pain and contrition. Judy did an expression of grim disbelief.

'What, and it's got your ears? I have headaches and they don't affect my ears. Is it something peculiar to you? Or a new plague that I'll be reading about in *New Scientist*?'

'I need an aspirin.' I went to the kitchen cupboard where I store my painkillers. I hadn't got any. 'I haven't got any.' I sat down again.

'You haven't got any because you didn't get any, and you didn't get any because you didn't pay any attention to me when I told you you'd run out.'

'How did I run out? There was a full box in there.'

'I had a couple.'

'*You* did? Why?'

'I had a headache. Now, I told Lynn I'd go into work this afternoon. So I'm going into work this afternoon, unless that's going to put you out. I told you all about it yesterday.'

'Oh yes,' I lied, nodding. I didn't remember that. Perhaps I didn't pay as much attention to her as I should.

It's not my fault, of course. Men will bear me out on this. Women don't tell you anything all night long. Then on comes a programme you want to watch and off they go, rattling away, asking you about frocks and wallpaper and other things you can't make sense of. It's almost as though they're interested in it all. I don't know how their minds work at all. Sometimes I hug Judy and half expect her to vanish, leaving a big powdery stain on my clothes.

She went to work and I went to the shops to get painkillers. When I got back I offered the woodlice some, but they didn't pay any attention.

'I know how she feels,' I told them, and they trundled across the draining board in search of bigger crumbs. I remembered what Jack had said. He'd said we'd murdered five people. He was obviously wrong. He'd got his wires crossed, which was bound to happen given that he was run through with them. I hadn't murdered anyone. I didn't have what it took. I got nervous just pushing woodlice off the draining board.

PART TWO

Sam, aged twenty

Chapter Five

— ◄ ► —

I

I'm Sam. I'm twenty. I've been twenty for more than eight months now, and it's been a short eight months. Time seems to be speeding up the older I get. I worry about that. I worry about a lot of things. Time used to run a lot slower. A year used to be a year and now it's six months. Time's devaluing. It's being hit by inflation.

'Take the time to think about it,' my mother used to say. Not about anything in particular. She just used to say it. She still does. She's got a stack of things she says that mean nothing to anyone else. I don't think they mean anything to her, either.

'In a bottle on the roof.'

'Because Y isn't Z.'

'You've got more books than Jack Robinson.'

'Take the time to think about it.'

So I took her advice. She says I never listen to her, but I do. I did about this. I took the time to think about time. It's going faster and it's leading us the wrong way. I read a lot. This is why my mother told me I had more books than Jack Robinson. I don't know who Jack Robinson is but if he's got fewer books than I have then he's in a bad way. I have a friend named Jack who has a small number of books – ones with bright covers, mainly, thrillers about soldiers outnumbered in the jungle, war stories for boys – but he's not called Jack Robinson. He's called Jack Ives.

According to my mother, Jack Robinson hasn't got much of anything. I have more shoes than Jack Robinson. I have more sleep, nights out, nights in, cheek and bad manners than Jack Robinson.

If I ever meet the poor bastard I'll give him some of my leftovers.

Trouble is, these sayings came from somewhere. They meant something at one time. Language has got all fucked up. Not in the same way as time, which is going too quickly, or the weather, which passes too slowly, but it's still in a tangle. We don't know what it means. We know what we mean by it, but we don't know where the words came from. Words can do a lot, properly applied. Words can do everything.

Everything is words. Everything is defined by language.

With training you can make words do different things. Point to different objects. Make those objects different.

I think that I can cheat death, to tell you the truth. I'm cutting through some things here. There's more to it than I'm letting on. This is fair enough. I had to work to know what I know. I'm not going to hand out any details for free.

I came to magic gradually. I used to read fiction. A lot of science fiction, when I was younger, along with the usual dragons and wizards nonsense. I grew out of it years ago.

In all fantasy novels there's a wizard and his name has one X and one Z and one C in it because all wizards favour the letters on the lower left-hand side of the keyboard. He has an apprentice from the town nearby. The apprentice is an adolescent boy as imagined by a nun; full of the desire to become better and go further and he's never masturbated.

The apprentice's father – a blacksmith – was killed by raiders led by a man with more Xes in his name than the wizard. The son wishes to learn magic so that he can go and beat the shit out of the bad guy and his henchmen. The bad guy is one-dimensional, his henchmen are just names.

The apprentice learns magic, goes on a quest, meets a maiden, doesn't fuck her and doesn't seem to want to, vanquishes the bad guys and has a chat with a dragon.

Not necessarily in that order.

I was twelve, heading into adolescence. I was reading these terrible novels, which seemed to have been transcribed from the minutes of role-playing games.

Don't get me started on role-playing games.

I knew that all the dwarf bullshit was of no literary value. I wasn't fooling myself. But come on, I was twelve and I could read books that claimed to be written for adults. My class-mates could barely read the instructions for videogames.

I wondered why I read this nonsense. I studied my motives. If this sounds calculating, fair cop. If there was any point to adolescent angst, it was to motivate you. It wasn't something to sit on the stairs and mope about. Here was this energy and this growth. What did I want?

What the heroes of those terrible fantasy novels wanted. What their spotty virgin readers, living with their parents at the age of forty, wanted. I didn't want to kill the bad guys. I didn't suffer from bad guys. They ignored me. My friend Jack was friends with bad guys.

I became friends with Jack when I was thirteen. I did it deliberately. I'm not going to kid you about that. I saw that he had a lot of friends of the unfriendly sort, and I learned what he was interested in – metalwork, mostly – and I pretended to be interested in it. I knew him a long time ago, my mother used to say. It's one of the things she thinks I didn't listen to. I don't remember Jack before we went to school. Once we got to school, I needed him. Having a friend with bad friends saves you a lot of trouble.

Don't go after the bad guys. Get them on your side. It's easier and quicker and they always fall for it. You only need two or three phrases to start a conversation:

'Call that a dog? That's not a dog. That's a fucking poodle. My dog'd fucking *murder* that.'

'Won't go as fast as the rally one, but it is the rally one. Got the same specs. They had to put a limiter on it or it wouldn't be legal on the roads.'

'Result. Course, if your lot had a defence it might have slowed us down. Still. Three-nil. *Result.*'

Once you know them, go out and drink with them. Out-drink them and they respect you. Get steaming and swear at everyone in the pub and they respect you. Get drunk and do anything and they respect you.

You have the bad guys on your side and you're not sure about the fair maiden.

I don't know about this. I put it down to teenage confusion, but the fair maiden hasn't come along yet. Perhaps I want something else. Perhaps maidens aren't my scene.

So, bad guys vanquished, fair maiden available but unused. So what was all the magic for?

What was magic ever for? Power. Power over reality,

because that's power over everything. Pointing bones and drinking potions, chanting cod-Latin phrases in the cemetery at midnight. All for the sake of power over everything.

I didn't want to be the apprentice. I wanted to be the wizard. I wanted to be the one the apprentice went to.

I threw away all of my fiction. Both my novels and my personal fictions, my stories about who I was. I gave them up. I looked at myself and kept the essence. I considered where I wanted to go and threw away everything that wasn't needed on the journey.

This was when I was thirteen. I was not a normal child. Not that I'm saying my family made me abnormal. I wouldn't want to give them any undeserved credit.

I didn't want stories about magic. I didn't want the illusion. I wanted the thing itself. And I knew it existed. I had seen it. We all have. Not stage magicians, with their Charlier passes and their double lifts. Not the David Copperfields or the Siegfrieds and Roys of this world, with their mirrors and tigers and cocoa-butter complexions. None of that was the real thing and so it was worthless. How could you believe in a magician who wore a *wig*?

There was real magic in the world. The texts aren't as difficult to come by as you might imagine. You mention to someone that you're interested in this or that, and they tell someone else, and you're quoted a price for a book that isn't generally believed to exist. The price is never much. I've got scars, true. I have done some things that would give a rent boy nightmares. I have done some things that a nightmare wouldn't put up with. It's all valuable experience. Everything is a lesson from the right point of view.

Little by little I came by knowledge. The real thing. Under

all of the rituals and cults, behind the mask, between the lines. There it was, the true magic.

It is not something you learn in a day. There's a price to pay. For every spell, a price. Little sacrifices. Cats and dogs. It's difficult at first and then you come to understand that a cat is a small price to pay for the ability to levitate.

Okay, I can't levitate, I admit. But I will cheat death. I can do that. I have the methods planned. I have the workflows sketched out and the critical processes shaded in.

There will have to be sacrifices. This is something that'll take more than dogs or cats. You can't keep the forces that be happy with the blood of domestic creatures. They prefer things higher on the foodchain.

There's no room for sentimentality in this business.

I have a library, or a bedroom. It'd depend on who you ask. If you ask me, it's a library. It has a bed in it, but then, so does the kitchen. My parents are sorting out the house. My mother has decided to decorate and my father is wearing old clothes and wishing she'd settle on a colour scheme some time before the next Olympics.

II

My father works in an office in Kingswinford. Kingswinford is a suburb of Dudley. People there think they're middle class but the middle classes don't sound like that. No one else on Earth sounds like people from the West Midlands. No one would want to. Listening to them you think: why don't they blow their noses? Why do they add extra syllables to small words? Fire becomes *Fi-ya*. Here becomes *He-ya*. To even things out they drop chunks of longer words: didn't becomes *Day*, wasn't becomes *Wor*. Curry becomes compulsory.

If I sound like I don't like the people of my home town, it's because I don't. I don't come from a better background, granted. But I will go to one. I'll leave Dudley behind.

People from Dudley never leave. They distrust other places. Other places have sunlight and pavilions, trams and bright nights, oceans and waterfalls. Dudley has a fountain that doesn't work.

Dudley people want Dudley and nothing else. Sunlight would give them headaches and rashes. Rivers would make them incontinent. In a shop like Harrods or Fortnum and Mason they'd be unable to find the tea towels and toilet rolls. Dudley women run to fat the way four-hundred-metre runners run a race; slow until the second bend and then hell for leather. At thirty, Dudley women expand like life rafts, get their hair permed and teach their children how to swear. Dudley men marry Dudley women, usually from the house next door, sometimes the next house but one.

Once in a blue moon someone marries someone from a different street.

This is frowned upon. They marry close neighbours for a good reason. Dudley people have special genes. They need them. In summer it rains and it's cold. In winter it rains harder and is colder. They need to get fat. Women do it at the age of thirty by eating cakes and pies and crisps. Men start when they're eighteen, building bulk with a diet of curry and beer. Dudley people need to be fat for the same reason Eskimos need to be fat. Thin people would die in a Dudley winter.

In the drizzle, Dudleyites queue at market stalls to buy tea towels. All but one of the market stalls sell tea towels. The inhabitants love them. Some collect tea towels. Others wear them. They queue outside the charity shops, too. Dudley has all of the charity shops, Barnardo's and Oxfam and twenty others, all smelling the same and all with assistants who look as cast off as the merchandise. People queue outside Poundstretcher and Poundshop in the hopes of getting a good offer on tea towels. If Dudley burned to the ground no one would care except for the manufacturers of tea towels, who would go out of business inside a year. The locals queue in the rain waiting to buy nothing from shops that don't sell anything you'd want. They stand swaddled in scarves and shell suits; they stand in their slippers in the street waiting for Shipleys to open so that they can have a cup of coffee and play the two-pence-a-play fruit machine. They push cheap cigarettes into their pasty faces and watch the same old clouds circle overhead as they have done, uninterrupted, for the last forty years. They queue and smoke and get fat without ever buying groceries. Then off they go, laden with tea towels, to get a kebab for tea.

It's like a part of Russia was placed in the centre of England. It's as though the Kremlin had thought: this place is too depressing even for us. So they got their scientists working in their bunkers far below the Siberian tundra and they found a way to transport the most miserable gulag to the West Midlands.

That's Dudley, and Kingswinford is an outskirt of Dudley – a crossroads on the way to Dudley. My father works there in an office above a hairdresser's shop. The hairdresser's is owned by someone called Denise, as hairdressers always are. Denise does special rates for pensioners. Somewhere below her shop is a lake of blue rinse and perming lotion. My father works for an insurance company, which is even less interesting than it sounds. When I was younger my mother would take me to see him at work. I'd stand and fidget and fiddle and fart, and my father would sit embarrassed and silent at his dull desk amongst his boring colleagues.

I tell you something, I'm never going to work in an office. I'd rather move to Tipton.

My mother doesn't work. She spends all day thinking of jobs my father can do when he gets home from the office. Then she tells him about them and he looks like he's thinking of better places to be. My mother likes to try different recipes from time to time, and we like her not to. She's good at root vegetables. Dudley women are. Give them a potato or a turnip and off they go, happy as Larry.

My mother invents well-known phrases. She just makes them up and claims they're centuries old. No one else has ever heard them. They're not in books of quotations or guides to linguistics.

I'd like to go and live with my uncle, Mickey Payne. He used to be something. No one will tell me what. He went to the Falklands and got scars. He comes round sometimes and he sees into me. Whatever I have, he has too. I think he knows what I'm thinking. I think he knows about the parchment, the ritual, everything. He tells me about things that my parents won't tell me: where to get a proper knife, how to use it. He left Dudley, joined the army, sent me postcards from around the world. Then he caught a live one in the Falklands and returned home with a face like a jigsaw puzzle.

He comes round and has a drink with my parents. I'm old

enough to drink at home but my parents disapprove. They say it's not suitable. My parents also disapprove of Uncle Mickey. He comes round and sits with a can of Kestrel and looks around the kitchen. It's too orderly for him. It's too bright. He sits there, a dark man in a light room, and he doesn't like it. He doesn't seem to like my parents. It's mutual.

He agrees with them about one thing, though. They all think I can do better for myself.

I could go to university and study. Something weird. Strange events in history, maybe. In the Middle Ages magic was fact. Magic was the truth.

This is the point. These things were *real*. They weren't things people thought they saw, and they weren't illusions brought on by tainted wellwater, and they weren't mass hallucinations, and they sure as fuck weren't anything to do with flying saucers.

I believe in magic, but flying saucers? Some beliefs are beyond a joke. In Kingswinford, people believe they live in a village.

My father was always at work. He went to work early and stayed at work late. I would see him just as I went to sleep, or just as I woke. At the weekends he would take us on long walks to places of no interest. He said this was rambling, and that it was enjoyable.

It was rambling.

We would trudge across fields, my father out in front, my mother taking second place, me some way behind, snagged on brambles or shoeless in mud. We went to the nearest available countryside, the closer edges of Staffordshire and Worcestershire, and then we ignored all that was scenic or interesting and walked across muddy fields for many miles.

My father liked to take us into fields already occupied by other inhabitants.

He liked to take us towards sheep, who would scatter, startled. He liked to take us through herds of cows speckled with their own dung. Cows upset my mother. As if sensing it, they would close in on her, making low noises, all innocent eyes and spindly legs.

He'd take us through fields that, he would assure us, didn't contain bulls.

It's not easy to run in mud.

His walks were in various places, and for varying lengths, but they had five things in common:

- There would be livestock.
- There would be an inconvenient fence, electrified or topped with barbed wire or both, that we would have to cross if we didn't want to go a much longer way round.
- There would be a swamp that we could not avoid.
- At some point we would pass very close to a sewage farm.
- They would go on much longer than you thought they should.

My father did enjoy them, in some strange way. I think he did. If it wasn't the walks he enjoyed, it was seeing my mother in distress. As he strode off across the flat fields, veering away from hillocks or rocks or rivers, she would take up the midpoint between him and me. She didn't want to let him get out of sight, and she didn't want to lose sight of me. He wouldn't walk any slower. He said that he went at a good speed. It would have been a good speed for a tractor.

I walked slowly. The walk would finish at around four,

although it would feel much later. If I walked slowly, I didn't have to walk so far. In those flat fields, as we passed signs telling us that trespassers would be shot, I had plenty of time to think.

There is no time to think any more. There isn't any time; it's thinner and running out.

I would sometimes see odd things: people who weren't there when I looked again, trees that changed position, fat, scrotal mushrooms arranged in peculiar patterns. I once saw a toad the size of a cowpat. It was a foot across, round and brown and flat. I bent down to look at it, as cowpats were one of the more exciting things we encountered on those treks, and it opened a pair of enormous eyes.

I was reflected in them, in my anorak, eight years old and possessed of little knowledge. It stared back at me, produced legs from underneath itself, and waddled off. Moving, it looked as it had when it was still, as though it was almost liquid and might burst at any moment.

That's one of my favourite childhood memories. I saw other things on those walks. Now they're the only things that make my childhood seem anything special. Everything else was normal. I went to school, I had grandparents, I had friends I grew out of and a family I was stuck with. None of which has any meaning. Anyone from Dudley had all of that. I learned of magic because I saw it. I saw things that could not be explained in any other way. I didn't see demonic dogs wielding sabres, but I saw enough.

Now that seems to be the thing that was my childhood, those walks I didn't enjoy. If I look back at all, it's there I look to: my mother flapping hopelessly at the cows who wanted to love her, my father a distant figure ahead of us, always on his way elsewhere.

III

Magic has demanded a lot of me. Not literally. I haven't had to cut anything off yet, but it has demanded that I change my attitudes. It requires me to be single-minded. It requires me to leave all else behind.

I haven't given up human company. I've got a few distant friends, and one – Jack Ives – close.

There are so many myths about rituals. They don't all require a black cat and a cemetery. I can think of half a dozen that don't. Nudity is optional but generally encouraged. But magic and puberty caught me at the same time, so I wasn't happy with nudity. My body was doing unexpected things and I didn't want anyone catching sight of it. I didn't see the need to involve other people in my magic.

People who gather for rituals are gathering, nothing else. They'd be just as happy at Tupperware parties.

Once upon a time I was getting ready for a ritual. I'd called Jack and he said he'd go with me. He was always happy to run through rituals. It didn't matter whether we were trying to summon Asteroth or knocking together a love philtre. It didn't seem to worry him that none of it worked. Though he could have done with a love philtre. If only for the sake of his eyesight.

It worried *me* that none of it worked. I knew how much I'd given – time, blood, all of that. I knew how much others had given. The books were full of warnings like the ones on film posters for '40s horror movies. 'Do not enter unless you are prepared for terror.'

You were supposed to enter. The warnings were there to entice you. So I went ahead and killed cats, chickens, dogs. Cats and dogs were easier to come by than chickens. Dogs were easy. Dogs aren't too bright. Cats were trickier. Cats don't trust anyone. It's very difficult to get a cat into a bag if it doesn't want to go there. Give a dog a biscuit and it'll follow you into a combine harvester.

I also used knives on myself. On the arms, mostly. Nothing that'll leave a scar. This time next year, there won't be a mark.

The sort of magic I choose as a speciality is commonly called black. I'm a dabbler in the black arts. You kill fluffy things to get on. You let scaly things be. I'm not the first to have tried this in Dudley. In one or two of the books about the black arts there is the story of a wizard who took up residence in Dudley Castle sometime in the twelfth century. The dates are vague. He moved in with two assistants and moved out the occupants. One assistant was a mason, the other is variously described as unfinished or incomplete. The books tell us that they attempted to discover the way to eternal life. In a departure from the usual storyline, they succeeded. The three of them managed to gain eternal life, or perhaps greatly prolonged life.

I'd settle for greatly prolonged life.

After a century or so of hanging around they got bored and left for foreign climes. There's a woodcut in one of the books, where the wizard and his two apprentices are stirring a vat of something undefined. As far as I know he was the first practitioner in Dudley, perhaps in the West Midlands.

There were witches but they were just old women. In those days they drowned them in the village pond; now we give them bus passes.

Since then the castle has been used by other dabblers, without any success. From time to time the zoo keepers – the castle is inside Dudley Zoo, and to get to it you have to climb over surprisingly small fences – find goat skulls, occult symbols, and less clearly magical paraphernalia like cider bottles and cigarette ends.

I wonder about the devotion of some acolytes.

I wondered about Jack. He seemed to be most taken with the sacrifices. He watched intently. He had some sort of fetish about piercing flesh. He mentioned nudity from time to time. I'm not sure he approached the subject with entirely pure motives.

Bad motives were good enough for me.

It wasn't that the invocations failed completely. I couldn't say that. I'd managed some successes. I'd revived the dead, for instance.

IV

A year ago, I met Jack behind Scratto. Scratto is a popular Dudley store. It has no shelves and no decor. It has rows of pallets holding boxes full of cheap foodstuffs. All of the products in Scratto have names closely resembling those of well-known brands. Mr Coupling cakes. Mick Donald's burgers. Zack Daniel's whisky. They look like they could be all right and they cost a third of the usual price. This is because they taste like shit. The other thing about Scratto is that there is no way out other than through the checkout. If you don't buy anything, you still get to queue.

We met at eight in the evening. Scratto was shut for the night, the pallets of dubious tat locked away.

'Why do they lock it? Who'd steal this crap?' Jack asked.

Jack was dressed in jeans and a rugby shirt. He didn't play rugby. The only thing he'd played at school was the recorder. He'd been rubbish at that, but then, so is everyone else. The only thing anyone can play on the recorder is *London's Burning*, and the only way you can recognize *London's Burning* when someone plays it on the recorder is that it's the only tune anyone learns.

Jack's jeans had been clean at some point in their life. I couldn't say the same for his rugby shirt. I don't think that had ever been clean. Jack was good at technical things: metalwork and computers. He used to have a slide rule at school. He claimed to know how to use it but, unless you're meant to use slide rules to hit other pupils with, I doubt that. He had the techie way of dressing: as long as nothing that'll get you arrested is in view, you're dressed. If you can bend it, it's clean. Colours are irrelevant.

Lots of techies became goths, when goths were at their least unfashionable. That way they knew they wouldn't have clashing clothes, because everything they had was black.

There were a lot of goths in Dudley.

We left the bright lights of Scratto behind and walked briskly to the castle. The castle is in the zoo, and the zoo is about as difficult to get into as a Gary Barlow concert. We went in through the gap in the fence behind the polar bear enclosure. There was no one around at that time of night.

One time, we'd bumped into thirteen Satanists, also using

the castle for a ritual. Jack knew one of them, and another worked in the record shop in town. They'd let us sit in on their ritual. They had a goat.

I was impressed at the time, but I've gone beyond the goat stage now. I wouldn't bother with goats now. They're smelly and difficult, like elderly relatives.

Jack led the way to the canal. There are canals all over the West Midlands, interlinked and locked. This one was stagnant most of the time. It was overlooked by three tower blocks a mile or two away. The tower blocks were about to be knocked down. They'd been about to be knocked down twenty years ago, and twenty years from now they'll still be about to be knocked down.

A tall wall of wet red bricks separates the canal from the edge of the town. We climbed the wall and dropped onto a steep bank of wet gravel. Gorse bushes held on to nothing. They pricked us as we made our way down to the mud and puddles of the towpath. Something jumped from the bank and into the water.

'Rat,' said Jack. More likely a coot, I thought. Whatever it was, it started to cross the canal but it was too dark to make out any details. It was the last week of November and the evenings had started to arrive before the afternoons had finished. It was only around half past eight, no later than that, and the canal water was dull silver, the gorse bushes black clumps. A quarter of the moon was visible, and one or two of the nearer stars.

'Cold,' said Jack.

'This isn't cold. This is winter. This is nothing,' I told him.

'Right, yeah, just a bit of a nip in the air? It's fucking

freezing. It's going to be minus five tonight. More than that. Less than that. Minus ten.'

'Why didn't you wear a coat?'

I had a long thick overcoat like something from the Crimean War. Putting it on made me think of soldiers overlooking empty fields of thick mud, while teams of horses hauled cannon into position. It had two deep pockets at the hips, and another pocket inside. That wasn't really a pocket, it was a place where the lining had come unstitched and hadn't been repaired. It left an opening six inches long leading to a pouch. In it I had a small bag of herbs, a penknife, a watch and a matchbox containing a woodlouse. I'd taken the woodlouse from under a plank that had been lying in a neighbour's garden. The watch was my father's. I had a digital one and a digital one wouldn't do. The ritual required clockwork. All the watch needed to do was stay in a pocket, so perhaps it wouldn't have made a difference. But I was skimping on some of the other ingredients, and I didn't want to cut too many corners.

The penknife I'd had for years. Like all penknives around the world, it had a small blade that was difficult to open and a large blade that was blunt. The herbs were mixed herbs, from the supermarket. I wasn't going to spend weeks drying and powdering shrubbery when you could get the same effect from a shelf.

The canals in Dudley and the surrounding area – Netherton, Oldbury, Stourbridge and the rest – pass through many locks and several tunnels. The Black Country is hilly and cold. The navigators strove to dig straight lines, but hills and valleys got in the way. They bored tunnels through crumbling banks of poor rock, using existing caves if they were conveniently placed. Long stretches of the canals run underground.

You can follow their line from above. Here and there, in small bleak fields behind warehouses and factories, you find small circular buildings of dirty brick. They're six feet high, no more than that, and perhaps ten feet across. They are topped by black painted railings, which curve in forming a dome. If you climb up, holding the railings, and look down you find there's nothing inside: a long dark shaft of nothing leading straight down out of sight. You're at the top of a ventilation shaft. Somewhere down there are the dark cold waters of the canal. If you drop a stone between the railings it'll fall and, after some time, you'll hear a splash.

The first time you do this, or see it done, the splash takes an age to come. It seems as though the stone falls miles.

Whenever you repeat the exercise the splash comes more or less immediately. It never seems to take so long again. It is as though these shafts, now unused, have only one trick and can only play it once. After a few more tries you stop dropping. You spot the brick enclosures now and then, from the top deck of the bus, perhaps. They're always in small fields of pale grass. They share the field with thin ragged ponies; the ponies, like the enclosures, always seem to be the same. It's as though one field has been copied onto the landscape several times over, fading a little each time.

We stopped at the bottom of the embankment and looked at the mouth of a tunnel, into which the canal ran. There was enough of a breeze for the canal to have small waves rippling along its surface. The light of the quarter moon fell outside the tunnel. It wasn't going inside. Neither were we. I'm not one for tunnels. I'm sure Freud would have found that interesting, when he wasn't thinking about fucking his mother.

The tunnel is cut into a rock face that rises sheer out of

the small valley. It's of some porous stone that is no use for anything. When the tunnels were excavated, the navigators would sneak away chunks of rock, thinking they could sell them to builders or sculptors. No one wanted the stuff. It crumbles under pressure; it will not break cleanly. Laid down as gravel, it becomes dust and blows away. You can't climb it because it will give way and change shape.

A hollow had formed close to the mouth of the tunnel. It was just large enough for the two of us to crouch inside. On our last visit we had arranged a small pile of bricks there but someone had scattered them. Between us we found enough bricks to put the altar back together. The rest would be in the canal under three feet of dirty water.

The details aren't as important as you'd think. If you read about magic, you get the impression that everything must be exact. Everything must be exactly as stated in the recipe. It doesn't work, of course. A cat won't always behave when you're putting a knife into it. A dog might bite you. Your apprentice might throw up. It might not be possible to get fresh basil; sometimes, you just have to make do with mixed herbs and initiative.

We knelt down either side of the altar. It wasn't solidly constructed and it wobbled. Jack folded his arms and closed his eyes and inclined his face. I put the matchbox, the penknife and the mixed herbs on the altar.

'This is the beginning, and the end.'

The words do seem to make a difference. You can skimp on the ingredients, but you need the vocabulary. You feel something with the words. It's as though something else is speaking through me. Something much bigger, much older. I told Jack about that and he told me not to be so fucking stupid.

'You can't lay the blame on other forces,' he told me. 'You're the psycho. Deal with it.'

He might have a point.

The castle has been used for rituals since it was built. I'm not big on history, but castles go back to what, the eleventh century? Earlier? They were rebuilt and extended for a few hundred years and then phased out. They're still there, though. That's the thing. History is under us, around us. It is us. And it doesn't go away.

Things don't stop happening. Nothing is finished.

'Here are our gifts,' I said. I opened the matchbox, leaving the cover to one side. The woodlouse began to climb out of the tray.

'Here is our pain.'

I opened the penknife's small blade. I used to keep it sharp. You need a sharp knife for this stuff, really you do. I kept an eye on the woodlouse as I cut Jack's left hand.

'Fuck,' said Jack. I cut the back of my own left hand and flicked the woodlouse back into the matchbox. It began to climb out again. I opened the mixed herbs and sprinkled them into the box. I intoned the names of a few minor demons. You don't need to know their names. They know yours. I guided Jack's left hand over the box and let him drip into it. I added some blood of my own. Then I put the end of the knife through the centre of the woodlouse, which stopped its escape attempts. Its antennae drooped and it curled up and died. I put a fingernail against its shell and pulled the knife free. I put the cover back on the matchbox.

'We return here.'

'Every fucking week,' said Jack.

'It's probably best if we keep to the script.'

He opened his eyes.

'It's probably the same either way,' he said. 'What's in the box?'

'Dead woodlouse,' I told him. 'Open it and have a look.'

'I've seen a dead woodlouse before.'

'This one isn't staying dead. In there, this one is coming back.'

He looked at me.

'I had my eyes closed. How do I know you killed the little fucker?'

'You know because you had your eyes open because you're sneaky. If you're going to peep, do it less blatantly. Just friendly advice, you understand. It's nothing personal.'

'So you stabbed it. Way to go, big white hunter. Now we've got a matchbox with a dead woodlouse in it. And you cut me. That's not normal.'

'You watched me cut you and you didn't do anything about it. I don't know if that's normal where you live, but round my way that's weird.'

'Round your way, everything's weird. It hasn't worked, has it?'

'I don't think so.'

I wasn't feeling too bright. It was cold and I had muddy knees and a bleeding hand. I felt sorry for the woodlouse. I opened the matchbox. The breeze carried off flakes of dried rosemary and shredded sage. The contents had settled to one end, a pulpy mass of wet red leaves. The woodlouse had sunk out of sight. I shook the box.

'It never works,' said Jack. 'Come on, admit it. You make it all up as you go along. You do all this performance stuff, waving the hands and kneeling at angles, and then nothing happens. You're making it all up, aren't you?'

'I'm adapting.'

'That's nice for you.'

He looked at the matchbox. The breeze was pulling thin red tendrils of damp herbs out of it. A hair's breadth of thyme stretched out, curved over touched the bricks of the altar. Another tendril folded itself out and joined it.

'Sam?' said Jack, looking less sure of himself. 'Is that supposed to be happening?'

'Yes,' I said. 'Our little friend is back.'

'He's put some weight on.'

'That's a vegetarian diet for you. All the nutrients you need.'

More tendrils – legs, we now knew – made their way out. A lot more. I don't know how many legs woodlice have, but it wasn't that many. Besides, these were big. They were an inch and a half long. They curved out of the mixed herbs on both sides of the matchbox drawer. They pushed the lid away. They looked as though they were made out of a mixture of shredded leaves and chitin. There was more of it emerging, glimpses of ragged shell, little twitches. It reared out of the mulch and chittered.

'Jesus jumping fuck,' said Jack. He was out of the hollow. I hadn't seen him move. I was standing next to him and I didn't remember standing. The matchbox tore down one side. The thing in there began to drag itself out. It seemed soft.

'I brought it back,' I said.

'That's not a woodlouse,' explained Jack. 'It's half fucking herbal.'

'It's healthy.'

'Yeah – considering it used to be dead.'

I couldn't work out the shape of the new arrival. It seemed to be asymmetrical. One side was overendowed with legs. There was no obvious front. It was, as Jack had said, half herbal. That's what you get for skimping on the ingredients. It opened an opening – I'm not going to say it was a mouth, and if you'd seen it, you'd know why – and chittered again. It was a horrible noise.

'I'm fucking off,' said Jack. He was already halfway up the embankment. The insect stopped struggling, half free of the box. It began to extrude antennae. I followed Jack.

By the time we got to his house he'd turned the whole event into something else.

'Dark down there,' he said. 'Gloomy. Damp and that. The wind blowing through the tunnel. I'm not ashamed to say it: I was a bit nervy for a minute there. Woof.'

I let him have that thought. It might have been dark, but it hadn't been so dark that you'd mistake a small insect for a swollen and pulpy one that chittered in its birth pangs. That had been a success. I'd got one right.

After that, eternal life would be a doddle. There was only a difference in scale; one life, against five. One woodlouse, against five people.

Just a matter of scale, really. That, and the fact that the people wouldn't be coming back.

PART THREE

Sam, aged thirty

Chapter Six

I

Jack was wrong. I'd never murdered anyone. It's not the sort of thing I'd do. I'm naturally timid or, as Judy puts it, a coward. I once ran away from a spider. This was back in my days on building sites.

It wasn't a small spider. I want to make that clear. It was a big hefty aggressive one. I turned over a board, getting ready to dig another length of trench, and there it was. It squinted in the light and trundled at me. It was all legs and teeth. I could *see* its teeth. Honestly. I climbed out of the trench and shouted to Spin. Darren saw the spider and ran off. Spin made signs that Darren didn't have time to translate. The spider made signs back at him. Then it ran after us.

My mother used to tell me that spiders were as frightened of me as I was of them, but I've never run at a spider in my life. They *always* run at me. I ran away from this one.

'Where are you off to so scared?' Mr Link asked us as we passed him. 'Is there danger of work in this area?'

The spider topped the edge of the trench and scuttled at him, gnashing its mandibles. He trod on it.

'There we are,' he said. 'What have I always said? How do

spiders get into buildings? Through holes. Through doors and windows. Buildings are about *solidity*. Buildings are about *uninterrupted lines*. If you have openings, creepy crawlies get in. And then lazy big girls' blouses, such as your good selves, run off and do no work.'

There. Mr Link could kill a spider and I couldn't. I'm not a life-threatening person. Unless I unplugged a life support machine by accident while I was trying to plug the Hoover in or something. I'll admit clumsiness, but that's different.

So Jack's accusations upset me. I kept remembering things he'd said while I was drunk. The gist of his claim was that ten years ago, when we were twenty, we had murdered several people in Dudley. This upset me. Even people from Dudley had the right to live. Not the urge perhaps, but certainly the right. He claimed that it had all been my idea and he'd gone along with it to avoid hurting my feelings, because he was 'sensitive that way'. He was clearly wrong. I'd have remembered murdering people. I could forget what Judy had just told me easily enough, but that was always about cushion covers or wallpaper, and those things forgot themselves.

I went to work with a head full of hangover and bad thoughts. On top of being accused of murder by my best friend I had to give a talk to my team. The council were going to subcontract the work. Another company was getting ready to buy our department out. I had to let my team know what this meant for them, while at the same time not letting them know what it meant for them. I also had to avoid mentioning that we were being bought out, although everyone knew about it already.

Companies keep buying each other. I've noticed this. Sooner

or later there'll be one big company, which everyone will work for. Then it'll have to buy itself out.

There were rumours at work. Clerks sent each other email. They met in corridors and whispered. The council did not approve of people talking to one another. The official line was that it led to rumours and supposition. Rumours and supposition were not allowed. Clerks were only barely tolerated. If the council could have replaced the staff with emails and memoranda, it would have done. Instead it used a different tactic. It put all of the stroppiest people in my team. Then, to fill in the gaps, it added the ugliest ones and left me to it.

My team of stroppy and ugly people had reached the meeting room before I got there. Of course, they would have had plenty of time. They wouldn't have been held up by work. As I entered they were talking in low, conspiratorial tones. I heard my name mentioned, along with some words you wouldn't use in front of your aunt. Not, that is, unless she habitually swore like a motherfucker. When they saw me they stopped talking and looked at me instead. A couple of them looked at me with vehemence, another one or two looked at me with terrible disdain. The others looked at me the way you look at a timetable on a windswept and unsheltered platform when you know no train is due. I stood in front of them and tried to look like I belonged there.

'Thanks for coming,' I said, 'I know you've all got a lot on. I just wanted to get you together to say thanks for all you've done so far, we appreciate it –'

'We're getting the sack,' someone muttered from the back of the room.

'This is just a little chat to let you know what's going on with the organization,' I said.

'Right then,' said Steve Timmins, a known agitator who had made his way to my team by doing something unspecified in the stockroom which had left another, meeker, member of staff needing counselling.

'Yes, Steve?'

'Are you going to tell us what's going on?' asked Steve.

'Yes. As I was saying, I've got you here to tell you what's going on with the department, if you're interested.'

'Of course we're interested,' said Steve. He had a creaky leather jacket and an oily quiff. He always wore black drain-pipe trousers. Either he had a lot of them, each with stains in the same places, or he only had one pair and wore them all the time. I wouldn't have put it past him to put stains on the same parts of several pairs of trousers. I wouldn't have put mass murder past him. I'd have put matches well out of his reach. What had he *done* in that stockroom? From time to time I'd hear people mentioning it in quiet voices in quiet corners, but I never got close enough to find out any details.

'I'm glad to hear that you're interested. Now, with regards to the department –'

'Interested, yes. But are you going to tell us what's going on, or are you going to tell us that something might be going on but that you can't tell us what it is or when it might happen or who will get the sack when it does?'

He leant back on his chair, which balanced reluctantly on its hind legs. I had an urge to give it a kick. He lowered his head and looked at me from under his quiff. I discovered that I didn't like his quiff. Then, I didn't like anything about him. I didn't even like his ears. It's not often I dislike someone so much that their ears annoy me.

'It's true that I can't give you all of the details at the moment,' I said.

'Well can you give us *any* of the details?'

I shook my head, readying an explanation.

'What are we in here for, then? I've got the filing to sort out and Kath needs to do something with her binders before they get out of hand. Why do we have to waste our time coming in here and listening to you not telling us something? You could not tell us without us being here. You could go home and not tell us when we weren't there. That'd save everyone time and trouble.'

There were murmurs of agreement from all corners of the room. I felt that the meeting might be slipping from my control. I thought back to my team leader training: a wet weekend in the Pennines when we had to eat worm omelette and slither down potholes holding hands and crying. What had they told us? It came to me. I ought to *isolate the troublemaker*. I should give an *indication of my authority*. I needed firmly to *set out the limits of acceptable behaviour*.

I had no idea how to do any of that. There were no potholes in the room.

'I can't tell you what I know,' I said.

'Why not?' asked Steve.

'Because it isn't something that you need to know.'

'Then why are we in here listening to you?'

'To put minds at rest and put a stop to any silly rumours,' I said. This was what I had been told the meeting was for, but I had an idea I hadn't been supposed to say so.

'Well how do you think you're going to do that without saying anything?'

'Why don't you write it on the whiteboard?' suggested Melanie, a large placid girl with an unfortunate hairstyle.

'I can't write it down. If I can't tell you it, what makes you think I can write it down? What would Ted Wiggins say if he saw me writing secret things on the board?'

Ted Wiggins was the head of several departments. No one was quite sure which ones, which seemed to suit him. I've noticed that a new sort of executive has evolved. It looks like the others, but it can't survive for prolonged periods of time outside of the environment of pointless meetings, preferably with other, similarly evolved, executives. Ted was one of this new breed. While he would never stoop so low as to speak to one of my team, there was always the danger that, on seeing a meeting in progress, he would join it out of force of habit.

'He can't write it on the whiteboard,' said Theresa, a woman who had been middle-aged her entire life. She had joined the council in 1914 so as to avoid being sent to the trenches. I wasn't sure which side she'd have been on.

'Why not?' asked Melanie.

'Because there's no markers,' said Theresa. 'Sandra from Purchasing had them for the Christmas cards. There's no markers and there's no wipes either. So he couldn't wipe it off. If he could write it. But Sandra's had the markers so he can't.'

'Sandra brought them back,' said Melanie.

'She didn't. I told her to tell me if she brought them back.'

'You were off with your leg. It might have been the veins.'

'No, I had the veins done before she had the markers. It must have been the toenails.'

'It was your leg. I remember saying when she brought them in. I said, you were off with your leg. Sandra said she wasn't surprised. I don't know what she meant.'

'You don't, with Sandra. Where's the markers, then?'

'They were all dried up so I chucked them in the bin.'

'Right. So, like I said, he can't write it on the whiteboard then,' finished Theresa.

'I wouldn't write it on the whiteboard even if there were markers,' I said. 'It's not something I feel I can write down.'

'Is it difficult for you to spell?' asked Melanie, deadpan.

'I can never spell millennium,' said Theresa. 'I always do too many Ls and not enough Ns. If I wrote it down now, I'd get it wrong.'

'Let's move on,' I said. 'Let's forget about writing anything on the whiteboard. Let's pretend the whiteboard isn't here.'

'If you'd lent it to Sandra it wouldn't be.'

I gave them all a look. I was getting ready to lose my temper. They quietened gradually.

'Right,' I said, 'I can't tell you what's going on. I can't write it down.'

'Why not mime it?' asked Steve.

'Like that thing with Lionel Blair and the thin woman,' added Theresa. 'I used to like that. I could never guess them, though. I like that one with Roy Walker. I used to like the sheepdog thing, but it's not as good now.'

'If we could just stick to the point,' I said.

'We would if we knew what it was,' said Steve.

'I can give you hints.'

'Not mimes?'

'Hints.'

'Well, if it's about UltraCrate putting in a bid to run us we know about it. We'll move into their structure and they'll charge the council. They'll probably start out renting office space here and end up owning the whole building. The first stage will be late this July and there'll be individual meetings with members of staff to discuss where they want to fit in. Not that it'll make any difference. There's an encrypted list on the server with the names of the staff we're keeping and the ones we're getting rid of. It needs two passwords, which were chosen by the Finance Director. The first one is "Debbie" and the other one is "Dallas". I can't imagine how he came up with those. Anything else we don't know?'

I was taken aback. That was everything I wasn't supposed to tell them, plus some things I didn't know.

'How do you know all that?'

'Everyone knows. Sandra told us the week before last.'

'I was off with my wrist,' said Theresa, 'so they rang me at home and told me. Didn't you know?'

'Of course I knew! I'm *supposed* to know. You're not.'

Another thought struck me.

'How the fuck did you expect me to mime all that?'

Steve smirked, Theresa flinched. The others looked on, hoping I'd lose my temper and do something they could talk about later.

'Jesus,' I said, 'the rumours in this place are unbelievable.'

'You should hear the ones about you,' said Steve, settling his chair back onto four legs.

'Me?'

'Not married, is the gist if it,' said Steve.

'Sandra reckons you're a poofter,' explained Theresa.

'Well, I've wondered,' said Melanie.

'I'm saying nothing,' said Steve, 'I wouldn't want to cause any trouble. I'm a quiet guy.'

'Is there anything else?' I asked. I wanted to get out of the meeting room and go and have a nice drunken rest in a hedge somewhere.

'They say you spend a lot of time with some bloke with pins in his dick,' said Steve.

'Would that be Barry Sheen?' asked Theresa. 'I saw him once, opening a supermarket.'

'I heard he had chains from his bollocks right up to his nipples,' said Melanie.

'What, Barry Sheen has chains from his bollocks to his nipples? He'd have to be careful. What if they got caught in the spokes?'

'Not him. Mr Haines' boyfriend.'

'Hold on. Let's stop this now. I don't have a boyfriend.'

'Would you like one?' asked Steve, raising his eyebrows.

'No! No. I'm not interested in that sort of thing. I'm straight. Jack is going out with a young lady, and if he has pins in his penis I haven't seen them. I'm not married because I haven't met the right person. Woman. Lady. Female human. Whatever they're called in here.'

'Only asking,' said Steve.

'Well thank you for your concern.'

'I said he was normal,' said Melanie. 'He's just ugly until you catch him right.'

I was speechless. I could only think of words that wouldn't help. I wished I was in a pothole, learning management skills with beetles up my jumper and water in my socks.

'Do you think he *really* murdered five people?' asked Theresa, and I fainted.

II

I had to do something. I arranged to meet Jack for a talk. I told him that I wanted to talk about his theory. I didn't want to meet him in the Messy Duck. I was wary of the pub. It had drinks in it, and I didn't want him drunk. Drunk, he was likely to run about telling people about the murders he imagined we'd committed. There was the chance that he'd go to the police and confess. Of course, if the people in my team knew about it, the news would spread without any help from Jack. I wondered how they'd heard anything about it. I wanted to nip it in the bud before we got in trouble. Because, the more I thought about it, the more I realized Jack really meant it. He honestly believed it all. People believe all sorts of strange things. They can justify anything: ethnic cleansing, boy bands, you name it.

Ethnic cleansing is troubling. It always seems to be applied in the wrong direction. If there *has* to be ethnic cleansing, why can't it be aimed somewhere useful? Against Scousers, say. They could level Liverpool and replace everyone in Brookside with parrots. They'd sound the same and look much better. No one would notice.

I arranged to meet Jack at the library. He wouldn't be able to drink there, and there'd be people around if he started freaking out. We'd have to keep quiet, too, and that'd help to stop him getting too excited. There would only be us, the librarians, and people who ran their own businesses queuing for the photocopier and asking each other if they had the right change.

The library was quiet, not surprisingly. It was untidily spread over three floors. Fiction on the ground floor, non-fiction upstairs and music in the cellar, arranged along wide shelves under blank white striplights. A staircase that creaked like a grandmother's hip led between the storeys.

I looked over the fiction to pass the time. I don't read a lot. I get bored. You're better off with a Playstation. Things *move* on the Playstation. Things are in colour. Books are still in black and white, and if you read them again, the story is just the same. I couldn't believe how many storybooks there were. Shelves and shelves of them. I went down the stairs to have a look at the CD section. I trod carefully on the stairs. The staircase creaked. The cellar was long and low. The CD cases were face-on, so that you could only see the first one in each stack. There were too many to focus on. I walked past the As and Bs. Allman Brothers, Beatles. Another few steps and I added Carpenters and Denver, John. It wasn't a cellar at all. It was a great big mausoleum for the works of dead musicians. I went back up the stairs. The staircase creaked. Librarians looked at me through their spectacles. They all wore pullovers that didn't fit, like it was a uniform. They hated noise. I wondered why they didn't do something about the stairs. Could you oil stairs to stop them squeaking? Could you breed a new sort of librarian, cross one with a llama so that they could grow their own pullovers?

Perhaps they did. There was a zoo in Dudley.

I was getting nervous. I think strange things when I'm nervous. I loitered between shelves of fiction and waited for Jack.

He was half an hour late which, for him, was half an hour early. The librarians eyed his facial jewellery. They'd seen students with nose rings and it didn't upset them. They gathered books and tugged at their pullovers. I caught Jack on his way to the staircase.

'You got here, then,' he said.

'Before you. Half an hour before you.'

'Yeah, well, you have to be early. You're uncomfortable otherwise. You're caught up in things. You're tied down. That's the difference there. I'm free.'

'You'd have to be. No one would pay for you. Shall we find somewhere to sit?'

'Go on then. I've got nothing else to do. Lisa's out tonight.'

I waited until we'd found a table before I went on.

'Have you told Lisa what you told me?'

'No,' he said. He looked as though he had more to say about that. He didn't say it. He looked thoughtful. That was worrying enough in itself. He wasn't a thinking sort of person. He had things on his mind.

'You do know it isn't true.'

He looked at me, and I knew I was wrong. He didn't know any such thing. He was full of it. His expression, the dark areas growing under his eyes, the way he looked at me; all of it said, he believed it. To him, it was true.

'What do you think we did?' I asked him.

'Murder,' he said, 'is what we did. Lots of times. We had blood on our clothes. We killed a woman with a cat. It was your idea, all of it. You and your fucking *magic*.'

That was too loud. Eyes turned to peer at us from behind inch-thick spectacle lenses.

'I didn't believe any of that magic stuff,' I told him. 'It was just, you know, gothy. It went with the March Violets and Play Dead albums. It wasn't real. We never *did* anything about it. I would know.'

'Yeah, well, I do know.' He sounded angry. 'I do know.'

'Think about it. How did we manage it? You lived with your parents. Didn't they notice?'

'My dad wouldn't notice me if I ran in on fire. And my mother only noticed whoever followed me home. I could have walked in there *carrying* a fucking body; I could have *slept* with corpses for all they cared.'

'You're not going to tell me we did that as well?'

'I didn't. I don't know what *you* did. You and your rituals. You and your calling. Calling. As if. You don't remember what we were trying to do, do you? Perhaps it worked. You told me we could live forever.'

I had a feeling as though the room had tipped, as though the view from the windows had changed. I had some sort of memory of a ritual. Something we'd done, when we were younger and wiser.

'You know,' he said, looking into my eyes. His left ear was sore at the top, red and swollen around another new ring. 'You got it then. I saw you get it.'

'Wait,' I said, 'you mean you've been sitting on this for ten years? Why bring it up now? You've had ten years to talk about it. I know it didn't happen. Magic, yes, rituals, yes. But murder? Come on. We were nobodies. We never did anything. I left Dudley and came back. That's all I've done. That's all we are. People from here. Where did this *come* from?'

'I didn't remember before. It's just come back. That programme we saw at your brother's did it. We killed people in some of those places. We buried them.'

The only programmes we'd watched were the Tweenies and a documentary about Dudley. I didn't think he meant the Tweenies.

'This is absurd. It's your subconscious trying to make sense of your life. You *want* to have done something. It's a film or a book or something. How could you not have remembered until now? And what about me? I can't remember it at all. Perhaps you should see someone.'

'The police?'

'I was thinking more along the lines of psychiatric help.'

He looked as though *I'd* accused *him*. A bit rich under the circumstances. He studied his fingernails, perhaps thinking about having them painted. Or removed.

'Why don't you try pushing it a bit?' he said.

'In what way?'

'You're trapped. There in your job, in your life. Trapped. You keep running over the same things. You and your inhibitions. You're shut in there. Why not try piercing? Break through?'

'How would that help? It hasn't done much for you.'

'It's done enough. It's opened my mind.'

'It's left the door open. Everything's coming in.'

'I'm a matrix,' he said. 'I'm open. Look at what Psychic TV say. Piercing is the start, it's putting the key in the lock. I'm receiving signals.'

'I don't know what you are. But I know we never murdered anyone. I'm a guy from an office. I watch television and go to bed. I don't want tattoos on my ears and screws through my genitals. I don't need to invent murders just to keep interested in myself. I don't need to colour myself in.'

'You think that's what this is? Me trying to liven myself up? Giving myself a new history? Fuck you, Haines. We did it. You're suppressing it. You just don't want to remember. I'm going to have a look at the local papers – the back issues. There'll be something in there. I'll prove it.'

'There's nothing to prove.'

'Well if you don't want to look, go home. I don't need you hanging around getting in the way.'

He meant it. He looked as serious as I'd ever seen him. I remembered what had happened at work.

'Have you mentioned this to anyone else?'

'Of course not,' he said. 'I'm a fucking accomplice. But I can't sit around remembering this stuff. It's there all the time, in the back of my head. I want it out. Go home. I'll look at the papers. If I don't find anything, then perhaps you're right. Perhaps you are. I'll see you.'

He didn't want me there. He wasn't comfortable with me, and I wasn't comfortable with him. I said I'd see him around and walked out, into the ongoing drizzle.

I knew he wouldn't find anything in the papers because we hadn't done anything.

But I did wonder how you could kill someone with a cat.

Chapter Seven

I

I didn't see Jack for a couple of weeks. It's not that I was avoiding him, I just wasn't going to places he'd go to. I thought Jack must have picked something up from one of his piercing lounges. Something had been driven into him along with a needle. Something had got under his skin.

At that time I hadn't seen the extent of his piercings. I knew about the eyebrows and the ears and the ones around his mouth that made him look like a marine crustacean. Those were obvious, and so were the flares of colour low on his arms. I didn't like to think about what else he'd had done. He was probably so run through with bolts and stays, wires and workings that he was influencing the position of magnetic North. There was something ritualistic about the whole business.

Without suffering, there is no growth, I'd heard.

I didn't know about that. I'd suffered, and I hadn't got anything much out of it.

I went to work and thought about nothing. The council offices were good for that. It was actively encouraged. There was a bonus scheme involved. If you were able to cope with the boredom then the sky was the limit. As a bonus, Steve Timmins got a job somewhere else and left. He was replaced by a sullen and silent young lady with a grim look about her and the sort of complexion you only get with a lifetime's diet of lo-cost beefburgers. Her name was Jane, the lady from the agency told me when she called. Jane with no Y. She could type ten thousand characters a minute.

'Any words?' I asked. 'Or just characters?'

There was a frosty little pause, then the sound of the receiver being carelessly clunked down on a desktop, and then the sound of a conversation. I only caught odd words – temp, sacked, suspended sentence – and then the lady returned.

'She is computer literate,' I was told, 'and has a certificate.'

I wanted to ask whether it was from the vet, but thought better of it. I had never met the lady from the agency, knowing her only as a voice on a telephone, and I didn't want to upset her in case it turned out that she was either nice or violent.

'Anything else?' I asked. 'Does she have any hobbies?'

'I'd imagine so. Is there anything else? Only we have a Michelle to find a place for, and frankly it's a bit of a struggle.'

Send her here, I wanted to say; that's where you send all the other hopeless ones. But I didn't, because I have a life-assisting cowardly streak. I gave Jane some filing to file and showed her where the emergency exits were in case the building caught fire or fell over.

'Thanks,' she said, and took her bundle of papers and oddments to the filing cabinets. She seemed to be fine with filing. Perhaps the agency was going to send us a few decent people for a change. I'd always thought, by the law of averages, they must have at least one on their books, although I had no proof of this. It was more a matter of faith.

There are a lot of employment agencies, and as a general rule you get what you pay for. Balanced against this is the consideration that for the price of two top-notch temps, you can get four or five shit ones from an agency with an office in a back alley in Stourbridge.

That's where the council got theirs.

It was a small agency, as many are. All you need to set up an employment agency is an office – which can be as small as you like – with a few chairs and a few desks and, most importantly, a smattering of young women in crisp blouses. I've been a temp – I was sent to the building sites via an employment agency – and I know what I'm talking about. In the office of any employment agency, there will be some desks and chairs, a couple of desktop computers (one showing a screensaver of stars moving jerkily towards the viewer, the other with a half-finished hand of Solitaire laid out), and four young women in crisp white blouses. When you arrive, none of these young women will be the one who deals with whatever sort of work you want to do. That will be dealt with – always – by someone called Sharon. Sharon will always be out of the office, and she will always be the person you need to see. A discussion will ensue, involving three of the four members of staff. The fourth will just nip out to do some photocopying although there is a photocopier in the corner of the office. It will be decided that in the absence of Sharon, you'll have to fill in this fifteen-page questionnaire and bring it back in when Sharon is available, shall we say next Wednesday?

Having spent three days doing your best to indicate why you'd rather not travel over ninety miles to work, without prejudicing your chances of employment, and having done your best to hint that you'd rather not work in a sewer or a rendering plant or on an oilrig five miles off the Norwegian shore without actually saying as much, and having failed to fill in even the top third of the blank page on which you are supposed to write any helpful or relevant work experience you might have, you go back in to the office as agreed.

The four young women in crisp white blouses are startled to see you. It had not occurred to them that you might return just because they told you to. They agree that you will need to talk to Sharon. Sharon is not in the office at the moment. She's gone to head office to talk to someone. A discussion will ensue, involving two of the four members of staff. One of the others will pop out to do some photocopying, despite the fact that there is a photocopier in the corner of the office. The fourth will telephone her boyfriend and begin to arrange her weekend.

It will be decided that in the absence of Sharon it would be a good idea if you did an aptitude test to see what sort of work you can do. You'll be escorted to an uncomfortable chair based on the tubular metal motif, installed in it, and given a ream of A4 paper. On the papers will be vast numbers of absurd questions – what is the next shape in this series, how many times does the letter J appear in this sentence, if a dog walked for three miles a day where would it be by Easter? None of these questions appear to have any relevance to anything. You write the answers in spaces which are either too small for the answers, or so large that you feel you must have misunderstood the question. You finish the test and hand it to one of the women in crisp white blouses. Disgruntled, she hands it to one of the others, who puts it to one side and taps at the keyboard of the computer not currently involved in playing Solitaire. She tells you that your scores are fine, they'll call you if there's any work.

You go home and wait for three weeks, and then they call you at four in the morning and ask whether you can get yourself five miles off the Norwegian shore, only there's this job cleaning out the sewers under a rendering plant based on an old oilrig.

Of course, this might just be me.

The good thing about the temps we got from the agency was that they didn't expect much. Even the tedium of entering meaningless information into pointless spreadsheets didn't upset them. They didn't want to do anything else. In fact, they didn't want to do anything at all. The temps had very low expectations, and the council always failed to live up to them.

It was strange. The council would happily throw money at projects with no hope of getting anything back, funding single-parent theatre groups and disabled access to coal mines, but they wouldn't pay enough to keep good temps. We did *have* good temps, but never for long. They were poached by other team leaders, offering bribes I was unable to match – longer lunch hours, more holidays, pleasant company. My team did not feature in the list of Best Teams This Week, any week.

Jane without a Y finished the filing and went for a cigarette behind the firedoor. I checked the cabinets. She had done very well. Our filing had never been straight. I had never felt much like doing it, and there had been a lot of it in a bothersome tangle. I wasn't sure what all of it was – old planning applications, things that ought to have gone to other departments, expenses claims we hadn't got round to, letters from pensioners complaining about the rudeness of those young fuckers, you name it. Jane had got all of it into order. On top of the filing cabinet there was a folder with a question mark neatly drawn on it. Inside, she'd put all of the things that didn't belong anywhere else. She was much too good to be doing filing, I thought. Knowing the alphabet put her ahead of two-thirds of my team and three-fifths of management.

I decided we had to keep her. If I could get one or two good workers I could get some results from the team. They'd get a bonus if they managed to be Best Team This Week. That would bring me to the attention of management in a more positive way than was usual. By the time Jane without a Y came back from her cigarette break, I had decided to take her on permanently. If Personnel got stroppy about it, I'd sort them out myself. I'm not a violent person, but it was a matter of principle.

II

Work finished. One minute I was on the telephone trying to get sense out of Personnel, and the next I was alone in the building because it was one minute after five. I made my way to the bus stop and waited for a bus. The next one that came was full downstairs, so I went upstairs. There was a lot of room upstairs, perhaps because of the group of youths smoking at the back just under the NO SMOKING stickers. There was a maniac in the top front seat, as usual. This one had a satchel, as usual. I have always wanted to know what they carry in their satchels but I have never felt at all like asking one of them. A wasp was also using the top deck of the bus for its own purposes, zinging crossly from window to window.

The only other passenger was my best friend, Jack. He saw me before I could escape down the stairs.

'All right,' he said, as though he hadn't spent our last few meetings accusing me of murder. 'What you doing, then?'

'Going home,' I said, sitting on the seat opposite his. The wasp rushed past me on its way to the back.

'Right,' he said. He had a carrier bag less roomy than it needed to be. Hints of shapes were edging from it.

'I had a day off,' he said, 'so I went to the shops.'

'Oh. Are you allowed upstairs with all that ironmongery? Only you might make the bus fall over if we hit a sharp corner.'

'Still hung up about my body, then?'

There was a stir of interest from the back seats.

'I have no interest in it at all,' I said.

'You're freaked out by piercing. You know why? It's not actually the piercing, at all. It's the body. It's *skin*. No wonder you've blocked out the murders.'

'I don't want to talk about that.'

'I bet you don't. You didn't mind talking about it at the time, though. Couldn't shut up about it. When you were coming up with this bright idea to live for centuries. You were fine about it then. Now you're just the mild-mannered team leader. Come on. Admit it. You must be able to remember some of it.'

'I don't know what you're talking about. Really.'

I turned and watched the factories as we passed them. One

by one they were closing for the evening, the lights going out and the steam dissipating. A canal wound between them, going nowhere important; cold anglers fished pointlessly from its banks. There were no fish in the canals. They had died out years ago.

'I'm sorry,' Jack said. 'I am. Really. If you don't remember it, then you don't. I didn't, until a few weeks ago. Then it started to come back, odds and sods. Perhaps you're right and I got poked too hard at the tattooists. Perhaps it's a dream. But I can *see* what we were doing. I can *feel* it. It's up here all the time.'

He tapped his head with a finger. There were sniggers from the back seats.

'I'd know,' I said, 'I would. I couldn't *not* know. It's not about blocking things out or covering things up. It's about *not doing* something. It's about doing something I couldn't do. I can't watch cookery programmes if they bone a chicken. I have to leave the room when there's a programme about vets on in case they unravel a dog. I couldn't have done any of it.'

'Whatever. We'll drop it. I'll say no more about it. Here, look, I treated myself today. With all of this on my mind, I needed a treat.'

'What did you get?' I asked, peeping at his bag.

'Presents for Lisa, mostly. A box of chocolates and a thing to put the remote control in so you don't lose it. A box of nails.'

'What for?' I asked, worried.

'Mending the shed,' he said.

Their shed had been losing cohesion for several years. Lisa would nag at Jack to mend it, and he would say that he'd get round to it. I'd always assumed he didn't mean a word of it.

'Got a hammer as well,' he said.

'That'll help. With the nails.'

'Got this in town,' he said, and rolled back his right sleeve. His lower arm was a mess of Celtic designs and reptiles. I don't know a lot about art, but I knew that wasn't it. In the crook of his elbow was what looked like a burn, a puffy red expanse of pained skin. Ignoring my better judgement, I looked more closely, and saw a design in the centre of the sore area.

'Fucking hell, Jack,' I said.

'Good, isn't it?' he asked.

'What is it?'

'Tattoo.'

He flexed his arm. Small spheres of blood popped from the damaged flesh. The design was unclear, perhaps because I was avoiding looking at it.

'I know it's a tattoo. It's either a tattoo or you've had your arm ironed to get the creases out. What's it a tattoo of?'

He looked at me.

'It's a street map,' he said.

'A street map? Where? Why?'

'It's a street map of Dudley,' he said, flexing the arm again. Thick veins pushed the reptiles out of shape, and a new set of bloody beads rose from his street map.

'Put it away,' I said, 'before someone asks for directions.'

There were catcalls from the rear seats. The wasp, sick of the smoke, passed us and worked its way towards the maniac in the top front seat.

'Repressed,' said Jack, 'is what you are.'

'Better than insane.'

We'd almost reached his stop.

'You can't keep avoiding me,' he said, standing

'I wasn't,' I lied.

He sighed. 'Look, Sam mate, we've been friends a long time. Haven't we? Don't let this mess us up. Come round and see us tonight. I won't say anything about murders, honest. Lisa would like to see you. Fuck knows why, but that's women for you.'

It was the best offer I was going to get. Besides, I knew he'd keep asking until I agreed even if it meant he went fifteen stops too far.

'I'll come round,' I said.

'Good man. When?'

'Seven?'

'Don't be fucking stupid, it's Emmerdale at half past. You interrupt that and she'll skin you . . . Make it eight.'

He moved along the bus, threw himself around the pole and onto the stairs. His overstressed carrier bag followed him down and out of sight. I spent the rest of the journey listening to the jeers from the smokers at the back, wondering why the wasp didn't sting them all to death.

III

Jack's bag of nails got me thinking. Whenever Judy came round, she informed me that my house was untidy. She was right but I didn't know what to do about it. I tried to tidy it sometimes but it resisted. It wanted to be untidy. Shelves would help it, I thought. Shelves would make it take pride in itself. I could pile stuff onto shelves, and then there would be

space on the floor for furniture. Anyone could make shelves.
You didn't even need foundations. A few planks, a few nails,
and there you were: shelves.

I ran into snags immediately. I didn't have a few planks.
The only planks in the house were being used as floorboards.
I didn't want to clear the floor to that extent. I had an
assortment of nails in a tin in one of the drawers under
the kitchen sink. It's a male instinct. There's a primitive
need to keep a tin of bent and odd-sized nails somewhere
in the house in case they come in handy. I picked through
the nails. Some were very long, some were very short. None
were the right length. None were straight. There were some
screws hiding among them. I put the top back on the tin and
thought about it.

I wanted to make shelves. It would make Judy happy,
or at least less vocally unhappy. It would be something
accomplished.

It was a short walk to the hardware shop, down a gently
sloping hill. I got a selection of planks and a smattering
of nails. It wasn't until I started walking back that I realized walking back would be difficult while I was carrying planks. For one thing, there was a hint of drizzle in
the air. It was difficult to tell, what with the pissing rain,
but there was a hint of drizzle in the air. I didn't want
to wait for a bus. The buses had never been reliable. I
once asked Judy why they bothered to put timetables in
bus stops.

'Got nowhere else to put them,' she said.

I started to walk. It wasn't as easy as the walk down the
road. The hill was gentle on the way down. It was hard on the
way back up. The bundle of planks became heavier. I thought

that this was because my arms were getting tired, and then I noticed that the planks seemed to be getting fatter.

This was because they were getting fatter. They were absorbing rain. I began to think that they were *attracting* rain.

I've noticed that rain doesn't wet everybody. Some people can walk through a downpour and they're dry. I walk through a downpour and keep most of it.

I got home and put the planks on the floor. They'd swollen. The string bundled around them was taut. I picked a knot loose and the planks sprang free.

They weren't just swollen. They were warped in all directions.

Never mind, I thought. This isn't a delicate job. Once they're nailed together they'll be forced to be straight. I found the hammer in the bathroom cabinet, where it had been for a year or two. Every time I saw it there I meant to put it away, but I didn't. At least I knew where it was. If I'd put it away I'd never have found it.

I approached the planks with the hammer and my new nails.

'Right you bastards,' I told them. 'Fucking behave.'

I selected the three that were going to be shelves, and the two that would be the ends. I did some rough measurements and then nailed the lot together.

They turned out surprisingly well. There were one or two bent nail incidents, and some unnecessary splitting on the part of one of the planks, but overall the materials showed less truculence than I'd expected. The head of the hammer only flew off once, and it didn't hit anything breakable. I heaved the new shelves upright and dragged them to the wall. They leaned in several directions.

'Don't,' I told them. I began to pile on the things that had been in piles on the floor, books and CDs, spare nails, old TV guides, cushions.

I hadn't bought any cushions. Judy must have sneaked them in.

I bundled as much as possible onto the new shelves. They failed to fall down. The weight of rubbish held them solid.

I put the remaining nails on the top shelf, in a saucer that had something dried in it. It seemed like a good place for nails. It wasn't as though they'd be giving me any trouble, I thought, wrong as usual.

IV

A few hours later I was waiting with a bottle of Macedonian wine outside Jack's house and trying not to look like a burglar. This made me look like a burglar.

I was waiting for it to be late enough for Emmerdale to have finished. I'd been waiting a long five minutes and there was a longer ten minutes still to go. I hadn't planned on being early. That was Judy's fault.

She'd thought about coming with me. I had to keep saying it'd be nice if she did. I wasn't much bothered either way to tell the truth. I saw her almost every night. This long-standing relationship business took up a lot of time. You couldn't skip a meal or stay up until four in the morning playing on the Playstation. It was like being a child again. It was like living with an adult again.

Not only couldn't you skip meals, you couldn't eat a lot of things you'd taken for granted up until then. There were rules about food that only Judy knew. You couldn't have chips two days in a row. They'd make you fat and spotty.

You could eat barrowloads of chocolate all day long, and that made you fat and spotty and gave you the runs into the bargain, but that was fine because chocolate was an approved substance. I knew what the rules for approved substances were: if Judy liked them, they were approved. If I liked them, it was best to keep quiet about it.

She'd been undecided all day. She called me at work and asked me whether it would be a good idea if she came along. She could talk to Lisa. She asked me what Lisa was like.

'Don't know,' I told her. 'Jack says she's lovely.'

'He'd know.'

'He'd be biased. She won't be as lovely as you.'

'I'm not lovely.'

'Of course you are,' I said, watched by my team. Judy and I played a few more rounds of that game, and then she rang off undecided.

Half an hour before I was going to Jack's house, she decided not to come. She didn't know Lisa and didn't know whether she'd like her. She had some things she could be getting on with.

She was looking at the new shelves when she said that.

'You're staying here?' I asked.

'Where else?' she asked, challengingly.

'Well, you usually stay at your mother's in the week. I thought you'd be staying there.'

'I thought I'd come round here instead. I've never been here when you've been out. I can get to know the place properly. You haven't got anything you don't want me to see, have you? Anything naughty hidden away?'

Christ, yes, of course I had. I had things that I could only look at myself when my stomach was at its strongest. What if she went through the videos? What if she looked behind the wardrobe? I didn't know what was back there but it made the spare room smell in the summer.

'No,' I said. 'See you later.'

Because I was worried about what she might uncover I left immediately. I called at the off-licence and got the bottle of disturbingly timberish wine, and then I got to Jack's too early. I didn't want to interrupt Emmerdale, other than by bombing the television company, and so I was hanging around, holding a bottle, trying not to look suspicious.

I didn't know Lisa. I'd met her, apparently. It had been after a few drinks and I didn't remember it well. I didn't remember her at all. It had been one of those nights that you can't recall without prompting. There would be gaps in my memory, and then Jack would tell me things I'd done. Slowly the missing time would come into focus, a black mass of terrible things and people I'd need to avoid for a week or two or forever.

I'd been wondering whether Jack was a reliable witness. I was wondering whether he might not be giving me memories I didn't have. He'd told me I was a murderer when I was drunk. He had a vested interest in getting me to remember things that he thought he remembered.

Perhaps, whenever I'd been drunk, he told me that I'd done things I hadn't done. Would I know? I wasn't sure. I remembered them, sort of. In an unclear way.

A small dog barked at me from behind a large gate. I told it to piss off, and that was the moment Lisa chose to open the door.

'There,' she said. 'I said there was someone hanging about.'

'That's not a pervert,' said Jack from behind her. 'Well, it is, but it's one we know. Hello Sammy boy. Coming in, then?'

V

Lisa and Jack were at a different stage in their relationship than Judy and I. Judy and I were going out together. Judy often came to my house, and sometimes stayed for the night or a few days, but she left most of her things with her parents. Sometimes she left her sense of humour with them, and visited me without it. We were a couple but there was nothing a lawyer could fleece you for. We went on holidays together, and that was the longest we managed.

Jack and Lisa had advanced to the living together stage. Lisa had given up the comforts of home for the discomforts of Jack. I knew what it would be like. There'd be empty cans in pyramids, plates that hadn't been washed hiding under chairs, fewer chairs than gadgets. There'd be a single bed with an ominous mushroomy smell and a stiff blanket. There'd be something in the fridge that had evolved from cheese and that moved stealthily every now and then. The freezer would never have been defrosted. There would be rumours of a hoover in a cupboard somewhere upstairs. Only the video recorder, the stereo, and the games console would be clean.

Something had happened, however. It was as though someone had removed the inside of Jack's house and replaced it with a new one. I knew that Judy had sneaked cushions into my house, and the odd throw or rug. Lisa had replaced everything. The last time I'd been there, after the party in Stourbridge, I'd been too drunk to notice.

'Where's your house?' I asked him.

'This is what it looked like. Underneath.'

I imagined the clean-up: skips laden with chunks of matted hair wrenched from plugholes, clotted lumps of waxy material gouged from under the microwave, shedding dried peas and fingernail cuttings as they went. I remembered clots of fur rolling under the bed like mad puppies. Had all of that gone? Where to? Who would have taken it?

'How long did it take?'

'Couple of days, really. Did it one weekend. Lisa came round, did the upstairs. I did down here. Swine of a job but it needed to be done. Coffee?'

'Have you cleaned the kettle?'

'Binned it. It had limescale. Looked like it had fucking Windscale in it. Spoons had to go as well. So, do you want a coffee?'

'Do you have decaf?'

'No, we have coffee. Decaf. What do you need that for? You need waking up, is what you need.'

'Leave him alone,' said Lisa, moving between us and taking the bottle of wine. She gave it an enquiring look. 'He's just joking, he's like this with everybody.'

'I know. He's always been unpleasant.'

'I don't know what I see in him.' She looked up at him, making me think of mad puppies for the second time in five minutes. She was little and perky, blond and curly. She seemed to be made of bundled energy, all fizz and attitude. They gave each other a long look. They were obviously delighted with one another. I wondered whether Judy and I looked like that. I was fairly sure I gave Judy the puppy look, but she gave me something far more businesslike. Lisa skipped past me to the kitchen, and her breasts did the same. They were little and perky, like her. I tried not to notice them. I thought of Jack getting his hands on them. It seemed unfair. I bet he has pet names for them, I thought. Judy's breasts didn't have pet names, and access to them was on a strictly limited basis.

'I thought you didn't like short women,' I remembered.

'What?' asked Jack, looking towards the kitchen, which was where Lisa had skipped to. 'Short? She is, really. Hadn't noticed. Kettle on, then?'

'Kettle on!' said Lisa, bubbling out of the kitchen. She hugged him and then vanished again. There was a lot of clattering.

'Dunno how she cooks,' said Jack, leading the way to the front room. 'Seems to do it by banging things together. All noise and swearing and then, bingo! there's your tea.'

'Does she use the microwave?'

I had fond memories of Jack's microwave. He'd got it cheap off someone in a pub. It had taken two of us to carry it home. It had been one of the first ones made, and it had lasted because it was very solidly built. Even then, the modern ones were compact things with panels that you touched to set them to defrost or incinerate. This one looked like a wardrobe on its side. There was a tiny door set into the front. It looked like the sort of door you'd expect to see in a submarine. The door was opened by operating two catches, which gave satisfying clunks. Then the door could be jemmied open without much effort, revealing a space the size of a shoebox.

'What's in the rest of it?' I had asked.

'Fucking lathes, by the weight of it,' Jack had said.

Under the door there was a dial, with a pointer. There was no scale for it to point to. Next to it was a switch. It looked like the switch that Dr Frankenstein regretted throwing five minutes after throwing it. Above it was a word in Cyrillic. Below it was a longer one. Plugged in, the microwave hummed ominously. You'd seal some unlucky foodstuff inside the tiny compartment, twirl the dial for the sake of appearances, and push the switch down.

Jack never pushed the switch. By this stage of the operation he would be in another room.

The switch would click into place, and that would seem to be it. Then, taking you by surprise no matter how often you used it, the machine would suddenly give a long fizzing hum on an unsteadily falling note, like a mechanical sigh. The light inside the compartment would flicker on and off, settling on a gloomy white glow. The kitchen lights would dim. The foodstuff would revolve, and microwaves that you could almost see would fill the air around the microwave. The air would hiss and light up. I was sure that if you stood in the right place you'd be x-rayed, revealed as bones. Jack was sure that if you stood in the wrong place you'd be cooked, reduced to bones. The air would crackle like the air under high-tension wires. Your hair began to move, all by itself, in waves. Your nose would dry up. A bell would ring and startle you, and the microwave would slowly wind down, the crackling air settling, the almost visible microwaves folding back inside the machine, the tiny light going out.

You'd approach it with some trepidation. You'd unplug the microwave for safety's sake and open the door. Whatever you had put in there would have become a wizened black thing the size and shape of a walnut. We tried all sorts of things – small loaves, eggs, fish, books, shoes, whatever would fit in there. We'd fire it up, the microwave would give out its Russian sigh

– zhhhhuuum – and Jack would go to another room until it was all over.

'It's gone,' Jack said.

'What is?'

'The microwave. Useless thing. Used to make all me rings hot. Prince Albert, nipples, the lot. With Lisa being done as well, it had to go. Too risky.'

'Where did you take it?'

'Skip.'

'Two skips,' said Lisa, frothing past with steaming mugs. 'Took two skips and then we still had to go to the tip. Two skips and a trip to the tip.'

The last was called over her shoulder, as she was already on her way to another part of the house. She left the mugs next to us.

'Does she ever sit down?'

'Not to my knowledge,' said Jack. 'Full of beans. Full of go. Perky, though. You think she's short?'

He looked worried. I told him she was fine.

I looked around the room. It had been decorated, I noticed. The walls had been done in some sort of textured paint and finished in a dull red. It reminded me of flowerpots. There was a new carpet, too. It was slightly too small for the room, which seemed strange. Everything else seemed to have been done with care and attention. There were new shelves, too.

They looked better than my shelves.

Lisa arrived from everywhere and sat next to him on the sofa. Even sitting still she gave the impression of motion. She seemed to be made of rubber bands and springs.

'So what do you do then?' she asked me.

'I just work in an office.'

'There,' she said, turning her attention back to Jack. 'Not everyone works in a factory.'

'Printers.'

'Printers, factory, whatever. The point is, you could get a job in an office.'

'Boring,' said Jack, who had never been in an office as far as I knew.

'Ignore him,' said Lisa, shuffling across the cushions. 'The last time he was in an office was when he was stopped by customs.'

'Customs? Where?'

'Airport, where'd you fucking think?' said Jack.

'I didn't know you'd been away.'

'Been a few places. You've been on holiday with Jude, yeah?'

We'd been to the Lake District.

'The Lake District,' I said. 'Walking.'

'There,' said Lisa, bouncing up from the sofa. 'I said so. All Jack wants to do is sit on beaches. I like to walk.'

I was sure she did. I imagined her hurtling off, only occasionally to be glimpsed as she made her way to the top of each of the nearby mountains before running back to see what was keeping you.

I realized that I was thinking about her quite a lot. I was imagining her decorating, walking, naked. I didn't think about Judy like that. I wasn't sure whether I ever had. I supposed that I must have done. Judy was something different, an ornament or a picture. She looked exactly right. She looked finished, but Lisa seemed more complete. She picked up the empty mugs and took them clattering to the kitchen. She returned with a large round tin.

'Biscuits!' she said, opening the tin and presenting it to us. It was full of those Rich Tea biscuits that are outlawed outside England on the grounds that they're too dull to eat. I took one and nibbled at it. It was like eating plywood. I thought of the woodlice at home, chewing their way through the joists. Perhaps if I got them some Rich Tea biscuits they'd leave the house alone.

I took another bite. Joists would have more flavour.

'I reckon he could do with piercings,' said Jack. 'Make him less boring. Liven up the office.'

'He might like it,' said Lisa. 'We could do him one tonight. Have we got anything sharp?'

'There must be something we could use. Hatpin?'

I hoped they were joking.

'Quick piercing to wake him up,' said Jack. 'Might help him with his memory problems.'

'I don't have memory problems,' I said.

'Must be me then,' said Jack. A silence settled.

'Do us a coffee,' said Lisa, and Jack went to the kitchen. I'd never seen him following orders before. I carried on gnawing my way through the biscuit.

'Have another!' cried Lisa, flying across the room and settling on most of the sofa. 'Go on, if you want one. We've got another packet.'

'Lovely,' I said, taking one. 'Another packet?'

'In the kitchen. He's probably eating them now. We probably won't get one. He's a little nibbler. Was he like that when you were at school?'

'I don't remember him eating, really. I remember him eating a weevil once. It was crawling across his desk, and he ate it.'

'Why?'

'To impress one of the girls. Laney Hansen, I think it was. Funny-looking girl. His taste's improved.'

'What did he mean about your memory? Never mind, he's back.'

Jack had returned, carrying three mugs. Lisa had carried three mugs of coffee in a way suggesting that it was easy, even if you did happen to be moving in several directions at the time. Jack carried three mugs in a way that suggested that two was the upper limit. Coffee sprang out of a mug, dropped through the air in a brown lump, and burst onto the carpet.

'Cloth!' said Lisa, zooming to the kitchen and returning with a cloth, which she used to make the stain larger. 'That'll fade,' she said, leaving the cloth where it was and landing on the sofa like a bomb.

I'd noticed that the carpet wasn't the right size for the room. There was a gap between it and the skirting board. I wondered why they'd left it like that, after they'd gone to the trouble of putting carpet edgers all around the room.

It was probably a style thing. I don't always get style things.

Lisa put the lid on the biscuits.

'That's enough of those,' she said. 'We don't want to get fat. Fatter,' she giggled, tweaking Jack's midriff. She took the biscuits away.

'Tell you what, mate,' said Jack, 'I'm not going to get fat on those fucking biscuits. Fucking horrible things.'

Lisa returned from the kitchen with my wine and three small glasses. She'd opened the wine, of course. She could have done it with her fingertips. Her hair curled and frothed and her little perky breasts trundled to and fro under her blouse. I realized that Lisa and Jack were both looking at me looking at her breasts.

'He was flirting with me!' Lisa said. 'Before you came in he was saying you had good taste in girls. That sounds like flirting.'

'He's done worse,' said Jack.

'I'm sure,' said Lisa. 'What have you been up to?'

'Oh,' I said, 'I used to be a bit of a tearaway. You know. Nothing really. Not by today's standards.'

Jack looked ready to disagree. I didn't want him to. I wasn't sure how she'd take sitting in the same room as a murderer. Alleged murderer.

I thought of a way to divert her attention. I asked whether I could use the toilet.

'I dunno,' said Jack. 'I've seen you after a drink. We'll have to replace the carpet. And the wallpaper.'

Lisa said it would be fine, and I went upstairs. The unaccustomed tidiness went up with me. The landing had been something you passed through on your way to bed. Now it had pictures on the walls. Prints of landscapes. The light at the top of the stairs worked, and it had a shade.

The bathroom shone. My reflection looked baffled at me from chrome surfaces and polished mirrors. A wall of white tiles behind an iron bath glowed like daylight. I touched them, thinking my hand would slide across them. I didn't think there'd be any friction. There wasn't. My hand glided with a quiet squeak. I felt a sharp pain and pulled my hand back. Turning it, I saw a thin cut across the palm. The cut widened as I opened my hand and began to bleed.

I didn't want to bleed on the clean carpet so I held my hand and turned the cold water on. A loose screw on the cold water tap gouged a little hole in my other hand, and that began to bleed too. I looked at the bright tiles and saw that their edges were raw and sharp.

All at once I saw a lot of sharp edges. There were loose screws poking from under shelves and out of the taps. There were splinters angling out of the shelves and cabinets. A careless razor blade lay on the bath, next to a wire brush.

I can't swear to it, but the edge of the toilet seat looked like it had been sharpened.

I thought of the textured paint on the walls downstairs, the long blades all around the living room walls. In the kitchen the texture had been more like sandpaper. I thought about the exposed carpet edgers. They'd looked like something a fakir would sleep on.

A wire was bent out of a wicker bin.

'Come on!' shouted Jack from somewhere else in the house. 'What are you *doing* up there? You'll go blind mate.'

Light flared from a million bright edges. It was more a booby trap than a bathroom. The bleeding stopped after a long while, and I looked at my cold hands. They were white and wounded. I took them downstairs, noticing the splinters on the banisters and the places where the varnish had been teased into ridges.

I wondered what their bedroom was like.

I sat back in the comfy chair. Jack gave me a look. He knew what I was thinking.

'That one's for visitors, really,' he said. 'Visitors can't settle on this one. Loose springs. Catch you sometimes.'

Lisa slid across the dangerous sofa. It twanged under her. On a shelf behind her were three small delicate glass bowls. They looked as though they'd break if you breathed on them.

One held paper clips. Another held needles. The third held what looked like coiled fuse wire.

'We'll need to go to the bottle bank,' said Lisa, looking at the empty wine bottle.

'Got some left over from Christmas?'

'Oh no, we just like to go. You can get your hand in sometimes. I could open another bottle. I've still got the corkscrew here somewhere,' and she slid her hand up her skirt.

My palms warmed up and began to bleed. Jack sat up, watching. With a noise like tearing cloth the corkscrew appeared.

'You okay mate?' asked Jack. 'Looking peaky.'

'Is it the wine?' asked Lisa, bounding towards me like a tiny avalanche. 'Was it off? I thought it tasted funny.' Her concerned face stopped about a millimetre away from me.

'I'm fine,' I said. 'Bit warm for me. It's been lovely. I'm a bit tired though. Might as well be off home. If that's okay?'

'You could stay here!' said Lisa, looking delighted. 'We could sort you out a piercing and you could stay here. The spare room is nearly finished.'

'Couple of rough edges,' said Jack. 'Been meaning to get round with the sander. Never enough time, is there? Not enough hours in the day.'

'I'll get some blankets,' said Lisa, leaning over. I had a quick view of her cleavage, a burst of lace and scarred flesh, a glint of metal and the raw edges of peeling scabs.

'I'll be fine,' I said. 'Really. I'll be better off in my own bed.'

I stood up.

'It's been lovely,' I said.

'You'll have to come again,' said Lisa, looking up at me. Her perky little breasts shifted under her clothes. I made it to the front door without being flayed alive.

'Well, if you're sure,' said Lisa. 'Been nice seeing you!' She blew a kiss from a safe distance and retreated to the kitchen.

'Yeah well mate,' said Jack. 'Been a blast. Bit of a biscuit, bit of a chat. Like being civilized. Tell you what, next time we'll go out and get slaughtered.'

I hoped he meant drunk. I said I'd see him soon.

The door closed. A little while later Lisa screeched, not unhappily. The screeches ran up and down the street, and I left them to it and went home to bed.

Chapter Eight

Jack called me the following Sunday. He told me that he had young Liam to look after for the day while his mother went shopping. Liam was two or three, Jack wasn't sure which.

'I've got him until eightish,' he said. 'Can I bring him round? I don't mind him breaking your junk.'

I thought about Jack's house. It wasn't a good place for a child. There were all of those sharp edges and little spikes. My house was unsuitable in a different way. It was unclean. The new shelves were overflowing, and the vacuum cleaner had choked to death a couple of years ago.

I think you have to empty them every now and then.

I like children, generally. I like elephants, too, but I wouldn't want one in the house. I didn't want Liam poking about. I was also wary of letting Jack into the house, given that he was convinced that we were serial killers.

I couldn't leave Liam in his hands for a day, though. If Jack was becoming unhinged, Liam might not have a nice day. Uncles could be peculiar, as I remembered. Any teenage girl could tell you that. I thought of Liam toddling into the bathroom. Would Jack have put away the razor blade? I didn't think so. I had a brainwave.

'Bring him over,' I said, 'and we'll take him to see Samantha. By the way, I notice that my niece is named after me, and your nephew is named after, well, who exactly? Not you, though.'

'My sister was a goth. So it's Liam Hussey, probably. No way they named that one after you though. I can't think of anything that could be named after you. New sort of flea powder maybe. New sort of underpants.'

'And this is how you talk in front of your nephew, is it?'

'He's not in here, he's fucked off upstairs. He's following Lisa about. I'll be over in half an hour.' He hung up.

I got dressed – it was Sunday, and as a rule on Sundays I don't get dressed until the evening, and that's only if I'm going out. I called my brother and told him we'd be over.

He didn't sound all that pleased about it. It's hard to tell with Tony, though. He doesn't have a happy voice. That might be my fault. I upset him once upon a time.

I'll tell you about that later on.

When Jack arrived I locked up and climbed into the van. In the back, a gloomy child eyed me.

'Hello,' I said brightly. 'You must be Liam.'

'I hope so,' said Jack. 'Otherwise I'm in dead lumber with his mother. '

He pulled out into the traffic.

After a short journey he stopped the van half on, half off the kerb not far from my brother's house. Caroline was watching us from an upstairs window. The neighbours were watching us from their windows, too. Jack took hold of Liam's hand and toddled him to the door. Tony opened it, looking as

gloomy as ever. Marital difficulties, if you really want to
know. Samantha peeped around her father. She looked at
Liam the way you'd look at a long and complex equation.
She looked at me in passing, then settled on Jack.

'Jack!' she shouted, stumbling out of the house and grab-
bing him by the knees. 'Jack!'

'Coming in then?' asked Tony. 'Caz is just getting ready.
She's been getting ready for an hour or two, so she should
be down before nightfall. I was doing the back garden.
Bring them through, being as it's a nice day. We can stay
out there.'

I hadn't noticed, but it was a nice day. The sky was a
startling blue and there were few clouds, none much larger
or greyer than an aircraft carrier. The wind was warm.

Tony led us to the back garden. It was one of those long
patches of scrubland that older houses have, ten feet across
but seemingly miles long. Mossy red brick walls ran down
its sides, ending at a collapsing fence in the far distance. A
scrawny lawn occupied the first twenty yards. After that
things looked wilder. A shed was leaning into itself. There
was evidence of gardening close to the house, a fork and spade
leaning against the wall, a set of shallow trenches. I gave the
trenches a professional examination. They looked fine.

A hutch stood on a trestle table. Something inside it looked
at me then scurried out of sight.

'Jack!' said Samantha. 'See the pigs.'

She dragged him to the hutch. It emitted squeals.

'Oh yeah, guinea pigs,' he said. 'I had some when I was
little. Friendly things. What's their names then, trouble?'

He hoisted Samantha into the air.

'That one's Jack,' she said. 'That one's not.'

'What's that one?'

'Not Jack.'

'Right you are then,' and he popped her back onto the lawn. 'This is Liam come round to see you. Hey Liam, don't hide round there.'

Liam had turned shy. Tony had started messing with his trenches. They looked very professional.

It's not as easy as it sounds, digging trenches. It doesn't matter whether you're doing them for foundations or just for gardening, what you want is nice straight sides and a good level bottom. The trouble is, soil doesn't like being in straight lines, it likes to be in a mess. It's happiest when it can get on a shoe and get itself onto an expensive carpet, but if that's not an option, it'll settle for settling. You have to dig at an angle and press the edges flat, compressing the soil. That holds it together. That's how to get straight edges on your trenches.

These were very straight.

'Did you do those?' I asked.

'Who else?' asked Tony. 'I had some advice about it though. Hadn't done any digging before. 'Cept at the beach, sandcastles and that.'

'Nice job,' I told him. He looked pleased.

Liam approached Samantha. She looked at him doubtfully. I could understand that.

'Jack?' she asked.

'No,' said Jack, 'this is Liam. He's come to see you. Tell you what, you see your guinea pigs?'

She nodded.

'Well let's call the other one Liam. Jack and Liam, that's easy to remember. Jack's the big handsome one, and Liam isn't.'

Liam didn't seem fazed by any of this. He was looking into the hutch. The guinea pigs – Jack and Liam – looked back at him, chattering. Samantha prodded him.

'Look at that,' said Jack. 'Women after him already. Must be in the blood. I can't walk down the road myself without women throwing themselves at me.'

'Throwing themselves under buses, more likely.'

'Jack!' said Samantha, giving Liam a playful shove. Liam giggled and suddenly sat in the soil.

'Liam mate, I don't think we want to sit in the dirt, do we? What's your mother going to say when I get you home?'

Jack hauled Liam upright and passed him back into Samantha's clutches. I leaned down to look at the guinea pigs. They were both brown and white and large. One had short fur, the other looked like an escaped beard.

'I thought they were smaller than this,' I said. Tony sometimes bought things off men in pubs. Perhaps someone had sold him a brace of beavers.

'I thought they were, too,' said Tony. 'I remembered them being about the size of hamsters. They're probably cross-breeds. Half bear or something.'

The guinea pigs looked at me and chattered to one another.

'This one must be Jack,' I said, choosing the hairier one.

'Jack!' agreed Samantha. Perhaps she'd call everyone Jack. I couldn't decide whether that would make life more or less complicated.

'No,' said Jack, 'the other one's Jack. This is Liam.'

'I'm going to do a run for them, for when the weather's warmer,' said Tony. 'Not enough room for them in there. Look at the size of them.'

'Are you going to do anything with the other end? Down there where that shed is?'

'Haven't thought about it really.' He leant on his spade and wiped his forehead. 'Don't know what's keeping Caz,' he said after a pause. 'She might not be down. Things to think about, you know.'

I did know. Family things. You never get clear of them. There I was, mortgage and job, amicable relations with the B&S Building Society, a fully trained trench digger and still I was as tied to my family as I had been when I was three weeks old and relying on them for everything. There didn't seem to be a week that didn't contain news of one or more relatives discovering worrying lumps or forgetting where the garden was. Cousins got married, sometimes to one another, and produced children. I had to buy more Christmas presents every year, but every year I got fewer back. I could only be sure of getting two presents. One of those would be from me, and it'd be something I wanted. The other one would be from Jack, and it would be something impractical – an empty budgie cage, say, or a heavy ring designed to be inserted somewhere tender. I didn't think I'd be getting a present off Jack this year. I might get something from Judy if we lasted until Christmas. I didn't know if I deserved to keep her. A night or two before I'd been comparing her to Lisa and she'd been coming second in all categories. OK in a big field, bad when there are only two competitors. I knew that Judy wouldn't be happy to know that. I wanted her to be happy. She was stunning. She was marble, alabaster, a figurine. I wanted to keep her somewhere and look upon her and perhaps knock out bad poetry. I wanted to adore her.

I wanted to tear Lisa's clothes off and fuck her on the kitchen floor.

I decided that these were different things – spiritual and physical, perhaps – and that because of that, I wasn't actually being mentally unfaithful. I thought of them in different ways. I've never been unfaithful. I've been around unfaithful people and it doesn't work. An affair doesn't work. It's like the killer whale they used to have at Dudley Zoo. It's just too big to fit in there and sooner or later it gets out and there's mayhem.

They really did used to have a killer whale at Dudley Zoo. It was called Cuddles and it regularly bit its keepers. It used to live in a tank about the size of the children's paddling pool in the park. Trembling wet-suited keepers would clamber into the pool to play a few games and emerge bleeding from huge bite wounds.

Cuddles the killer whale was the most popular attraction in Dudley Zoo.

Anyway, that's what affairs are like, large mad fish in very small tanks. The very least that will happen is the carpet getting wet.

After an hour or so Tony began to drop hints about getting on with the gardening.

'If you cleared off I could get on with the gardening,' he said.

'We'd better be getting off then,' I said. 'It'll be time for Liam's tea soon. What're you having?'

Liam ignored me.

'So long then, princess,' Jack said. 'I'll be back soon. Shall I bring this little fellow to see you?'

'No,' said Samantha.

'And what about Liam?' he asked, giving me an evil grin.

'Jack!' said Samantha.

'Liam,' said Jack. 'I'm Jack. I'm taller than Liam and more charming.'

'Jack!' said Samantha. I was still unhappy that it seemed to be her favourite name. What was wrong with Sam? That was a terrific name. Jack was the sort of name you'd give to a donkey, and not necessarily a favourite one.

'Right then, fair enough. I'll see you. And you too, Tone. Kisses to the missus.'

Tony said goodbye to Jack, gave Liam a pat on the head, waved vaguely in my direction and turned his attention back to his trenches. Samantha went and peered at the guinea pigs, and they peered at her.

I said goodbye to her.

'Jack!' she said.

The drive back was terrifying. I'd imagined that we'd been having a nice afternoon, or at least a less obviously horrible one. Meeting the family, doing the garden – a spot of real life like you find in sitcoms, where problems last half an hour or less. Everything seemed to be on an even keel.

If anyone could break the spell, it was Jack.

'I had to talk to someone,' he said out of the blue. I looked at him. He was looking straight ahead, keeping his eyes on the road. He was looking where he was going. I didn't think I wanted to go there. Usually, he paid no attention to the road. He'd glance at it once in a while, then fiddle with the radio or the heating. He was looking at the road so that he wouldn't have to look at me. He was going to spoil my afternoon.

'I had to tell someone,' he said. 'I couldn't cope with it any more. The things I remembered . . .'

I looked at Liam, strapped into a child's seat. He'd found

something interesting in his nose and he was busy distributing it around the back of the van. He wasn't interested in the conversation. So, Jack had told someone. It didn't have to be a disaster.

'Who?' I asked. Probably Lisa, I told myself, and she'd know he was mad. She'd have assumed that he was drunk or something. She was mad herself. Just as long as it wasn't one of his drinking friends, like Eddie Finch. Eddie would have sold his grandmother to Idi Amin for a good story. It would be fine, I told myself, as long as it wasn't –

'Eddie Finch,' said Jack. 'I told him all about it. Everything we did.'

There you go, I thought. That's the worst that can happen.

It wasn't, of course. That was just the start of the fun.

PART FOUR

Sam, aged twenty

Chapter Nine

—◆—

I

It was November. The nights were getting colder and darker.
I had a thick coat, a scarf, gloves, and layers of underclothes.
Jack was wearing the leather jacket he always wore over old
faded clothes. He didn't have any gloves. And scarves were
out of the question.

There was a full moon. We were at the end of the old
railway tracks leading to Dudley Port, an area of flat sand
where the railway tracks end. There was nothing else there.
There hasn't been anything there since the last century.

There is now.

Jack was carrying a small sack, and in the sack were a
few body parts. Some fingers and a few toes. Things that
weren't too wet. We'd learned the hard way that tongues
made a mess when you removed them from their owner,
and they made a mess all the way to the burial ground.
Because fingers and toes have more hard than soft in them,
they bleed out quickly. They're also light. You wouldn't
want to carry an arm all the way across town. We steered
clear of genitalia. We weren't perverts. We left eyes where
they were, too. In horror novels, eyeballs pop out without

much effort. Someone hiccups and their eyes are in the soup. In the real world, they don't come out intact. We experimented with a spoon but it really didn't work. We tried using a vacuum cleaner, which worked but the eyeball vanished up the tube and into the cleaner. Neither of us felt like going through a vacuum cleaner bag. So we settled for fingers instead.

We needed to bury the body parts at the end of the tracks. That was in the parchment. Something of each victim had to be taken and buried there. The parchment was very specific about some things. The end of the railway line was specified. Jack asked to see the parchment every now and then, but he wasn't at a suitable level. He was good for carrying body parts and bumping off victims. He hadn't got the hang of much else. This was the fifth and last victim. Five was the specified number. It had been foretold.

A dog barked somewhere. I'd noticed that a dog always barked somewhere at this time of night. The railway lines passed through a deep entrenchment. I wondered who'd put it there. Who'd have a job like digging trenches? I was heading for better things. We passed through a short tunnel. We hadn't got a torch. The first time, we'd been worried about the tunnel. It was less than a hundred yards long, and dead straight. You could see light at the other end, unless you were going through it at night. Then it was very dark and quite frightening.

I'd decided we couldn't take a torch. It would be too obvious. It'd be visible for miles. The castle overlooked the railway lines. We didn't want a rival gang of satanists or cultists getting involved.

In the tunnel, it was darker and colder. The wind blew

straight through. Most of the railway sleepers had gone, and the ones that were left tripped you.

'Bollocks,' Jack said. 'Dropped the bastard.'

He fumbled about in the dark. Something scuttled towards us and stopped. Jack found the sack and we went on. The railway lines led into a wide area of open sand bounded by black trees. The sand was of the wrong consistency. It was loose on the top and difficult to walk in. It was packed solid and soaking wet underneath and it was difficult to bury things in. The railway tracks led halfway across it and then stopped, next to nothing. Perhaps there had been buildings here at one time. Perhaps there once was a pork scratchings factory, full of pigs with eczema. We stood at the end of the line. There were some sticks by the end of the rails, which we'd left there previously. They were three feet long and solid. They weren't much use for digging. We used them for digging.

After the first burial, Jack had wanted to bring a shovel. 'Why not take a spade? I mean we're digging holes.'

'We can't carry a spade. What if we got caught with it? What would we tell people it was for?'

He wiped his hands on his jeans, which didn't make anything cleaner. 'What if we get caught with a bag of fingers? "Sorry officer, they're spares. I like to carry some with me in case I lose one."'

He held out his arms, hands close together.

'That's a point,' I admitted.

'A *point*? If we were caught carrying a spade we could say, been gardening. Been to work on the building site. Leant it to a mate and I'm taking it home. What's this constable going to think? Oh yes, carrying a spade, must have been out burying bodies? Course he fucking isn't.'

'It's written. We take nothing with us. We use what we find.'

'Oh well, fair enough. It is fucking written. *Where* is it written?'

'On the parchment.'

'And can I see this parchment?'

'You'll see it when the time is right.'

'Oh good. I was worried about that. Because I wouldn't want to see it when the time was wrong . . . Is that a dog?'

'Shadow.'

'Looks like a dog.'

'It's a dog's shadow, then. A dog left it here. Happier now?'

'Oh yeah, fucking delighted. Ghost dogs on the railway tracks.'

'I think Andrew Eldritch has that line under copyright.'

'Yeah, well he can fuck off.' Jack picked up a stick and began to dig with it. I took a stick and joined him. The shadow edged closer. Jack was right. It was a small dog, dark brown and fat. It eyed the sack Jack had put on the floor.

'Here, fetch,' said Jack, throwing his stick. The dog ran after it. 'There's a good shadow. Always nice to see an obedient shadow. Some of them are right buggers.'

'You were right,' I said, 'it was a dog. I admit it. No need to gloat.'

'I'm not doing it because I need to. I do it because I like it.'

'You do it because you rarely get the chance.'

The dog returned, dragging the stick. It looked at the sack and sidled closer.

'Who wants a bone then?' asked Jack. 'Who wants a little

finger bone? Well, you can't. These bones have to be buried. It is *written*.'

I kicked the dog. It yipped and ran off.

'Nice one,' said Jack. 'You could have kicked me. I was the one pissing you off.'

Sometimes he's almost perceptive. To prove it, I kicked him.

II

I showed him the parchment a week later, in his bedroom. His mother was in the bathroom, singing. Among other things. I didn't want to think about Jack's mother in the bath or anywhere else. It wasn't that she was ugly or fat. She was, but that wasn't it. She was his mother.

'Sit on the bed. And turn the light down.'

'Why?'

'It's an old parchment. It's been in the dark a long time.'

'I know how it feels. Will I be able to touch it?'

'Of course not. It's valuable. It's a scrap of the past. Now, sit still.'

I let him see the wallet the parchment stays in. I opened it so that he could see the folded parchment in its plastic cover.

'Oh, wow,' he said, leaning forward. 'Woo. It's a piece of paper, folded up. It could be a page from the *Herald*. We're murdering people because of that, are we?'

'It's a parchment,' I told him. 'It tells us what must be done. And we aren't murdering people. We are converting them into a different type of energy. We are using their underlying potential.'

'Oh excellent, we're doing them some good. I'll have to remember that when we're in court.'

'We're going to live very long lives if we get this right.'

I wasn't sure about that. I knew what the ritual was for, but I wasn't sure if it would work on both of us. Perhaps it'd affect someone else altogether. That's the trouble with magic. It's about as reliable as a builder's estimate.

'Terrific. What are we going to do?' Jack said. 'What's the procedure for living a very long time? Do we have to pretend to be our own children so that people don't get suspicious? Do we have to get the opposite of Grecian 2000 and make ourselves go grey? Do we have to give our houses to ourselves every fifty years? It's going to be tricky.'

'Granted, dying would be easier. But it's not often thought of as the best option.'

'No, it's usually thought of as the only option.'

'Yes, well this time it isn't.'

He watched me put the parchment in my pocket. There was a silence. We'd started to have silences. We were spending a lot of time together, mostly in the dark. We were at the far end of adolescence. I wondered whether Jack was a virgin. I presumed he was. In Dudley there are girls who'll shag anything for a bag of chips and a kind word, and they aren't too fussy about the kind word. That wouldn't do it for Jack. He'd want a big romance, I thought. We sat on the bed. I wondered what he was thinking about. He'd had his eyes on me while I was putting the parchment away. He'd watched my legs. I was wondering what he was thinking.

I didn't want him getting fixated on me. He needed to find a girlfriend. Perhaps I could persuade someone.

If he'd just get the hang of soap it'd help.

'What's that?' asked Jack, looking at the floor. His floor was covered with piles of magazines – a collection made up of ones about motorbikes, airguns, and a stack of those magazines for men that men buy in case there's some real porn inside – and assorted dead clothes.

Jack's mother isn't big on tidying. She understands what the word means, but she doesn't know how to apply it to the world. Jack's father isn't the father he used to have. His first father left with someone else, as they do. The latest father has a motorbike and no road sense. Jack will outlive him even if the ritual doesn't work. Jack had lived alone with his mother for a long time. They'd reverted to her maiden name, Ives. When Jack hit adolescence she started dating. Carbon dating, to judge by her looks. She didn't marry the new fathers. She just got drunk with them for a few weeks and then cried when they failed to stay.

I tried to time my visits to avoid those stages of her relationships. It wasn't easy. They were the longest and loudest stages. In some of the relationships, they were the only stages.

I wondered about Jack. He'd lived alone with his mother for many years. There hadn't been a father figure. Statistically, he was likely to display feminine traits. Statistically, he was likely to develop strange fixations.

I didn't think he was developing feminine traits. His bedroom looked anything but feminine. A woman would have cleaned it, or thrown in lit matches and hoped for the best.

Strange fixations were another matter. I moved slightly away from him. I didn't want my apprentice getting a crush on me. There's this idea that crushes stop when adolescence does, and it isn't the case. It's just that you can put them in context. You've been there before and you know the way through. Jack put his feet on the bed.

'What are you doing?' I asked him.

'There's something down there,' he said. 'I saw something.'

'What, a patch of clean floor? Perhaps you could move some old socks there. If they aren't moving by themselves.'

'Something is moving by itself.'

'Oh?' I looked down. There was nothing there that I could see, but then there could have been anything hiding amid the debris.

'There,' said Jack. Something scuttled under a magazine. I didn't see it clearly, but it looked too big to be an insect and too small to be anything else.

It had a lot of legs. It looked like the woodlouse I'd raised from the dead. I put my legs on the bed. I wasn't keen on insects.

'It's that thing,' Jack said. 'The one you killed then brought back. It's followed us.'

'It was a woodlouse, not a homing pigeon. Keep things in perspective, Jack. This is a different thing.'

'So how come you've got your feet on the furniture?'

'I know it's a different thing. I don't know whether it's a friendly different thing or not. It might sting or something.'

I tried to spot the insect. Given its size, it was good at hiding.

'If you had a clean floor we might be able to see it,' I said.

'I don't want to see it,' said Jack. 'I've seen enough of it. If there are parts of it I haven't seen that's fine with me. What's it here for?'

'Perhaps it wants to read about airguns.'

'It's probably looking for you, mate. You're the one that resurrects woodlice. It probably wants you to put it in touch with its mother.'

'I'll put it in touch with its maker if I catch it.'

The insect emerged from under a discarded shirt several feet from where we'd last seen it. It looked to be part woodlouse and part cockroach. It had a touch of something else about it. Rottweiler, maybe.

It had mossy growths growing on its carapace and seemed less symmetrical than most insects. I couldn't count its legs. It waved long antennae in the air then moved towards us.

Jack hadn't spotted it.

'It's down here,' I told him. 'It's coming this way.'

He looked at the insect.

'You've given us a plague of insects,' he said. 'Nice one.'

'What do you mean, a plague? There's only one.'

'How many do you want? One is enough. It's a plague of fucking beetle and it's your fault, so you sort it out.'

'How?'

'Tread on it.'

'These are new shoes.'

'All the better, they'll still be solid. Go on, flatten the fucker.'

Jack had backed to the wall. The insect was heading directly for the bed, or as directly as it could with all the junk on the floor. It stopped to examine an abandoned plate and then moved on. It reached the point where it would have been under the bed if it kept crawling. It stopped.

It chittered.

'Oh fuck, it's that thing,' said Jack. 'I fucking knew it. You've brought it back from the dead and now it's after us.'

'It's about an inch long, how bad can it be?'

The magazine the insect had first vanished under caught my eye. There was something wrong with the cover. There were insects on it. Several of them. Big ones. They looked similar to the one that was standing by the bed.

'How many offspring do woodlice have?' I asked.

'Why?' asked Jack. He hadn't seen yet.

'Idle speculation,' I said. I thought about the woodlouse I'd resurrected. Sometimes woodlice had eggs gathered under their shells. They carried them about until they hatched, like good parents. I hadn't checked the underside of the sacrificial woodlouse. It hadn't seemed important at the time.

I wondered whether I might have caused some collateral damage.

A large faded poster of Raquel Welch wearing what looked like the skins of two small rabbits was on the far wall. It was moving. Thin feelers felt the air around it. Flat leggy bodies emerged from behind it.

'Jack?'

'What?'

'How many insects does it take to make a plague of insects?'

'One. I've told you that.'

'Right. In that case we've got plagues of insects. There are more of them.'

'More than what?'

'More than ten. They're all over that wall.'

Jack looked. 'Oh fuck,' he said. He turned pale and hauled his legs close to his body. He looked at the ceiling. I looked up too. There was nothing up there.

The one that was looking up at the bed chittered. Answering

chitters came from various places around the room. The insects that had crawled from behind the poster dropped to the floor one by one.

'They can't climb very well,' I said. 'Their legs are all wrong. They can't get up here.'

'Cool,' said Jack. 'Excellent news. We can stay on the bed. They get the rest of the room. Nice one. The first time you get something to work, it fucks my room up.'

'We're safe up here,' I said. 'We can flatten them one at a time. It's not a problem.'

'No, it wouldn't be. It's not your room.'

'We can deal with them,' I told him. I took off a shoe and tested it for weight. It felt solid. I looked at the first insect. It seemed to be looking back at me, but it was difficult to tell. It had compound eyes and it seemed to be looking everywhere.

'Let's see how solid they are,' I said, leaning over. I raised the shoe.

A crack appeared along the back of the insect. Its carapace split into two and opened. It emitted a nasty little noise and unfurled a pair of transparent, veined wings.

'Oh fuck,' I said, and flattened it with the shoe. I raised the shoe.

It wasn't going to be chittering again, that was for sure. It had turned into a greenish paste.

A low sound came from all around the room. It didn't sound very cheerful. I'd never heard angry insects before. Now I could hear a lot of them all at once.

That's the trouble with magic. It can make angry insects.

The sound rose around us.

'What the fuck is going on?' asked Jack.

'I think they're upset.'

The sound stopped. The insects stopped moving. I saw the carapaces of two split and open. I watched them unfurl their wings.

'Upset?' asked Jack. 'You're sure they can't get up here?'

A buzzing filled the room. It sounded like hornets. A pioneering insect left the floor, held up by a blur of whirring wings.

'Not absolutely sure,' I said, priming my shoe. 'Not one hundred per cent sure.'

Another couple of insects flew from the floor. They were no steadier in the air than they had been on their legs. I knew that woodlice couldn't fly.

The last of them rose from the floor. There seemed to be a lot of them hanging in the air between us and the door. They looked large and numerous. Perhaps they'd been eating old socks.

A chittering joined the humming. It rose to a peak.

I wondered why Jack wasn't complaining. I risked a quick look away from the insects. Jack was huddled on the bed, arms around his legs. He had the thousand-yard stare of a combat veteran.

The chittering stopped. I looked back at the insects and saw them just before they landed on us.

Jack let out a girlish screech and flew from the bed. I dropped my shoe. I felt something slide down my collar. I hauled off my top.

A series of sharp pains let me know that the insects were unfriendly. They'd invaded my clothes. I couldn't even see them. I undid my belt and removed my trousers. I threw them to the floor and jumped on them. Anything still in there wasn't getting out in one piece. I watched Jack doing the same thing, dragging his clothes off and dancing on them, stamping the life out of whatever was in there.

His underwear was dirtier than I'd imagined.

The bedroom door opened. The chittering and buzzing stopped. Jack's mother entered the room, wearing a towel and a grim expression. She looked at us.

'What have you two been doing?' she asked. 'It sounded like there was an orgy going on.'

She looked at us again. It struck me that most of our clothes were on the floor. Jack was only wearing his underpants. I wasn't wearing much more than that myself.

I had cleaner pants, but I didn't think that was going to count in my favour.

'There were insects,' Jack said. 'All over us.'

There was no sign of the insects. I found my shoe and picked it up. A mess of greenish fluid and cracked chitin covered half of the sole. I showed it to Jack's mother. She looked at it.

'Insects?' she asked. I nodded.

'Big ones,' said Jack. 'Foreign ones. Mexican cockroaches. I've read about them. That's what it was.'

'Mexican cockroaches? Spanish fly, more like,' said his mother. She gave us a look of disgust and closed the bedroom door.

III

That's the trouble with magic. Unexpected things happen.

Sometimes you need to change plans unexpectedly. It's a cutthroat business. You have to be ready to adapt.

That happened when we killed Mrs Bolton.

She was our first victim. I knew we couldn't take weapons with us. The parchment said so. You would find something there, and that would do the job. Everyone had knives, water, electricity, string. There would be something you could use. Jack objected to this, naturally.

'Well what if we took a penknife? That's just for sharpening pencils with.'

'Then why would we be taking it with us?'

'To stab her.'

'Then it'd count as a weapon.'

'Oh, would it? That's my plan fucked then. How about if we took half a brick? Half a brick isn't a weapon.'

'It is if you hit someone with it.'

'Well what if I took one and you didn't know about it? Would that count? You could find it there then.'

'We don't take anything with us. We use something we find and we take part of the body with us when we go.'

'Well it beats going to the school disco. I still think I could have something, though. If you didn't know I was carrying it.'

We were on our way to see Mrs Bolton. She lived alone, which was helpful. She lived on the Russells Hall Estate, which was also helpful. No one there would pop round to see what the matter was if we made too much noise. They only popped round to the neighbour's house when the neighbour was out at work. Walking there, we didn't pass anyone except for bored teenagers. They swore elaborately and at some length.

'Ignore them,' I said. 'We'll outlive them.'

'There'll be more of them,' said Jack. 'Teenagers are like that.'

We reached the last house in a row of identical houses.

'Here?' asked Jack.

I nodded. 'Number fifteen,' I said.

'Who is it?'

'We don't know her. I know *about* her. Mrs Bolton. Old woman. Forty, fifty, you know, old. Lives on her own, except maybe for one or two cats.'

'Cats?'

'Cats. Furry things, about so big, eat fish and purr. They do have them in Dudley, don't they? In tins perhaps?'

'I meant, do we have to kill them too?'

I was surprised by that. We weren't into random cruelty.

'Christ, no,' I said. 'What do you take me for? The cats live.'

'Right,' said Jack, relieved.

'Now, the cover story.'

'What cover story?'

'This one. We've broken down. We want to use the telephone. You've hurt your leg. Can you limp?'

'Like this?'

Jack tried a few paces. I've seen more convincing limping. Still, Mrs Bolton was old and old people will fall for anything.

'It'll have to do. If I'd have thought about it earlier I'd have bruised you, given you a kick or two. That'd help.'

'Not me, it wouldn't.'

'Too late now anyway.'

'Hold on, how did I hurt my leg? We broke down, we didn't crash. What happened to my leg?'

'Right, forget the leg.'

'What's happened to this forward planning?'

'It's adapted to the situation. That's the sign of good planning. I'm ready for all contingencies.'

'You're ready for a padded fucking cell. So, we've broken down, we want to use the telephone, then what?'

'We get in and split up. The one she's not looking at grabs whatever looks most likely to kill her and hits her with it. After that we can both join in and finish her off.'

'And if she makes a noise?'

'Don't let her make a noise. Hit her really hard.'

'You're sure about this?'

'I am. I've studied the signs. She's going to a better place.'

'Not too difficult, if you start from Russells Hall Estate. Then we get to live forever?'

'We'll run through the theory of it another time. For now, let's get this one done.'

'No problem. After you, then.'

'After me,' I said, strolling to the door of number fifteen and knocking loudly on the door.

IV

Mrs Bolton stood in the centre of her front room in a sea of cats. Jack was pretending to telephone for assistance, having actually dialled a random 0898 number. I was attempting to get on Mrs Bolton's blind side without putting my feet on any cats. I wanted to get there so that I could kill her without distressing her unnecessarily, but the cats were making it difficult. They kept looking at me with large round reflective eyes as though they knew what I was up to. It was also difficult because Mrs Bolton had the sort of uncorrected squint you wouldn't normally expect to find outside of documentaries about third world countries where the nearest hospital is eight hundred miles away and the only surgeon died the year before last. Her eyes looked away from each other as if they were afraid of her nose. They might well have been. It was a frightening nose, with tufts of hair and a sticky drip that never fell dangling from its tip. Her left eye looked left and her right eye looked right. It was impossible to say whether both eyes were in working order or, if not, which one was. She had an apparent field of vision of 270 degrees. I thought that the best way to take her by surprise would be from the front, as she couldn't possibly focus there. I couldn't say so.

Jack said: 'Car. Yes, the distributor. It's fallen off,' to which the reply seemed to be an orgasmic moan. I circled Mrs Bolton, searching for something to hit her with. Cats rubbed my ankles. They rubbed Jack's ankles.

'They like you,' said Mrs Bolton. 'They're such good judges of character. Bless their little hearts.'

They said owners grew to resemble their pets. It was true. Mrs Bolton was covered in cat hair, and she stank of cat piss. She was wearing a number of cardigans, each of them clogged with fur.

I spotted a huge vase resting on a small round table and homed in on it. It looked heavy. It should do the trick. I reached out for it.

It was heavy. I tried to lift it. It stayed where it was.

'And the spark plug,' said Jack, 'that's split.'

'Do you want a cup of tea?' asked Mrs Bolton.

'Yes please,' we both answered. We didn't know who she was talking to. She was looking at both of us, and we were on opposite sides of the room.

'I'll get the kettle,' she said. As she made for the door I tried to take advantage of my position. I hauled at the vase and it moved. I got a grip on its neck and lost it. It swivelled from my grasp and fell among the cats, causing consternation. It had been heavy because it had been full of water.

It became empty. The floor became wet. The cats became lively and vocal.

'What!' shouted Mrs Bolton, turning from the door, all cardigans and indignation. 'Cat murderer!'

She flew at me like a knitted rocket. I fell among the cats. She fell on me.

'Sam!' cried Jack. He dropped the telephone and grasped Mrs Bolton by the neck, turning her over, freeing me.

'Don't strangle her,' I said, standing and shaking cats from my arms. 'We have to use something here. That's part of it. We have to use something she owns.'

Mrs Bolton lay on her back struggling, wild-eyed. But then, Mrs Bolton had been wild-eyed before we'd met her. We couldn't be blamed for her facial problems. Jack held her down.

'Do something,' he said. 'She's gone mental.'

I couldn't find anything to use as a weapon. The television was too heavy and its flex was too short. Mrs Bolton began to gather breath for a scream.

'Fuck,' said Jack. Mrs Bolton looked offended. She paused, and then opened her mouth.

'Fuck,' I said. I picked up the largest and slowest of the cats, a fat black thing like an overstuffed cushion, and dropped it over Mrs Bolton's face.

Her scream was muffled.

I put my hands on the cat and pressed it firmly over

her face. Her feet scrabbled on the floor. Her slippers fell off.

The state of her feet . . . I mean, honestly, we were doing her a favour.

She struggled harder.

The fat cat purred. It was having a nice time. The other cats gathered and watched. They began to sniff at Mrs Bolton's outlying regions. They had always liked Mrs Bolton as a source of food, and now she was becoming a different one.

Mrs Bolton's struggles gradually abated. The fat cat purred and unleashed a contented fishy yawn. The telephone dangled, and a tiny voice told tales that you wouldn't tell your mother.

V

We took one of her toes with us and buried it at the end of the railway lines. The cats got the rest.

VI

My uncle, Mickey Payne, used to talk about the old railway lines. He told us he had some trouble there once.

'You've had trouble everywhere,' my father said. My mother was upstairs. She doesn't like Mickey. He's a bit rough. He's got scars on his hands and his face. He told me he was in the army and they were on active duty and someone rolled a grenade at them.

You think about things like that, things like grenades, and

you think about what they're for and killing five people is nothing anymore. Killing five people doesn't come close. There are people out there making flame throwers, nerve gases, improved strains of Ebola, faster-acting Lassa. I haven't done anything on that scale. All I did was kill five people. That's nothing.

I wonder whether Mickey killed people when he was in the army. He wasn't in action when he was injured. His squad were walking to the pub and someone rolled a grenade at them. The four of them stood and looked at it and then, that's as much as he can tell me. Whatever else happened, happened out of real time. The next thing he remembers is the hospital.

'Dishy nurses,' he'll say, sitting in my father's chair. He always sits in that one. I think my father is afraid of him. I'm sure he isn't really my uncle.

I asked my father, 'Who would throw a grenade at Uncle Mickey?'

My father said he'd try to get a list together when he had a spare month.

I think about it. What did Mickey do afterwards? He left the army.

'Hands were no good after that,' he'll say, sitting in my father's favourite chair, a cigarette in one hand, a cheap beer in the other. 'Shot to buggery.'

He doesn't swear the way my friends do. He just *swears*, it's just what he does. He can't speak without swearing. I imagined him swearing at the men who'd rolled a grenade into his patrol. He would never say where it had happened.

'It didn't make the news,' he'd say. 'The brass wanted it out of the papers. Look bad on them, see. Look bad on the rest of them.'

My father didn't believe it. He didn't say so, but I could tell. I think Uncle Mickey could tell, too. I think he knew. When my father was there he'd keep talking about it.

He said he'd been in trouble by the old railway line.

'There's a tunnel there,' he said.

This was last Sunday, and it had been weeks since we'd been there. The ritual was done. I looked in the mirror every day and I didn't look any older.

I suppose you notice it happening, getting older? Or is it something that creeps up on you?

'You know that tunnel?' he asked. 'Dark as a black cat's arsehole at midnight.'

'Never been down there,' I said.

'Oh?' he said, raising what was left of his eyebrows. Most of the right one was missing, and there were scars running over his nose and down to his jaw.

'No,' I said.

'Right,' he said. He couldn't have known anything. There were only six people involved, not counting myself. One of them was Jack. The rest were dead.

'I don't go out much,' I said.

'I'd try and get used to it,' he said. Ash fell from his cigarette and landed on the carpet.

'Clean that up,' my father said after Mickey Payne had gone home. He lived somewhere in Tipton. 'Don't let your mother find it.'

My mother stays away from Mickey Payne. I know the bigger picture, I know the history that we all fit into, but I don't know all of my parents' history. They have stories hidden away.

So do I, by the way. I've had to tell a few lies. It comes

with the territory. I've told Jack one or two. I've told myself a couple. Seems unfair not to if you're lying to everyone else.

VII

After we buried the last part of the last victim, we watched the dog for a while. It kept out of reach.

'It wants the bones,' said Jack. 'Dogs like bones.'

I looked for something to throw at it. There was nothing available. The mud was too muddy and Jack was too heavy. The dog circled us at a distance then eventually moved off, scrambling up the embankment and vanishing into the shrubbery.

'All done,' I said. 'That's us finished. Now all we have to do is live forever. That wasn't so painful, was it?'

'Could have been worse,' agreed Jack. 'I don't feel any different though. Should I feel different?'

'You should look different, never mind feel different. This is only eternal life, not a miracle.'

'Yeah well. Ask me again in two hundred years.'

Jack gave the grave a last look and then followed me through the tunnel. I knew he'd be all right. It was nothing he couldn't cope with. He'd enjoyed the deaths, as far as I could tell. He might not be stable, but I was fairly sure that he wouldn't tell anyone what we'd done.

PART FIVE

Sam, aged thirty

Chapter Ten

I

I called work on Monday morning and told them I wasn't feeling well. Which wasn't quite true. I was feeling fucking awful.

Eddie would have our names in print. The whole story would be in the local paper, all because of some insane thing Jack had come up with.

I brushed my hair in the wrong direction and went to the newsagent before I shaved. If my name was in the paper, I didn't want people recognizing me. This was Dudley, and if people thought that I was a mass murderer they might ask for my autograph. Perhaps Eddie would have treated the story as a joke. Perhaps his editor would have turned it down. I presumed he had an editor. I bought the *Pensnett Herald* without looking at it and skulked home.

Everyone seemed to be looking at me. Perhaps that was because I was skulking, unshaven, and had my hair brushed the wrong way. I got home, locked myself in, and unfolded the paper.

The story was on page one. Well, the first part of it was. There was more of it on pages two and three. It was interrupted by a full-page advertisement for a furniture warehouse, and then returned on page five. Page six was the letters page, and that was full of the usual grumbles ('I fought in three world wars . . .', 'Why do young people go to London? We have everything you want here in Pensnett . . .'). We weren't in the classified ads or the sports pages, just those four full-page spreads. I had another look at them. The first time I hadn't read them. I'd seen them, but it hadn't got into my head. My brain wasn't able to accept the information.

I gave it a nip of whisky. That calmed it down.

I don't normally drink in the morning, but normal rules didn't apply. It wasn't a normal day.

On page one there was a headline.

DUDLEY MURDER COUPLE MURDER FIVE.

Under that was a photograph of Jack, next to a photograph of me. Mine was an old school photograph taken on the one day in my life when I'd brushed my hair the wrong way by accident. The photo of Jack was recent. In case there was any doubt as to who the murderers were, our names were printed in what looked to me like ninety-point type. Below that was some of Eddie's more excitable prose.

On page two was Jack's confession. He'd assisted in the murders of five people. Parts of them had been buried in various places in Dudley. There were photographs of some of the places. I knew them, as they'd been in the documentary that had started Jack's delusions.

On page three was a map of Dudley, with the MURDER SITES marked, and the SHALLOW GRAVES noted.

On page four was a list of other famous Dudley-based killers, including a paragraph about Cuddles, the killer whale. It also mentioned James Whale, who spent part of his life in Dudley before going to Hollywood and not coming back.

While he was there he directed *Frankenstein* and *The Bride of Frankenstein*, both starring Boris Karloff. The article included Frankenstein's hapless creation in its list of Dudley murderers.

I had another nip of whisky. The whole thing was ridiculous. Jack was mad. They'd dig where he said the bodies were buried, find nothing, and that'd be that. This time next week, I thought, it'll all be over. I could do the digging for them, if they liked. I was good at digging.

After a week we'd only be featuring on the letters page. Then that would be that. Some good could come of it, I realized.

Fame gets you free drinks in a Dudley local.

I had another nip of whisky. I imagined being in a pub, a week later, with people buying me whiskies.

'So how did it feel?' they'd ask.

That's a terrific question. If a reporter ever asks you how it felt when your family melted or you were diagnosed with leprosy, put your finger in their eye – any finger, although obviously lepers may have fewer to choose from, either eye – and ask them how that feels.

I had another nip of whisky. I was upset at some level. That would be why I was thinking cruel thoughts about lepers and reporters and melting families. I was upset and slightly drunk. But then I realized there was no need to be, because Jack would soon be found out.

What would happen to him? Would he be taken away somewhere? I didn't know what happened. From my own observations I'd developed a theory that violently unstable people were given supervisory jobs in care homes for quietly unstable people, while dangerously unstable people were given bus passes and made to spend their lives orbiting the West Midlands.

Still, Jack would have to undergo treatment, if not imprisonment. He'd be carted off somewhere and given the sort of drugs only available in secure institutions and school playgrounds.

That would leave Lisa with no one to look after her.

Suddenly, the day seemed to be full of bonuses. In a week I'd be having free drinks and there would be the chance of consoling Lisa. There would be jokes from my friends and I'd be able to sell my story to the national press; failing that, to Eddie Finch.

The telephone rang, disturbing the pleasant thoughts. I answered it in case it was work, calling to make sure I was at home ill.

'Yes?' I said.

'Sam,' said a voice. I couldn't place it.

'Yes?'

'Are you drunk?'

Drunk seemed a strong word. Then, whisky seems a strong drink first thing in the morning. Perhaps I was drunk. I recognized the caller's voice.

'Tony,' I said. 'I'm not drunk. I'm off work ill.'

'They told me that. You're not off work because of this thing in the paper, then? You're not off work on account of you're ashamed to go out?'

'This is all something Jack's made up. He's off his head.'

'Is that why you brought him round to see my daughter? My wife?'

Tony's voice was harder than usual. It was flat and solid. He sounded worse than angry.

'You bring this maniac to my house and let him talk to Samantha. You let him play with her, and you knew what he was like? How do I know it's not true? I know what you were like back then. Dressed in black, reading all of that Crowley rubbish, hanging around the cemetery. For all I know you did what he said. I know you're capable of it. I know exactly what you're capable of.'

He listed some things I'd done wrong, a few indiscretions. Family things. He told me that I wouldn't be going to their house again, with or without Jack, guilty or not guilty. He said that it would reflect badly on Caroline and Samantha. I tried to explain what was going on but he said he'd heard enough and rang off.

I rang back but it was busy, and it stayed that way.

Strange. A few days ago I had been thinking that you never got away from your family. Now my brother – as close to my family as I was going to get – had severed all ties. My family had got away from me. My best friend was mad, and my girlfriend was moody.

I gave up taking gentle nips of whisky and started swigging it instead. I lay on the living room floor for a while and watched a woodlouse struggling up the wall. I discovered that drinking whisky from a bottle while prone results in a noseful of painful liquid.

I began to shake.

I was still doing that when the police arrived.

II

There were two of them. One male, one female, both younger

than me. The female one had police eyes, a look of equal parts distrust and dislike. The male one was doing his best to have police eyes, but the expression wasn't finished. He looked like quite a cross puppy.

'Yes?' I said.

'Police,' said the female one.

'Really?'

She ignored that. 'Can we ask you a few questions?'

'Come in,' I said. 'Coffee?'

'No thanks. I don't think this will take long, do you? It all seems cut and dried.'

'Oh. Yes. Come in, then.'

I led them to the living room and sat down. They stood over me. The male one looked at my shelves and suddenly got the expression he'd been trying for. He wasn't impressed with my shelves.

'Did you make those?' he asked.

'Yes. Didn't take long.'

'No, I wouldn't have thought so. So. You've seen the papers? You know this Mr Ives? Only he seems to know you quite well.'

'I know him.'

'Have you been drinking?' asked the female one. 'I'd say it was early to be drinking. I suppose you have a lot on your mind at the moment? With all of this murder business?'

I nodded.

'Well. Let's see what we can sort out. I'm PC Stiles and this is PC Fields. We just want to have a little chat. Nothing to worry about.'

'Nothing at all,' said Fields. He smiled.

'I see,' I said. This seemed to be a new approach. Nice cop, nice cop. Fields sat on the free chair. Stiles moved to stand directly in front of me.

Nice uniform, I thought. Fits well.

'Now. We've been sent by our boss, Inspector Moore. He's concerned about this story.'

'It doesn't reflect well on the area,' said Fields.

'It doesn't reflect well on us,' said Stiles.

'And it doesn't reflect well on you,' said Fields. 'I can see you'd be upset by this whole thing. We're obliged to look into it, of course. Inspector Moore is going to follow up a few things. Have a look what's gone on.'

'How long have you known Mr Ives?' asked Stiles.

'Since we were children.'

'How would you say he was? Mentally?' asked Fields. He flipped open a notepad and poised a chewed pencil over it.

'I wouldn't know. I know him, but he seems sane. Until recently. This is all new.'

'What's all new? Confessing to murders?'

'Yes. To my knowledge he hasn't confessed to murder before . . . He didn't murder anyone. I mean, neither of us did.'

'We wouldn't have thought so. Our problem is, the story is in the papers. People want to know what we're doing about it.'

'Pressure from above,' added Stiles. 'Politics. Influence.'

'When we spoke to your friend Jack, he seemed quite earnest,' said Fields. 'We do get people who confess to things, as a hobby. As a pastime. They tend to be strange.'

'Single,' said Stiles.

'Male,' said Fields. 'And while Mr Ives is male he isn't, technically, single. He seems to be in a relationship. It might be a strange relationship, and they might have strange hobbies.'

'Pastimes,' said Stiles.

'Of course, what people do in their own homes isn't any of our business.'

'Unless they're dismembering the lodgers or cultivating crops of narcotics.'

'But as we all know, people have strange ways. This is a multicultural society. We can't assume that because people behave differently, they are criminals.'

'Correct,' said Stiles. 'That would be my point, too. Sometimes people confess for strange reasons.'

'So what would you say Mr Ives' state of mind was?' asked Fields. 'Would you consider him more likely to murder people, or just to confess to it? Perhaps for reasons of a mental nature.'

'After all, body piercing suggests a need for self-violence. That might also reveal itself in false confessions.'

'You don't believe him, then?' I asked. They'd made it clear, but I was drunk and I wanted to be sure. Perhaps I was already out of danger.

'Course not,' said Stiles. She took a small step back and relaxed. 'It's not something we enjoy in the West Midlands police force, people confessing.'

'It's not that we want to frighten you,' said Fields. He was lying, of course. They wanted me to know that I'd be in for a hard time if they thought Jack was serious.

'Now,' said Stiles. 'You say that Mr Ives imagined all of this? His confession is false?'

I nodded.

'I need a verbal response, Mr Haines. Are you saying that Mr Ives made a false confession?'

'Yes.'

'That would seem to be that.'

Fields snapped shut his notepad and put it away.

'What happens now?' I asked.

'That's all,' said Stiles. 'We have a look at the places Mr Finch mentioned in his articles, if we think there's anything to go on. To tell the truth, there are no records of anyone going missing at that time. If five people are murdered, they're missed. No one missed anyone ten years ago. So that seems to be fair enough.'

'Inspector Moore will, of course, investigate further. He's very thorough.'

'More thorough than you might want, I sometimes think. So we'll be off now. We may be back in touch, but I doubt it. You can keep your passport. You're free to go wherever you want.'

'Now all we have left to do is rough up your friend Mr Ives and dump him on some wasteground.'

'He's joking,' said Stiles. Until she said that, I hadn't doubted it.

III

I sat down heavily and realized that I was sober. That didn't seem fair, after I'd put the time and effort into getting drunk. I didn't think the hangover would pass me by. That would turn up later in the afternoon. You can't outdrink hangovers unless you do the full Hendrix.

I wasn't satisfied. Something was wrong. Not just the accusations and the police popping round for a conversation loaded with veiled threats. If Jack was mad – I don't know the technical terms, so mad will have to do – it was new. He'd always been more or less sane.

Apart from the body piercing. But then, a lot of people go in for body piercing. It's not unusual. Many people observe their own genitals and think, that'd look cool with a nail in it.

I don't think like that. I think, a nail in that would hurt like fuck.

In any case, body piercing wasn't enough to make someone mad. It was more of a quick way to spot students. Whatever had happened to Jack had happened in another way.

He'd told me that he'd started thinking about it after the documentary we saw at Tony's house. I'd seen the same documentary, and it hadn't made me believe that I was a murderer. It must have been something else. There were programmes that made me want to commit murder. Most of them seemed to be on early Saturday evenings. But none of them made me think I'd already done it, because the person I most wanted to murder was on the TV at the time.

How do they become famous? These people who can't do anything. Where do they come from? You see them from time to time in guest spots on variety shows. Then suddenly there they are with an eighteen-week run of a forty-minute extravaganza with the usual dancers and guests who all turn out to be famous for being well known and mediocre. Bad boy bands fragment into four or five bad presenters; dismal soap actors become dreadful singers. Some vanish, and you think they've gone for ever. Then it turns out that they're club DJs making more money than some corporations. I would sit there on a Saturday watching this parade of nothing and a red mist would descend. I would become agitated. I would imagine slapping them. I don't think you could ever get tired of punching Jeremy Beadle. You could do it for months without the amusement value wearing off.

So television did lead me to think violent thoughts, true, but it didn't make me go out and act on them. I was too busy staying in and watching television.

Jack had got his ideas from somewhere. The documentary had clearly helped him along, but that had been a catalyst. Something else must have been involved. I flicked through the *Pensnett Herald*, hoping that something might spark off an idea.

If Jack had got his ideas from somewhere, I needed to know about it. If Jack was in trouble, I ought to do something about it.

Besides, I didn't seem to do anything much. This gave me something to do. It would give my life some excitement.

I thought about that list of Dudley-based murderers. Perhaps there were more. The *Herald* didn't go in for extensive research. Eddie certainly didn't. He went in for extensive drinking. I could start with the history of it all. Perhaps Jack had read something and forgotten he'd read it.

I didn't have any books on my shelves. I didn't have any books at all, come to think of it. I didn't get on with books. I'd have to go and find some.

I decided to start my investigations at the library. You couldn't get much more exciting than that.

Chapter Eleven

I

It took me some time to get ready to go out. I was sober but no one had told my fingers. They thought I was still drunk. They wouldn't work properly, which created difficulties while shaving.

I always think about growing a beard when I'm shaving. Women don't know how lucky they are, not needing to shave.

Of course, some of them do need to shave, but as a rule I don't mention it to them. That's one of those little rules for easier living. Don't tell women they have moustaches, they won't thank you for it.

So every day I have to go through this ritual, foaming up the face and scraping at it with a blade I ought to have changed three months ago. But razor blades are one of those things that fall off shopping lists, a category that also includes bin liners and toilet rolls. It's a lot of scraping to go through and sometimes I get a sore neck. I tried an electric shaver but the batteries went flat and batteries don't even get onto the shopping list. I tried shaving last thing at night, but that didn't work. I'd develop stubble around lunchtime. The sort of people whose job it is to sit in offices disapproving of things would look at it, disapprovingly.

It took me a long time to shave that day. Bristles appeared in areas I'd cleared. My hands were less steady than they might have been. They'd have been good for people shaking collecting tins.

I reached the library early in the afternoon. I must have missed the lunchtime rush as the building was deserted apart from three librarians waiting for life to come and find them. I went directly to the non-fiction department. The stairs had introduced a couple of new creaks into their repertoire.

The top storey was brightly lit but otherwise dull. I thought it'd be best to start with the Local History section. If Dudley had a history, I wanted to know about it. To my surprise, I learned a few interesting facts. Interesting if you live in Dudley, that is.

Firstly, Dudley wasn't always the dullest town in the world. Up until the eighth century it wasn't even there. There was a hill, and a lot of forest. Then along came an Anglo-Saxon wanderer, passing that way for unknown reasons. Perhaps he liked the look of the clouds.

He found a clearing, and settled there. Other people turned up and settled with him. His name was Dudda – not an unlikely name, many people in Dudley have names like that even now – and the Saxon word for a clearing is Leah.

The clearing in the woods miles from anywhere became known as Dudda-leah. Over the next few centuries this was knocked down to Dudley, for ease of use. Strangely, many residents of Dudley favour the old pronunciation, and still attempt to use it whenever possible.

In around 1070 AD the Midlands were knocked about by

the French. A French nobleman, not highly regarded, by the name of Ansculf of Piquigney built a castle there.

Some time after that – the dates are vague at best – royal approval was given for a market in the town. It's still there, and it still hasn't got anything you want, unless you want tea towels, transparent greetings cards and the overwhelming smell of fish.

The market caused Dudley to grow, in the same way that a melanoma causes a freckle to grow. The castle passed from lord to lord with a gap of several years that the history books didn't explain.

In due course, Henry VIII was crowned. Henry wasn't satisfied with being king and killing women who couldn't bear him children. He also wanted the lords to have more power. So it was that the lord of the castle at the time – John of Dudley, the lord finally having come to terms with having Dudley as part of his name – was granted a long list of supplementary titles, perhaps by way of compensation.

These included Earl Martial of England, Viscount Lisle, Duke of Northumberland, Earl of Warwick, and Baron of Somerie and Tyas.

I couldn't help noticing that all of those titles involved places other than Dudley.

John Dudley's long list of titles didn't do him much good in the long run. Henry was given to mood swings. During one of them he had John Dudley beheaded at Tower Hill. Which put Judy's mood swings in perspective. She was far worse. She'd never let you off with a beheading. First you'd have to guess what you were being beheaded for.

My theory about French architecture was flawed. Dudley Castle didn't collapse without assistance. Parts of it were

demolished during the Civil War. A fire took out the resi-
dential areas in 1750.

In the 1930s, the latest Lord decided to construct a zoo
around the castle. The castle sits on top of a hill overlooking
the town and the zoo covers the flanks of the hill.

I was taken to Dudley Zoo several times when I was young.
It was alleged to be a treat. My parents would drag me
up long inclined paths, past empty cages. Sometimes things
hidden in dark corners would whine. Chimpanzees wanked
joylessly over dangling tyres. Giraffes attempted to reach
above the cloud cover. In the reptile house empty enclosures
were marked:

CHAMELEONS – EXPERTS AT CAMOUFLAGE

A small lake in a larger enclosure held a crocodile, lying
still in the water, looking for all the world like a log. Closer
inspection revealed that it was a log. The crocodiles had been
shipped somewhere warmer.

A pen held giant tortoises, although I never saw them
emerge from their shells. Over the years I formed a theory
that the tortoises were tortoise shells.

Close to the exit a pets' corner had been constructed, with
goats and rodents to fondle, allowing the urban populace to
develop the sorts of diseases normally only found in rural
areas. Every path led up, and it would be raining. If it hadn't
been raining, we wouldn't have gone to the zoo. We'd have
gone for a walk in the countryside instead.

That was the history of Dudley, from its birth to the present
day. Founded by a man called Dudda, invaded by the French,
and home of few notable people.

The notable people were listed. James Whale, the director
of *Frankenstein*. Cuddles the killer whale, no relation. A

handful of rock groups that managed to get into the charts:
The Wonder Stuff, Ned's Atomic Dustbin. A handful that
didn't: Head of David, Belch Pop Frenzy. A local computer
company that did well back in the days of the ZX Spectrum,
Hardboiled Games, whose games featured a lot of magic,
black and otherwise. The heroes used magic. The villains
used magick.

I used to be interested in magic. I'll come clean about that.
Jack was right, I used to be into black magic. It was fun, in
the gloomiest sense of the word. I used to wear black clothes.
I used to drink black drinks. I was a goth, and I still have
some miserable records. Punk groups used to release singles
and albums on variously coloured vinyl – the UK Subs hardly
ever released a black vinyl album. Goth bands, on the other
hand, only released black vinyl albums. They would only
have used coloured vinyl if there had been a colour darker
than black.

Hardboiled Games released a lot of games, technically
accomplished ones for the time. There were only two people
in the company – this was in the early 80s, before computer
games were big business. One of them was into magic.
Or rather magick, as they preferred the Crowleyan spell-
ing.

He'd been involved in rituals at Dudley Castle. They used
to sneak in at night and fail to invoke demons. Their games
involved rituals, spells, and all sorts of fun stuff. In a short
press release, quoted in a book about industry in Dudley,
one of them mentioned a wizard who had once lived at
the castle.

I thought about that gap in the dates in the history books.
I'd heard something about a wizard at the castle. It must have

been one of those things you learn about at school. At the time you sat looking out of the window or noticing bra straps and getting the erection which would not properly subside for another five years. Somehow, snippets of information stuck with you. It must have been in a forgotten history lesson that I'd heard about this twelfth- or thirteenth-century warlock.

If I'd heard about him at school, Jack would have, too. We'd been friends at school. Perhaps that was where his strange ideas had come from.

The history books didn't mention anything about wizards. They went into a lot of detail about crop rotation and the Spinning Jenny. I replaced them on the shelves and went to look in the supernatural section.

I didn't put the books back where I found them. That's what librarians are for.

I found the supernatural section without too much trouble. Initially, I was thrown off the scent because it wasn't called the supernatural section. It was called mysticism, and it had subsections – astrology, ufology, shamanism, and hundreds of others.

People would believe anything.

I don't want to appear dismissive of new age mysticism. That would be unconstructive. But it is all rubbish. There aren't any shamans in England. You weren't a Cherokee in a previous existence. You didn't help to build the Great Pyramid of Cheops. You weren't on the Titanic. If you had a previous life, you were gullible in that one too. Crystals are pretty stones and aliens are not swapping secrets with the US government.

There was magic in England, but it wasn't that kind of

magic. It was the sort that needed feeding. On the American Plains, perhaps shamans did run with the wolves.

In the English forests, the wolves slinked from between the trees and ate you, your baby and your wife. Between the trees in an English forest, a long time ago, a clearing grew. A castle was built and occupied by a succession of lords.

At some point in the thirteenth century a wizard came along and took up residence. I learned this from a ragged cloth-bound book the size of a coffee table. Nasty pictures lurked inside. It ran through some of the legends of the Dudley area – the mad wife of Oldbury, the beast of Pensnett, and others – and gave several details about the wizard.

It said that he arrived at some point early in the thirteenth century. He travelled with two henchmen.

I'll quote the article. It'll save us all time.

II

It went like this:

In the earliest part of the thirteenth century – some accounts claim in the first year – a new arrival came to the town of Dudley. He was a warlock, travelling with two companions. One, formerly a stonemason by trade, acted as his bodyguard. The other is variously described as crippled, or misshapen, or wrongly made. He seems to have been more a familiar than anything else.

The lord of Dudley stepped aside for the warlock. His repute came before him. It was said that he could work wonders, curing ailments and healing broken bones. It was also said that he preferred to cause ailments, and shatter bones. A deal was struck. The lords of Dudley would gain ownership of the town for ever, if the warlock and his strange companions could have the occupancy of the castle for a score of years.

Fear and greed together did their work. The lord moved out; the warlock and his companions moved in. For weeks the townspeople were alarmed by strange lights and frightful noises. What happened next cannot accurately be chronicled. The project of the warlock was one of the oldest – eternal life. There in Dudley, many dark powers could be tapped, for Dudley lies at the point of the map furthest avoided by ley-lines. It is a site of grim power.

It is said that the warlock, or his companions, sacrificed five of the townspeople and buried their bones – or some of their bones, as the accounts vary – here and there about the place. All of this was by way of being a ritual, and at the end of the ritual the strangest thing took place. Eternal life was granted, by whatever dark forces were invoked.

The score of years became a century. The lords of Dudley watched the castle from the town, generation after generation waiting to regain their rightful seat. The townspeople grew more afraid, becoming pale and stooped, given to strange ejaculations and wild humours. A time came when they gathered, taking torches and what weapons they had, and stormed the castle.

They found it empty. The trio of immortals had fled. Where they went is uncertain, although many tales seem to mention them in passing.

What is sure is that five skeletons were found in the

castle, each of them missing some digit – a finger here, a toe there.

The castle was reoccupied by the then Lord of Dudley. The occupancy was an uneasy one, and in the eighteenth century, after many generations had suffered unsound nights, the castle's living quarters were destroyed in a fire.

The cause of the fire is uncertain, but it is not by any means inconceivable that a miserable lord, fretting at night in the cold stone chambers as the strange sounds that originated centuries since rang through the corridors, took a lantern and flung it to the floor, seeking to end the misery once and for all.

III

You can see why I gave magic up as a bad idea. It was all rumours and hearsay. The fire probably started because the Lord of Dudley was smoking in bed. I was interested to hear that the townspeople had stormed the castle. I wondered whether James Whale had been bearing that in mind when he filmed the climax of *Frankenstein*.

There was a woodcut on the facing page. It showed the wizard at work in his laboratory, or wherever it is that wizards work. His assistants stood on either side of him. One held a tool of some sort, with a long handle. I couldn't tell what it was. I don't know why it never occurred to medieval illustrators to learn to draw. All of the people in woodcuts have the same face. These three had the same face. The illustrator hadn't bothered to depict the malformities of the malformed one. I wondered what they might be. There was a lot more scope in those days. Eight hundred years ago everyone was malformed. To be noted for it, you'd have to be spectacularly malformed. It couldn't just be ginger hair.

Although the story was clearly rubbish, I had a feeling that Jack must have read it. I'd never seen Jack reading, but I assumed he could do it. Some things matched what he claimed he'd done. There had been five murders. They had buried parts of the victims. It had all been part of a ritual to gain eternal life.

That tied it in with Jack's dementia. That seemed to be enough matching points. I left the library proud of myself.

Detective work was a doddle, I thought. I'd been researching less than two hours and I'd found the source of Jack's inspiration. If I went in there for a week I'd probably find the cure for cancer. I thought about changing jobs. I could make it as a private investigator. I could have a filing cabinet with a whisky bottle in it, and a secretary who'd ignore my wisecracks.

I thought better of it. I was already a team leader. Give it another five years and I'd be in line for a promotion, maybe a payrise. I decided to go to work the next day. I needed to head off the rumours.

I did buy a bottle of whisky, though. I thought I had something to celebrate. After all, I'd solved one mystery already.

If I went on at that rate, I'd have all the answers by the weekend.

Chapter Twelve

I

I woke up with a hangover. It wasn't the sort of hangover you wanted to wake up with. There were worse things to wake up with – a dead dog, say, or your mother – but this was bad enough. For one thing it was too big. It was bulging out of me in all directions. For another, I couldn't remember how I'd got it. I'd been celebrating my detective work and then without transition it was morning, and the alarm clock was going off, and I'd got one of Oliver Reed's leftover hangovers living in my head.

I sat up. I was on the living room floor, dressed. The television was on. The alarm clock wasn't going off, I realized. The noise was coming from the television. It was a morning programme with a boisterous presenter and a clamorous crew who couldn't just do their jobs and keep behind the cameras where they belonged. All of them were shouting, all at once. I reached over to turn the television off and my hangover tilted like a ferry with the bow doors open. I was sweating, heavy drops of bad-smelling liquid rising through my pores and running to the tips of my shivering fingers.

What had I been drinking? I knew about the whisky, but

there must have been something else involved. Not lager. This wasn't a lager hangover. Those were gassy, this was poisonous. Something settled in my bowels. I managed to turn the television off. I'm not used to being distressed by household appliances. It's not dignified. I looked at the clock on top of the television. I was going to be late for work. I went upstairs in about the time it would take any other person to climb the Wrekin. I wanted to go to bed until the alcohol had left my system, but my system wasn't that forgiving. It wasn't going to let me sleep through it. If I tried to lie down, my system would simulate funfair rides and I'd be sick at length and volume. I gave the bedroom a look of longing and went to the bathroom instead.

In the mirror my reflection looked like a premonition of my death. The eyes were hiding far back in shadowy hollows. Something like a beard had sprouted overnight. My hands were too shaky to risk shaving. I have an electric shaver that runs off two batteries, and I had two batteries for it. I'd had them for six years, and they'd been flat for five. I looked at my reflection. I opened my mouth and had a look in there. No teeth were missing but the tongue had been carpeted. It was done out in furry red and yellow, like the flock wallpaper they used to have in Indian restaurants. By the feel of it someone had put underlay down first. I watched my reflection sway, then held onto the sink. A wave of nausea lurched from my stomach to the back of my throat. A little clot of something I'd eaten last night popped into my mouth, tasting like it had spent the night in a Sumo wrestler's jockstrap. I swallowed it. I wasn't going to spit it out. I was well brought up even if it wasn't. I washed as much of myself as I could stand to touch, feeling temperature changes going through my body.

I drank a lot of cold water from the tap and felt no better. I followed the water with more Nurofen than the instructions recommend. Something in my bowels changed position with a loud, liquid noise. I was in for a bad time, which didn't seem fair. The hangover made me feel like I was four years old, ready to cry. It wasn't *fair*. I dried myself and went to the bedroom. I found a clean shirt and put it on, making it unclean. I felt leprous. My skin felt as though it was about to slough. I half hoped that it would, then I'd have a good reason for not going to work.

There are two sorts of people when it comes to sick leave. One sort never takes any, struggling in to work and getting in on time even if they've been mauled by leopards after a mistake at the zoo. The other sort take sick leave once or twice a week and never seem to be ill, perhaps because of all the rest they're getting while sick people do their jobs. I'm the first sort. I'd rather be the second sort, but my parents used to send me to school with measles or tonsilitis or whatever else I had, and it became a habit.

My parents weren't the best parents you could have asked for. I found a tie on the wardrobe floor. That was a bonus. It's not often that my ties make it back to the wardrobe, they usually make a nest under the bed along with yesterday's socks. I put the tie on and thought I was looking something like sensible. I dressed my lower half and put on my shoes.

The laces were tricky, but I managed to get them tied. Not in a bow, but at least they wouldn't fall off. Possibly not for weeks.

I found my wallet and some change in the pockets of the trousers I'd spent the night in. I went back to the bathroom and had another look at my reflection. I'd got washed, I'd got dressed, I'd taken medicine, I must surely look better.

I looked like shit, and I was going to be late for work.

I reached the bus stop after the bus. But I was in time to see it pull away from the kerb. I caught the driver's eye and waved as I ran unsteadily to the stop. He waved back cheerily and drove off, changing gears in that bus-driver way, first to third and then pick one at random and stick with it to the terminus. An old woman watched me miss the bus. She was standing under the shelter with a shopping bag on wheels. It was tartan. Her face looked like someone had screwed it up. Her hair looked like someone had fucked it over. I was going through one of the hot flushing stages of my hangover, brought on by my ten-yard sprint for the bus. She was wearing a coat made of some sort of itchy-looking wiry wool with a pattern of zigzagging lines that your eyes couldn't focus on. The coat ended far enough above the pavement to reveal that she was wearing Derry boots. She had on a headscarf and a neckscarf.

'You missed that bus,' she explained to me. I don't know why old people have to tell you these things. Perhaps it makes them feel better about going through wartime rationing. I looked down the road for another bus, although there wasn't one due. I made a mental note to sort out driving lessons.

'I say, you missed that bus,' said the old woman. I grunted in a way that was meant to indicate my unwillingness to engage in a conversation.

'Gone, that one has,' she added.

Jack had claimed we'd killed an old woman. I was beginning to see what the motive would be.

'Gone up the road. Be at the next stop by now, I shouldn't wonder.'

She peered up at me.

'Won't be another for half an hour,' she told me. 'Used to be every ten minutes down here. Half an hour now. If one comes. I was here last week and there wasn't one all day. You'll be late for work. '

She fell silent. I was hoping that she'd fall under the traffic, but silent would do to be going on with. A thought struck her.

'Even if there is one,' she said, 'it'll be full. You won't get a seat. They might not let you on at all. They don't all come down this road now, you know. They changed them.'

I looked at my wrist. My watch wasn't on it. I remembered taking it off before having my quick hopeless wash, and then I'd got dressed, and then I'd left the watch in the bathroom. I had no way to judge the passing of time. It was like being in one of my Historic Peculiarities lectures.

Learning about Historic Peculiarities involved learning about human beings. If animals had history, they weren't telling anyone about it. The lectures tended to focus on the more morbid parts of history. We spent a lot of time learning about torture. For a long time, people torturing other people would make use of household things, screwdrivers and pliers, electricity and water. Then the idea of psychological torture came up and interrogators began locking people in cells with no lights and no windows and no clocks, no way to judge how long they'd been there. It sent people insane. Time fell apart for them. Time ran in odd directions, like a three-legged dog.

Waiting for the bus with the old woman and no watch, I went through all of that. As a bonus for fans of the older, more direct, forms of torture I had my hangover. For what seemed like hours I stood pouring sweat into my unclean shirt and releasing farts into my horrible gusset, all the time buffeted by the old woman's dismal predictions.

'None of them know how to drive,' she said. 'Not been here ten minutes most of them. Give them a bus each, they do. No one gives pensioners anything.'

Someone might give a pensioner a punch in the throat, I thought. There was another long wait. To while away the time I shivered and belched. The next bus was crowded, and I had to stand, wedged up against a young man in a sharp suit. The old woman didn't get on the bus. She stood at the bus stop, watched it go, and then walked off. She was a bus stop vulture. It was the first time I'd had sympathy for hypothermia.

I was late getting to work, but I told everyone I'd been in a meeting and that seemed to do the trick. I left my team to their spreadsheets and switched on my PC. What *had* I been drinking? Usually I don't want to get drunk, I want to have a drink or two then go to bed. The trouble is that there was another plan, and I didn't know about it until I'd had a couple of drinks. The hidden plan went like this: *Drink everything in the house*. Then I'd go to bed and wake up with a hangover. But this wasn't that sort of a hangover. This was the sort that suggested serious drinking. It implied that I'd gone out of my way to get drunk. I must have finished the whisky off. Then what? There had been a bottle of sherry I'd had for years because no one drinks sherry unless it's out of a bottle in a brown paper bag in a shop doorway. I must have polished that off too. I must have gone through all the drinks in the house.

Now all the drinks in the house were going through me the way Hitler went through Poland.

I'd got drunk with the whisky, and then I'd got the sherry out, and then I couldn't remember anything until I'd woken up with all my clothes on. I thought about that, watching the figures in my spreadsheet flicker. I had lost chunks of last night. There were holes in my memory, and I was frightened by what might have fallen through them.

II

Back in the days when I worked on the building sites there were lots of things to remember. Trenches had to be no wider than they were deep. You weren't to stand in front of diggers or 'dozers. You weren't to shout at young ladies. The number of cigarette breaks in the day was limited to the number of available cigarettes. If inspectors came and asked you anything, you said you didn't know and the man who did know was at another site.

I remembered all of that. Mr Link praised my powers of recollection.

'You're a credit,' he said. 'Most students we get here have taken so many drugs that they have trouble saying "trench", never mind digging one. But you have a terrific memory. And that's fine. You've got a full set of arms and legs. That's fine too. I'm not an equal opportunities employer. The government says I have to be, and I say I didn't vote for them and they can piss off. If Stevie Wonder asked for a job here I'd show him the door and he'd bump into it. So I'm happy that you have all the necessary faculties, relating to unskilled manual labour.' He said that before Darren and I got our wires crossed. After that, Mr Link stopped praising my powers of recollection. Instead he dissed me at length.

It wasn't my fault, not altogether. We were working on a site outside Oldbury, one of those towns you get where you can't find the town centre. You get to a suburb, an outskirt, with a small shop that's equal parts off-licence, tobacconist, and porno merchant. There's a pedestrian crossing and pedestrians crossing it, interrupting the traffic. There's a bingo hall with an enormous billboard, and an edge-of-town supermarket. There are roundabouts and ringroads and traffic islands scattered about as though someone had been selling them off cheap. You drive around a few, searching for the rest of the town, and find yourself at a motorway junction. The signs say Oldbury is behind you. You go around the next island, which is huge and insane and dotted with traffic lights, none of them in sync with the others. You head back to where Oldbury must be and somehow miss it again, ending up on the road to Birmingham with nowhere to turn round and a bus overtaking you so that it can block your way at the next stop. You turn round in someone's drive and head back, through the elaborate system of islands, heading this way and that, but wherever you go, signs say Oldbury is behind you, where you've just come from. Eventually it dawns on you, as you pass the edge-of-town supermarket and the small shop and the pedestrian crossing, that *this* is Oldbury. It's a town without a centre. The rest of it isn't there, and there's no point looking for it. This *is* Oldbury. It really *is* behind you. It's behind everywhere, because it stopped ten years ago and no one thought to build a middle.

We were putting up an office building on the east side of

town. As the van passed through the outskirt that turned out
to be the town, a bus pulled up in front of us and we had to
wait while it unloaded. Darren and I were in the front, being
by now the old hands. In the back, jostled by the picks and
shovels, were two new lads, both ex-students. Darren looked
at the passengers alighting from the bus.

'Bloody hell, Sam,' he said, 'check this out. None of them
is *normal*.'

He was right. Everyone clambering slowly from the rum-
bling bus had some sort of defect. To a man they were blind, or
had club feet, or walked with an unusual gait, or had withered
arms, or swore repeatedly at the air, or all of the above. They
emerged from the bus and wandered randomly, into the shops,
into the bushes, into the road, into each other.

'Must be a special bus,' I said.

'Sunshine bus,' agreed Darren.

It wasn't sunny, as it happens. It wasn't a special bus, either.
It was an ordinary bus, and they were ordinary Oldbury
residents. Oldbury residents were inbred in a way that would
make Alabamans feel queasy. The gene pool was stagnant and
polluted. Darren and I learned to send the other ex-students
– Damien and Marcus – to the local shop for supplies, i.e.
cigarettes.

The first day there, after a hard morning of deciding where
to put the trenches, Darren and I went to the shop. Until that
job, going to the shop had been a perk. It got you out of the
way of any work. There was a chance that while you were at
the shop, someone else would do the work. We went to the
shop. There was a counter with no one behind it, and the
usual stock, smoking supplies, magazines, sweets. I looked
over the magazines. The selection was strange. The top shelf

was what you'd expect. What I didn't expect was that the next three shelves would be the same. I hadn't seen so much pornography in one place before. I looked at the remaining shelf, and found that it held true crime magazines. Other than the titles, they looked exactly like the porn. Darren leafed through a magazine and, in the interests of research, I looked over his shoulder.

'Jesus,' he said.

I didn't know what he'd found a picture of. It looked like liver gone wild.

'What is it?' I asked.

'I don't know. I don't think a doctor would know. I don't think its *owner* would know. It looks like a kidney.'

'I thought liver.'

'Well that's unanimous then. It's something internal. What is this, *Surgeon's Monthly*?'

It wasn't *Surgeon's Monthly*, if there is such a thing. It was called *Pure Dirt Fantazia* and it would have made a surgeon throw his hands to his face and call for help. Darren replaced the magazine between *Big Women* and *Asian Secrets*.

'Just ciggies then,' he said, approaching the counter. It was still deserted. He leaned over it. There was a till, one of the old ones with buttons that had to be pushed about a foot to make anything happen.

'Hello?' he said, quietly. From behind a door behind the counter came the sounds of someone approaching. The door opened and a young woman came through. She looked as normal as anyone in Oldbury, which is to say that she had the right number of eyes and fingers. The eyes were slightly crossed and the fingers were partially webbed, but at least they were all there.

'Is it waiting?' she asked with a strong but unidentifiable accent.

'Sorry?' said Darren.

'No, not,' she said. 'Cigarettes? Is it them?'

'Camel,' said Darren. 'Forty, cheers.'

The girl looked at him.

'Is it cigarettes? Not. Not cigarettes today. Tuesday, Wednesday, cigarettes. Not today please.'

'They're there,' said Darren, pointing to the shelves behind her. She looked at his finger as though she was considering biting it.

'Tuesday, Wednesday, cigarettes. Not today. No cigarettes today.'

'Is there anyone else here?' Darren asked.

'Him also,' she said, pointing at me with her batrachian hand.

'Him also want cigarette, today, not Tuesday please,' tried Darren. She gave him twenty Embassy.

'Take them,' I whispered.

'How much?' he asked.

There was a definite gleam in the girl's eyes as she said:

'Prices to be found in listing in drawer. Also codes for greetings cards.'

By the time we got back to the building site, Damien and Marcus had marked out the lines of the trenches with wooden staves.

'Nice job,' said Darren. 'Tell you what, lads, next time we need some fags getting in, you can go. Be a bonus, seeing as how you've done so well.'

'Cool,' said Marcus, not knowing what we were letting him in for. Damien nodded. Darren and I looked over the lines they'd laid. They looked fine, good and straight, meeting at right-angles, no curls or jiggles or anything else that would give Mr Link a headache. We forgot one of the things you have to remember on a building site, which is: *don't take anyone else's word for it.*

That afternoon Marcus and Damien went for cigarettes and Darren and I started to dig. We started at a corner – we always started at a corner because you could judge the position from there – and slowly moved away from one another. By the time Marcus and Damien returned, in strange moods and with the wrong number of packets of the wrong brands of cigarettes, we'd dug a long way. Darren was doing an end trench, which was shorter than the one I was doing, and he'd almost got to the next corner. I was lagging slightly but I wasn't worried. Mr Link would be pleased with the progress. Usually, on the first day at a new site, we didn't do anything. The weather would be wrong or there would be confusion about the land or there would be a field of cows where the building was supposed to go, and none of us felt comfortable with cows. They were big and bulky and made strange noises.

Things seemed to be going well. We packed up early and drove past the small shop and the edge-of-town supermarket that wasn't on the edge of town.

'There's nothing but porn in that shop,' said Damien. 'Filthy.'

'The way the people here look, they *need* porn,' said Marcus.

'They need more genes,' said Damien. 'Are you volunteering?'

'Not fucking likely. They'd probably get them by eating you alive.'

'Better than having sex with them,' said Darren. A bus arrived and disgorged another cluster of misshapes and Darren swung the van around them.

A day later Spin joined us. He'd been on holiday, but Darren couldn't tell us where. The mime was uncertain.

'Portugal?' he guessed. 'Istanbul? Miami? Saundersfoot?'

We finished the trenches, and they were long and deep. Mr Link was due to visit, soon. He knew we were in good hands with Darren and Spin.

I should have realized something was wrong when Damien and Marcus marked out two more trenches. They were inside each end of the rectangle we'd already dug out and stretched right across it. I was surprised, at first. Mr Link didn't approve of interior walls. He didn't disapprove of them as much as he disapproved of doors and windows, but he was wary of them. Looking at the foundations, we were going to have a long building, with side walls and end walls, and then a few feet inside the end walls another pair of end walls.

'Are you sure this is what we're supposed to be doing?' I asked.

'It's on the plans,' said Marcus. 'We've checked them.'

I asked Spin about it and he gesticulated an answer.

'Spin reckons Mr Link is moving into new areas, architecturally,' Darren translated. 'This is similar to his previous theme, that of massive empty cuboids, but now he's working with joined massive empty cuboids. It's by way of being an extension to his oeuvre, Spin reckons.'

'How can you tell all that from him waving his hands about?' asked Marcus, who wasn't used to Spin.

'It's easy, really,' said Darren.

'Why don't you know where he went on holiday, then?'

'Proper names are a different thing. You can do gestures for *holiday*, or *travel*, or *cat*, or anything really, but names are abstract. I haven't worked out the way he does names.'

'How do we know what he's called then?'

'Who says we do? Does Spin sound like a proper name to you?'

Spin nodded, alone.

'He did a spinning thing with his hands, so I called him Spin, and he liked it. So he's Spin.'

Spin nodded again. Marcus looked back at the trench, unconvinced. We began to dig out the two new sections Damien and Marcus had marked out.

Mr Link arrived an hour later. It became apparent that there was something wrong.

'What the buttery fuck do you think you're up to?' he asked us all, looking at what we'd done. 'What the fuck have you *done*?'

'We've nearly got the foundations done,' said Darren. 'If it's going to make things difficult, being this far ahead of schedule, we can slow it down with the scaffolding.'

Spin shook his head when scaffolding was mentioned, and either crossed himself or told us something. Marcus, who had gained his degree in psychology, moved smartly away, putting on a limp and mingling with the people of Oldbury.

'Oh, I think we can cope with being ahead of schedule,' said Mr Link. 'Seeing as how you've made a complete pig's ear of it. Now, how do we like our buildings?'

'Square,' three of us said and Spin mimed; 'Square, flat, straight and empty.'

'So what are those other trenches for?'

'Cavity walls?'

'No. Those trenches are in the wrong places. But also in the right places. Who marked it out?'

'Don't ask me,' said Damien. 'I've only been doing this a week. I was out getting the cigarettes, and let me tell you, that's a job and a half in this town.'

'Is it a town?' asked Mr Link, momentarily distracted. 'I thought it was funny that they'd given a name to a traffic island. Not as funny as building two buildings in the same space, though. Now, how am I going to put up two warehouse-style office complexes when I have enough end trenches but half the number of side ones?'

I looked at the foundations and realized what we'd done. We'd set two sets of foundations overlapping one another. They weren't overlapping by a small amount, either. They were overlapping for about a hundred metres.

'Ah,' said Darren. 'I don't suppose you drew them on top of each other on the plans?'

'Well of course I did, what am I? W H bloody Smith? How much paper do you think I have? I drew them in different colours. Two rectangles. How difficult can that be to follow?'

'Erm,' said Darren.

'We can put one of them there,' I said, 'and set another one over here.'

'Over here? Next to the road? *In* the road? In a bottle on the roof? Where were you thinking of, exactly? Because the one we *do* have foundations for has its foundations – and some of another building's foundations, well done there, that's the sort of extra touch that always cheers me up – right in the middle of the plot. So, how will we sort that one out then?'

The answer to that turned out to be, by working all night.

I thought about all that two years later, while I was waiting for my hangover to leave me alone. It seemed to fit. What if we'd gone ahead and built two structures into the same plot? Would it have worked? Could two structures coexist?

Could both Jack and I be right, at the same time? His truth and my truth, in the same space? Could he be remembering some of the truth, and I forgetting it? These thoughts swirled in my head, gradually settling.

I realized that I'd been thinking nonsense. Jack was off his head. The days on the building sites were safely in the past, and the past was over with. None of that could touch me now. None of that was still around.

III

My hangover diminished. By midmorning it had become a slight queasiness and a hint of a headache. I felt well enough to talk to my team. I remembered that Steve had left, and Jane from the agency had turned out to be bright.

My team inhabits a set of desks at one end of an open-plan office. It's open-plan so that everyone else in the office can see how badly my team is doing. From time to time Ted Wiggins would drift by on his way to or from a meeting, and look at them with evident disappointment. I wasn't worried that my team never produced anything – this was the council – but a bad team might seem to mean a bad team leader. I didn't want to get in any trouble. I looked over what they were doing. Melanie was busy playing Minesweeper, which we allowed on the computers as it was less interesting than a spreadsheet. Theresa was sitting next to Melanie and looking perplexed.

Theresa was of the generation before computers. She might
have been from one of the generations before that. She would
forget her password, or how to switch the computer on, or
what to do with it once it was switched on. She couldn't do
anything with computers except delete files she didn't want
to delete. The more important they were, the more likely
she was to delete them. She deleted system files, hardware
drivers, spreadsheets, whole screenfuls of EXEs and LOGs
and INIs. There would often be someone from IT standing
close to her desk, looking weary. Today it was Nigel, a lanky
gawky boy who looked about fifteen. He blinked in the glare
of the office lights, eager to get back to the IT cubbyhole so
that he could browse porn sites and look up the schematics
of Klingon battlecruisers.

'No,' he said, 'there's no need to do that. Don't press the
delete key. That's the one that deletes things. That's why it has
"delete" on it. It means, this is the key for deleting things.'

'What, this one?' asked Theresa, pressing it. A list of things,
highlighted blue, rapidly shrank.

'Yes, that one. That's the one *not to press*,' said Nigel, with
heavy emphasis.

'I see,' said Theresa, tapping it. Each time she tapped, Nigel
flinched.

'So if you could not tap it, that might help. Leave it alone.
Pretend it isn't there. Now, your password. It's Theresa, like
it was yesterday. Like it always is. It's your *name*. Shall I write
it down for you?'

Theresa didn't recognize sarcasm, which was just as well. I
left them to it and checked the other desks. Three were vacant.
That couldn't be right. There were two spare, and Jane should
have been at the other.

'Where's Jane?' I asked.

'Jane who?' asked Melanie.

'Jane who was here yesterday. The girl who knew how to do something.'

'Gone.'

'Where?'

'New team leader at the end asked to borrow her and she went over there. She's staying there now. Team at the end, behind Contracts and HR.'

'She was all right,' said Nigel.

What did he know about women? He was a computer freak. The only women he saw were kissing Captain Kirk with their faces painted blue. I wasn't going to let Jane go to another team. This was all down to Jack. If he didn't keep saying that we used to murder people, I wouldn't need to get drunk, and then I wouldn't have had the hangover, and then I'd have been watching my team instead of waiting for God to kill me and end the suffering.

'Which team?' I asked, looking over the ranks of desks.

'At the end,' said Melanie.

I made my way along the office. I wanted to stride, but it doesn't suit me. I think it's my knees. They aren't striding knees. I passed the other teams and arrived at the end set of desks. I could see Jane, hunched over a keyboard, copying data from nowhere to nowhere else. A man stood over her with his back to me. He was wide and it wasn't fat. He looked solid. He had a solid neck. He had very black hair. I didn't know how to catch his attention. I'm not the sort of person who can just butt into a conversation.

'Hello, Mr Haines,' said Jane. 'I'm over here now.'

'Who authorized that?' I asked. The new team leader turned

round. It was Darren. I should have recognized that hair. It still looked unnaturally black. I still thought that he dyed it. He looked at me with little surprise.

'I heard you were working here,' he said. He looked at my tie. I didn't think I'd knotted it very well. He gave me a friendly punch on the shoulder.

'I think I've poached one of your team. Saw her down by the coffee machine and I thought to myself, there's a bright girl. So I made enquiries, as you do, and that was that. Hope that's OK with you, only I've not been here long. I need a good team. You've been here for ages. I bet you've got a cracking team sorted. Anyway, I need pretty girls in my team.'

Jane smiled. If I'd said she was pretty she'd have gone to a tribunal. Some people can get away with anything.

'Oh, they're not bad,' I said. 'I can do without one or two. Jane's new to us anyway. I'm sure she'll do well with you.'

'It's a turn-up, isn't it?' he said, 'both of us here. How's things, then?'

'Fine,' I managed. 'When did you start?'

'A few weeks ago. I was only moved into this section yesterday, though. I had the interview months ago but it's the council and they lost the forms and didn't get back to me and anyway, they're an equal opportunities employer so I didn't think I had a chance. I can see why they took you. Low IQ and that. I expect you're balancing out my high charm and abilities with your low ones.'

He was smiling. I realized that he was pleased to see me. I was pleased to see him, too.

'Heard from Spin?' I asked.

'Not heard from, no. He's been in touch but you don't

hear from him as such. He did fine in local radio, they liked what he did. He's moved on now. He's got a job on the local news, on the telly. I haven't seen him, but my brother says he's all right. He got a break. While he was on the radio he got talking to someone, in the way he does. They had some money left over and let him do a TV documentary. He put together this little thing about Dudley. Stupid thing to make a programme about it. I don't know anyone who saw it.'

'I did see a programme about Dudley,' I said, and told him about the one I'd watched at my brother's house with Jack.

'Is he the one the rumours are about? I've heard loads since I've been here. Nice to see you're making an impression. Spin would be glad to know he'd caused such a stir. Anyway, the television company liked what he did with that documentary, and they gave him a job. He presents the news now.'

'What? Spin reads the news?'

'Yep.'

'Actually reads it out?'

'Couldn't say, I haven't seen him.'

'I saw it,' said Jane. 'I saw it this morning.'

'What's happening then?' I asked, thinking of Eddie Finch and the local newspapers. 'Summer fete in rain disaster? Local man saves hamster?'

'No,' said Jane. 'Nothing really. There's an outbreak of scabies in Kingswinford. You were on, obviously. But the police are saying it's all a misunderstanding and that people shouldn't burn your house down or anything.'

'Oh good,' I said.

Darren gave me another friendly punch. 'Tell you what,' he

said. 'If I were you, I'd be thinking about compensation. The press did a false story about you. But I suppose it's difficult to prove it was false.'

'You must be able to prove it,' said Jane. 'After all, there aren't any bodies. There would be, if you'd been out killing people.'

'Bang on,' said Darren. 'They didn't bother looking for any evidence, did they? Not a thing. Just whoomph and the story's out. If it wasn't that you work for this lot, you might be out of a job. With the council a criminal record's probably a bonus. They'll give you a rise.'

'They'll give you a car,' said Jane.

'You still on the buses?' asked Darren. 'God, you're aiming low, you know that? You're a graduate. Peculiar History, he did,' he told Jane.

'Historic Peculiarities,' I said.

'And that,' he said. 'Bright enough, good at digging trenches, good with people. Here he is, a chance to make some money out of the local press. But he's not the sort to rock the boat. Fair play, I say. Too many people around just go for what they want. Well, I need to be getting on with things,' said Darren. 'I'll see you around. Come on then, trouble, I'll need you to do the filing.'

He put an arm around Jane and led her away.

I thought about what he'd said. He thought I'd leave things as they were. He thought I'd let things lie. He didn't think I'd want to rock the boat.

I did want to rock it. I wanted to overturn it. I could live with being less likeable. It might make me more liked.

I was upset by Jane's attitude. She also thought that I wouldn't do anything about the story.

I'd prove the pair of them wrong. I'd thought of something else I could do.

That night, I thought, I'd go and do some more detective work.

PART SIX

Sam, aged twenty

Chapter Thirteen

I

A long time ago, I went to the pictures with Jack to see a double bill of superhero films. These were films so bad that they didn't get to go straight to video. Instead they went straight to celluloid and were banished to a bare handful of dismal cinemas in the smaller and wetter towns of Britain.

The cinema was mostly empty. A parent told an offspring to shut up, repeatedly. An offspring failed to shut up. A group of young teenagers on the far side of the auditorium tried to work up the nerve to say something audible. A drenched, miserable family sat two rows from the screen and didn't say a word.

On the screen, an actor who couldn't act played Thunderboy. Thunderboy looked to be about thirty, and not as fit as you might have thought would be necessary for a superhero. We were watching a double bill of Thunderboy movies. I don't think they made a third one. It was hard to see why they bothered with the first one. I didn't see the credits, so I don't know who was to blame. I wasn't paying attention when the credits rolled. I had to keep asking Jack who was who and what they were up to. By the second film I could manage by myself. The plots weren't difficult to follow. In the first of the movies – *Thunderboy* – the titular hero learned of his hidden identity and, after the usual identity crisis, vanquished his arch nemesis. In the second – *The Return of Thunderboy* – our titular hero did the same things all over again. Inept special effects failed to make him appear to leap into the air and fly. In a trice he could change from his street clothes into his hidden costume. His hidden costume looked as though it had been bought from an Oxfam shop. So did his special effects.

The acting tended to the wooden. The leading lady never led anything else. The first film was so bad that you didn't think there could be a worse one. The second was worse. We would have left, but it was still raining outside, and it was a small town, and there was nothing else to do. And Jack was managing to enjoy the films.

That was the first inkling I had of his innate masochism.

II

We weren't in Dudley. We'd gone on a camping holiday to Avebury, where there was nowhere to camp. After trying a few hopeful-looking fields, and being chased off by heated farmers, we'd found a field with only a couple of hundred hippies and druids in it a few miles out of town. There, we pitched our tents and had a day or two of warm weather, when we saw the sights and I lost my head. I'll come back to that.

Then the rain, which had been missing us, turned up. Compared to Dudley, which is on a hill among other hills, Avebury and its surrounds are flat. The landscape is seven-tenths sky.

From the third day onward, it was seven-tenths rain.

The holiday started in the rain, of course. We left Dudley

on a coach – neither of us could drive in those days – at six in the morning. Rain drummed on the roof and ran down the windows. Being penetrative Dudley rain, it managed to find ways in through the bodywork.

Half an hour later, we were under clear skies. The coach didn't stop, all the way to Avebury. It felt a much longer drive than it could have been. There was a toilet on the coach, and it didn't flush properly. There was a hostess on the coach who came round with a trolley of desperate pies. She winked at Jack. She winked at everyone else.

'I'm in there,' said Jack.

'It's a twitch,' I told him. 'She did it to me.'

He raised his eyebrows.

We were driven across Salisbury Plain. Plain is a good word for it. I don't think I've seen anything less interesting, and I grew up in Dudley. Jack looked out of the window. The armed forces own large expanses of Salisbury Plain. They'd have to. There are only large expanses.

Jack was looking for exciting hardware. 'There,' he said, pointing at nothing. 'An APC.'

'A what?'

'Armoured personnel carrier.'

'It's a bush.'

'It's camouflaged.'

'It's fucking good camouflage,' I told him. The couple in the seats in front turned and looked at us with disapproval. We'd got used to it. The road across Salisbury Plain ran in a straight line for what felt like days. After a couple of hours on the steppe we passed through Salisbury, which was a town made of narrow roads and gift shops. After an hour of Salisbury we emerged onto more of Salisbury Plain.

'How much of this is there?' asked Jack. He'd stopped pretending to see military tech. If there was any, he wouldn't be able to see it. That's the way it's designed.

Much later, we arrived at Avebury.

The holiday was my idea. It was easy to talk Jack into it. It was the school holidays, and there was nothing else to do. At that time, I had started thinking about time. I was thinking about the ritual, but I hadn't told Jack about it. I wanted to see if he was trustworthy. I thought that if we spent some time away from other influences I might get a better idea of his nature. If I went ahead with the ritual, he'd have to help me murder people.

I thought that camping would be cheap and easy, so we borrowed a couple of tents.

'We could share one,' Jack had said. I explained some things to him, mostly involving personal hygiene. It wasn't a discipline he favoured. We each took a small tent, a sleeping bag that would turn out to be too hot to sleep in, and reading matter. He took a few commando novels, and I took an interesting parchment I'd found. I crammed a few tins of beans into my rucksack, and Jack crammed a leaky Gaz stove into his. Neither of us remembered to take matches.

You can get used to cold baked beans.

There were thousands of hippies and travellers in Avebury. They were all over the standing stones and ancient sites, fucking them up for those of us with a genuine interest, dropping roaches and burning things down, tripping too far out and pummelling the stones.

I know what those places were for, and it wasn't for attracting the loving vibes of the earth goddess or catching the multiple eyes of the guys from Arcturus. Those were bloody places, all of them. There is always an altar. There are bones under every ancient monument. There was no love involved, and, take it from me, there never was an earth goddess.

After pitching the tent we walked the mile or so back into Avebury. The town had a few shops, all selling monument-related bits and bobs. One or two did a sideline in groceries. The first day was frighteningly sunny. The sky was a shocking blue, especially if you came from Dudley. Walking to the stone circle – I had taken us there to go to the circle, and Silbury Hill, and West Kennet, and all of the other sites that have been discovered because any sort of mound can be seen from thirty miles away – we passed clumps of travellers. They had loose clothes and dreadlocks, and they'd be on the road until they turned twenty, when Daddy would get them a plum job at the bank. They sat around in circles playing tin whistles and didgeridoos, handing round thin spliffs and pretending they owned the place.

'This land belongs to the people,' one of them droned to her companions, as they gave us evil looks. We weren't dressed like the people, apparently. We didn't have the people's haircut.

'We're the people,' said Jack. 'We're the clean people, here to bring you soap.'

'There's no need to be confrontational,' said another.

Of course there was. There was every need. The people who understand ancient sites can't get near them now, not without forking out for a didgeridoo and a white-boy's Rasta hairdo. And the travellers have got it all wrong, they are all one hundred per cent wrong. This land *doesn't* belong to the people. This land was for the exclusive use of a favoured few.

The people should all fuck off home and leave the land in the hands of the powerful.

When we want the people with us, we'll ask them along. One by one, say, to be gutted at harvest time. Until then, they should get back in their minivans and go home and stop pretending to be anything out of the ordinary.

They saw some of that in my eyes and left us alone. Magic has its uses. Jack followed me to the centre of the circle. It was wide, and the sarsens were flat thin things far taller than ourselves. There's always a legend with these places: once there were seven sisters, and so on. There would be cautionary tales – no two people would count the stones and arrive at the same total, the stones line up with the stars, and all the rest.

Obviously, stoned people couldn't count stones. That went without saying. And there are enough stars for hundreds of them to be in line with anything. Those are coincidences, by-products. They're the sarsen equivalent of Teflon.

This is what the stones were for:

You would be taken there, in the middle of one of the more important nights, by men from the village. You had known them all your life but did not know them now. They were different men by night. Men are like that. They force-fed you a drink that tasted of flowers and then spun you around in the centre of the stone circle. You would be dressed in a white robe, the hem rising and circling you, making a white wheel in the night. The men would stand, with their knives, and they would not be the men you knew at all. And then in they would come, with a whirl of the blades and the blood would be black and from outside the stones would come the howls of something awful and immense, the rational world now shrunk to this one stone circle, everything outside it dread chaos and disorder, the sky rent by the howls of a rapacious and ancient god.

That's my theory, anyway.

We stood in the circle. Nothing happened. We walked around the circle. I touched one of the stones. I expected a feeling, some connection to the past. It felt like a stone. Jack was looking the way a husband looks when his wife takes him to the shoe shop. We sat in the shadow of a stone.

'I'm not getting anything,' I said. I wanted to tell him about the parchment, and the ritual we could use to live forever, but I didn't think he was ready for it. The sun was warm and we hadn't got anything to drink. After a while we walked back past the tepees and VW campers.

Tepees, for fuck's sake. Didgeridoos. As though any dead culture would do. They didn't know the names of their own gods. They couldn't play anything as complex as a lute or build the simplest round hut.

Jack managed to convince a shopkeeper he was eighteen, and bought us a two-litre bottle of acidic cider. That night, serenaded by the sounds of far Australia, we drank it. I talked to Jack about my plan to live forever. He said it was a good idea. I said we'd have to kill people. He said that was fine. The cider ran out much later, and we went to our separate tents. Later that night, I heard Jack being sick. He could never take his drink.

III

Properly speaking, *The Return of Thunderboy* is not the sequel to *Thunderboy*. It's a continuation. It's half of the story, and without it, the first half makes no sense. In the first movie (these aren't films, not by any stretch of the imagination) Thunderboy discovers his powers, which include the compulsory ability to fly without mechanical intervention and the taken-for-granted superhuman strength. He also discovers that he can control the weather, up to a point.

His weather powers mainly involve thunder. Much stock footage of black clouds is inserted between shots of inept actors.

In the second movie Thunderboy discovers that he can travel through time. He does this, travels back twenty years, finds himself as an ineffectual teenager, and gives himself the power that will make him Thunderboy.

It's circular. It's a single plot, disguised as two films. At first I thought it was an unexpected clever touch. Later I thought it was laziness.

Jack sat and absorbed it all. The mismatched dubbing, the creaking seats, the small-town bad boys frightening no one but themselves; all outside his perception. He saw nothing but the movies.

He found his magic there.

IV

He had to. There was nowhere else to find it. Every site in Avebury was crammed with poncho-wearing crusties, with their organic reek and their communal babies. Silbury Hill was off-limits. A barbed wire fence was coiled around its base. It was a strange little hill, short and conical with a flat top.

It got a flat top because lots of those land-loving free-roaming types used to stand on top of it, sometimes having a bit of a dance and then sitting around for a tune or two on the old tin whistle.

Travellers don't know any good tunes. They're all on weed, and weed makes you listen to Hawkwind, or Rush. One of them will have an untuned acoustic guitar and they will play the first two bars of *Wish You Were Here* cyclically, eternally, because they're not adept enough to play anything but the rhythm part.

We looked at Silbury Hill, walked around its base, made a detour to avoid a herd of cows – my mother's fears turned out to be genetic – and arrived at a long straight road. Haze rose from fields of dry grass. All of the farmers seemed to be growing straw or stubble. Across the road, a thin track led across a bleached field. Weary travellers in loose trousers trudged along it in both directions. The sun made its way to the centre of the sky and stayed there for three hours.

There was a barrow up there. Not the garden sort, the sort they used to erect around dead people back in the days when gods had bad tempers. We went to look at it. The path was of loose, sandy soil and large round stones. It led directly away from the road and then took a right-angle to the left. After half a mile it took a right-angle to the right. Then it went upwards, as though it wasn't hard enough going already. It went up onto a grassy rise.

I felt a tingle of anticipation. The stones had been stones, the hill had been closed. But this would be something else. The haze rose from the fields and surrounded us. It did cruel things to vision; Jack flickered in and out of existence. The fields rose and fell like the sides of a sleeping dog. A small hill in front of us rose sharply, pale green and stubbled. Thistles stretched from it. I shook the haze from my head. Jack became constant again, the fields settled down. The path led between the thistles, which had been real after all. Sweat crawled down my scalp. Something was afoot. We crested the ridge and there it was, the long barrow, and on it a horde of people babbling about the earth goddess and the right to roam and there it was, as expected, the sound of the first two bars of *Wish You Were Here* being played with exacting incompetence.

There was no magic in Avebury. It had been hammered flat by the sandals of too many shambling summer-holidaying students.

The visions in the fields had other causes. I had sunstroke. I spent the next two days in my tent.

On the third day – the copyright on this one *must* have gone by now – I rose. I could hear the sounds of many fingers tapping on the canvas. It grew dark, and a chill fell upon me.

Looking outside, I found that it was raining. Jack was sitting glumly in the entrance of his tent, watching puddles join forces. The last time I'd seen the sky it had been blue, and the sun had been jammed in the centre of it, balanced right at the top. The sky had been huge and the air had been on its way to solidity. Swinging your arms, you could feel it sliding through your fingers.

Now the sky had dropped two hundred feet, and it looked like a dishcloth. A constant rain fell. The ground was flat, so the rainwater gathered. It made inroads into my tent.

'It's in mine,' said Jack. 'My books are fucked.'

'They were fucked before. Have we got anything to eat?'

'Beans.'

'Have we got any matches yet?'

'Of course we fucking have,' he said, looking at me strangely. 'What's up with you? You've made no sense all day.'

'I've had sunstroke.'

'You've had no fucking sense, is what you've had. You were with me when we bought the matches. Remember? Remember buying the cider?'

I remembered that.

'I remember you vomiting,' I said.

'Right, but I threw it up and got it over with. I swear you've been drunk for two days. It's your metabolism or something. It's only this rain that's snapped you out of it.'

'That's because I've been suffering from sunstroke. Rain cures it.'

'Does it bollocks.'

'No, it doesn't cure bollocks. If you want those removing we'll need the penknife. If I haven't had sunstroke, why am I hungry?'

'Because you've been too pissed to eat for two fucking days, that's why. And you've done some right fucking wittering while you've been at it. We've had the field to ourselves. The rest of them were frightened they'd catch something off you.'

I hadn't noticed that the field was empty.

'It was probably the rain,' I said.

'They went yesterday, while it was sunny. While you were wittering. Like a little old woman, wittering away.'

'Well they heard a weather report and had to get back to Surrey or wherever they come from.'

'Whatever. So, beans?'

'Beans. And we can have them hot?'

'No.'

'What about our matches?'

'They're in there,' he said, pointing into his tent. I leaned far enough out of mine to peep in. The floor had been invaded by water. The rain had made inroads into my tent. It had made motorways through his.

'This is a fucking disaster,' he said. 'Why did I agree to go on holiday with you?'

'My good looks and charm?'

'You paid for the coach. That was about it. What the fuck are we going to do out here in the middle of nowhere in the fucking monsoon season?'

'Go to the cinema?' I suggested, and that's what we did.

V

A grim usherette with a lit cigarette and a face like the one Mother Theresa used to save the wear on her best one walked up and down the aisle with a tray of melted ice creams and warm Coca-Cola. The rude teenagers fell silent as she approached. The children of the family in the second row began to pester their parents for warm sweets. The offspring that would not shut up asked its parent for something.

There was the cheering sound of a slap.

There was no intermission. During the film, halfway through a scene, the lights came on and the image became unclear. This upset no one except Jack. Jack was distressed. He had been enjoying the movies, for his own strange reasons. I had theories about that:

One. Jack wanted to have a different identity. He wanted the one he had, and he also wanted another one that could be hidden under his everyday clothes. In Jack's case, that's an accurate description. He wore the same clothes every day. Under those he wanted to be someone more colourful.

Two. Jack wanted to be something out of the ordinary. He wanted to fly.

Three. Jack wanted to get the girl.

None of those seemed impossible. I knew Jack was interested in tattoos. Well, he had magazines about tattoos. It was more likely he bought them for the pictures of naked women, like everyone else, but there was a slim chance that he was interested in the tattoos.

Body piercing was something else he'd mentioned. Some sects believe that body piercing aids magic. It depends on the magic. I want to impose my body on the world, not the other way around.

Getting the bodywork touched up was easy. Learning to fly would be more difficult. Thunderboy did it by hanging from wires in front of a rear-projection screen, and even then he looked uncomfortable.

Getting the girl was something Jack would have to work out by himself.

The usherette dropped her cigarette butt on the floor and trod on it. It smouldered. She leaned over us.

'Ices,' she said, using the tone of voice you'd use when you were telling someone you'd accidentally reversed over their dog. 'Drinks.'

'No thanks,' I said.

'I'll have a coke,' said Jack. She handed him a battered can.

'Fifty,' she said.

'How much?' asked Jack.

'Fifty pence. Is he foreign?' she asked me. 'Help him with his money.'

'Here,' said Jack, handing over money. 'Thanks.'

She inspected the change at length.

'That should do,' she said. 'Right you are, then.'

She shuffled away. Jack sipped warm cola and the lights went down, or rather off. There was no dimming, the lights went out and the movie had never stopped. Jack settled down and fell back into it. I went to the toilet for a break.

To get there, I had to walk back out into the lobby. In a tiny refreshment booth a fat youth eyed his charges. The toilets were through a swinging door with loud hinges. Behind that, a corridor led to GENTS and LADIES.

A chart on the wall said that these toilets had been cleaned and inspected. There was a place for the cleaner to sign their name, and a place to put the date. The most recent date was five years old. The most recent signature, on closer inspection, turned out to be that of Mickey Mouse. I paddled across the cracked tiles and did my best to see what I looked like. There was a mirror but it had interference. It was cloudy and stained. I looked like a ghost. I splashed back to the auditorium and waited while my eyes got used to the darkness. I spotted Jack and sat next to him.

He was still wrapped in the movie. It was the second one, and there wasn't a lot of it left. Thunderboy had been back in time and given his younger self the secret identity that would turn his younger self into him. He'd fought off the ranks of large but dim henchmen, and now he was on his way to save the girl at the last minute. I hoped it was at the last minute. Sitting in a wet tent no longer seemed such a bad thing.

Jack watched avidly as Thunderboy took to the air. I looked at the cables that were holding him up. Perhaps magic is all like that, after all. Perhaps it's all misdirection. You don't look at the cables, you look at the flying man and make the effort to believe.

It was too much of an effort.

That was where it began, if you ask me. That was where Jack's body-modification thing was sparked off. He was watching those terrible movies and he was thinking about colouring himself in, about having a hidden identity. He'd end up, years later, run through with ironmongery and tattooed from head to foot.

Perhaps that was what the piercings were about. Perhaps he was future-proofing himself, turning the nerves off, getting set up for pain. Perhaps he saw more than I saw, all the time.

(That could be true. I never did find magic. I don't know how long I'll live. All mirrors look like that cinema mirror now, all of them faded and faint. These days I always look like a ghost. I don't know whether or not I'm getting older. I think Uncle Mickey knows something I don't. I'll try to ask him, one of these days.)

I sat in the cinema, knowing that I could manipulate Jack into carrying out the ritual, knowing that he would take my word for all of it. I thought I was in control. You don't see how wrong you are, sometimes. I was looking for magic and Jack had found it, in a pair of cheap movies. He sat there and watched Thunderboy fly to the rescue while I just sat there, seeing the wires.

PART SEVEN

Sam, aged thirty

Chapter Fourteen

I

When I got home I found some old clothes to wear. Detective work could be a dirty business, and I didn't want to get any new clothes dirty. I'd only have to wash them. I could throw old clothes away.

I knew this because Judy mentioned it on a regular basis.

'You can throw those old things away,' she'd say. 'You can buy new clothes.'

I could buy new clothes, but it wasn't my idea of fun. That was a point the two of us differed on. I thought shopping for clothes was something you did to get clothes. She thought it was fun in itself. She could do it for days.

I looked at the article in the *Pensnett Herald*. Jack had gone into a lot of detail about our imaginary crimes.

They are imaginary. Honestly they are. We didn't do anything. I'd know. I'd tell you.

Jack claimed we buried parts of the bodies. He mentioned the old railway tracks outside the town. He was very specific. There was an illustration accompanying the article, and it showed the alleged burial site.

I knew how to prove he was wrong. I could go to where the

bodies were supposed to be buried and dig. There wouldn't be any body parts there, and that would be that. Proof. I put a trowel in a plastic bag and took it with me. I thought a shovel might be difficult to sneak through town. I could be there and back in an hour, although the digging would take longer.

It was a mild day. The drizzle was in mist form, hanging rather than falling. I joined the old railway tracks at the edge of town and followed them to Jack's imaginary burial site.

The route led along a deep entrenchment and through a tunnel. I'm not afraid of the dark, but in the tunnel I was worried. I felt someone watching me, though I couldn't see anyone. I couldn't even see myself. It was dark in there. That's the way of tunnels. After that short dark walk, the old line ended at a wide flat patch of sandy soil. I got the trowel from my bag and realized that it would take a long time to dig up the whole area. It was easily twenty feet across, and twice as long. The trowel seemed very small. I looked over my shoulder. I still had the feeling that someone else was around. The railway line was in a deep trench. There were trees and bushes along the tops of both sides. Someone could have been hanging around in them. I decided I was being paranoid. No one would be hanging around looking at abandoned railway lines. The news was a day old, and there was nothing to see.

The feeling wouldn't go away. It had settled in for the evening.

I looked around. Not far from the railway line, a stick had been pushed some way into the ground. It looked like a marker.

I decided to dig there. The stick was rotten and fell to pieces when I tried to pull it free. I squatted and began to prod at the

earth with my trowel. The soil was wet and heavy. It clung
to the trowel in unhelpful clumps. When I tried to shake the
clods loose, they showered me with mud. I shook the trowel
more vigorously and lost my balance in a strange, slow way.
I fell into the mud in slow motion.

As a rule I only fall over in public. It's something to do with
people. The more of them able to see me, the more likely I am
to trip over things that aren't there or pratfall on black ice.
The more of them that are in earshot, the higher the chances
of me making an involuntary noise on my way down.

I made an involuntary noise. The ground was wet. Dudley
ground always is. I stood up after a ridiculous struggle. The
mud was fond of me, and didn't want to let me go. I hauled
myself free of it.

I thought of my involuntary noise. It had been high-pitched.
I was glad no one was there to hear it.

But I had the feeling that someone was, of course. I looked
at the trees. Nothing moved there. I looked at the ground. I'd
give it another shot, I decided. I swore at Jack, who wasn't
there to hear me. If I didn't find anything, that'd do. I wasn't
going to dig the whole area up to prove what I already knew. I
knelt in the mud where I'd been digging before and carried on
digging. I pulled out the few short sections of the damp stick
that had been marking the place. They were clearly very old
and rotten. I put them to one side and dug a little further.

There was nothing there. The stick hadn't been marking
anything. I looked at the remains of it. The three little
sections that had been under the ground looked different.
The other part had crumbled, rotted right through. Those
sections looked more solid, rotten in a different way.

I picked them up and cleared the mud from them. Two of

them had joints at each end. The third, smaller, piece only had a joint at one end.

It had a fingernail at the other one.

I wondered who would have put a fingernail on a stick. I knew some people had strange hobbies, but that was the first time I'd heard about that one.

Then it clicked. The fingernail was on the end of a finger that had been buried under the stick. The three little sticks were finger bones, what you'd get if you severed a finger at the knuckle and then buried it until the soft tissues decomposed.

What you'd get, for instance, if you needed to take something of the body with you after the murder. If you needed something to fuel the ritual.

I dropped my trowel and held onto the finger. I walked away from the burial ground. I didn't want to go through that dark tunnel again. I could climb up the revetment and make my way to the main road that way. I'd have to cross a hundred metres of wasteland, but at least it would be light. I reached the top of the trench and blundered through the wet bushes. The trees had low branches that caught me low down. I emerged from the shrubbery and saw the wasteland. Something rose from a chunk of concrete and approached me. It was a man, I noticed.

'Mr Haines,' a voice said. 'Here's a turn up. Here's a thing. I hope you don't mind if we don't shake hands. I think you've met some of my little friends. I'm more.'

More? More than what? What did he mean, and who were his little friends?

'Inspector Moore,' he explained. 'I think we'll be arresting you now, if you don't mind.'

II

He held out a transparent plastic bag. I looked at it.

'If you could put the finger in there,' he said. 'Good of you to dig it up for us. We could have been down there for weeks. I asked for a methane probe but they wouldn't authorize one. That leaves manpower alone for the job, and manpower means me. Excuse me complaining. You aren't going to try running for it? Now would be the time.'

He had a crumpled, sorry face. He was middle-aged but his face was ten years older. It drooped from his skull. His eyes were bright. In that face they looked like stars. He wore a battered felt hat and the traditional long mackintosh. His shoes were bright. The mud was steering clear of them. I dropped the finger bones into his bag.

'Not going to try running? Oh well,' he said, disappointedly. 'I came here to see whether there were any signs. Digging, that sort of thing. There weren't any, and then you turned up and made some. I should read you your rights, ideally. I can never get it right. I always think that your rights stop when you murder someone. So I don't tend to read people their rights. I tend to treat them quite badly.'

It was like being threatened by a teddy bear.

'I don't know anything about this,' I told him.

'No, I wouldn't have thought so. I seldom meet people who know anything about anything. They were somewhere else, with someone else. They never met the people concerned. Sometimes that's down to lapses of memory. I can usually help to fill in the gaps. The car is over there.'

I turned to look where he was pointing. Something flew into the small of my back, directly over one of my kidneys.

I dropped to my knees and wondered what had hit me. I thought I might have been shot.

'I do apologize,' said Moore. 'I thought you were about to make a break for it. I may have applied a little too much force. If you'd like to fill in a complaint, there'll be time at the station. Will that be necessary?'

'No,' I said. My lower left side ached. I stood.

'I thought not. Now this,' he said, raising the plastic bag containing the bones, 'belongs to someone who has something to complain about. The car really is that way.'

I looked at him.

'Go on,' he said. 'I won't thump you again. Not until we're at the station, anyway.'

He kept his word. The car turned out to be a dull Volvo. It didn't seem to suit him. I'd have expected a Jag or a crumpled Escort. He drove it at an ordinary speed, with me sitting next to him in the passenger seat. He stopped at traffic lights. I could have got out. I didn't. I didn't have anywhere else to go.

III

At the police station I was led past a crowd of uniformed people who couldn't be bothered to dislike me. So they ignored me instead. Moore led me into a room where three chairs surrounded a desk. A cassette recorder sat on the desk. A video camera in a high corner had a red blinking light on it. Moore told me to take a seat and then left me to it.

I looked at my watch. It was six thirty. That wasn't even

late. That was hardly evening. I wondered what time I'd be going to bed. I wondered where, too.

The room was painted that old institutional shade of pale green. At one time, back in the sixties when the architects all thought that concrete walkways were the next big thing, someone in government bought a huge shipment of pale green paint. Thousands of gallons of it. It had been earmarked for use during the war, if fighting broke out somewhere pale green, but the war ended inconveniently and the paint went into storage.

For years it sat in enormous hogsheads, safe from prying eyes. Then a civil servant, with nothing to do now that the war had left the country bankrupt, came across a docket noting the contents.

He bought the whole supply from the government for six-pence, waited six months, and sold it back to the government for thousands. The government, suddenly flush with pale green paint it had already possessed, passed the lot of it to local councils.

They used it to paint the inside walls of hospitals, schools, police stations and prisons. They painted council offices pale green. If it had been weatherproof they'd have painted roads with it.

In some places it's still there, always in high rooms, applied directly to unplastered brick walls. In the centre of the dead-flesh coloured ceiling will be a white globular light. Inside the light will be the bodies of fifty generations of house-flies.

It's cold paint and it hasn't faded because it hardly had any colour in the first place. When you're in among it, you're either in trouble or in a shitty job. It's bad news paint.

I sat and looked at it. It was all over the walls and the ceiling. There were no windows. I'd expected a mirror. There was always a mirror in the room when Kojak interviewed suspects. On the other side of the mirror would be another room, from where the mirror would be a window, and in there Stavros would be busy taking notes and waiting for the scriptwriter to give him a funny line.

The door was wooden and edged, top and bottom, with metal strips. There was no handle on the side of it that I could see. A peephole in it was open. No one was looking at me.

The floor was of even cement. The table and chairs were loose. The room held several smells. There was the expected smell of cigarette smoke and the unsurprising smell of sweat. There was another, sharper, smell, something like human flesh going off.

It was coming from me. I was muddy and sweating. I was also frightened and confused. I knew that I hadn't killed anyone, and I didn't think that Jack would have.

I assumed that Jack was in a room similar to the one I was in. They'd want to talk to him. He was the one who'd confessed in the first place.

That was where I got stuck. Jack had confessed to something we hadn't done. Jack had made it up.

But there was that finger. That had been solid enough.

Perhaps Jack had planted it to help his confession along. Which meant he must have got it from somewhere. From someone, really. They're not the sort of things you find lying around, fingers. They come with owners and the owners want to keep them.

Removing them takes a good twist with a pair of pliers, and you have to keep a grip. It's better if there's someone else to help. They can hold the wrist steady and you can twist the finger off. Once the skin tears it pops free without a lot of bother.

I didn't know about any of that. It arrived in my head the way a bullet would. I had no idea where it had come from.

I'm being honest with you here. I have secrets, and I'll be keeping them. There are things you don't need to know. I'd never killed anyone. Honestly.

The bones had been too old, I realized. They were years old. Jack couldn't have acquired them recently. If they were ten years old, that would mean he was right. But he wasn't right. He couldn't be.

I saw a finger being popped out of its joint, and a dead woman with cats sitting on her.

It must have been the newspaper reports. Jack must have been talking to me when I was drunk. Perhaps he was playing an elaborate joke. Perhaps the next person in a uniform would turn out to be a strippogram.

I thought not. It was too elaborate to be a practical joke. Besides, I didn't want to see Moore naked. His little friend Stiles would be all right. Perhaps she'd be along to question me.

When would they be in? I'd been there hours. I was nervous and I needed to go to the toilet on several counts. The smell of cigarette smoke made me want a cigarette. I looked at my watch. I'd been there about eight minutes. Time was in a state. That made two of us.

I tapped my fingers on the table. It made me think of fingernails and I stopped. My scalp itched. The red light on the video camera blinked. Did that mean they were filming me? I tried to remember if I'd done anything incriminating

while I'd been there. It had only been eight minutes. I couldn't
have done much.

I'd picked my nose, but only to pass the time. It hadn't been
what you'd call productive. I'd scratched my scalp. I'd rubbed
drying mud from my hands and crumbled it onto the floor.
None of that could get you hard time.

Being implicated in murder could, of course. That was held
to be bad. If they were talking to Jack he'd be confessing. He
had a history of it. He had form. If Jack was confessing he'd
be including my name. He told Eddie Finch that it had all
been my idea.

I looked at the watch. Another minute had elapsed. It had
done it very slowly. Time was doing interesting things.

I had a lot of time to study it.

At eight-thirty I was escorted to the toilet by an expression-
less uniformed man built like a Soviet shot-putter. I washed
using a tiny bar of filthy soap and cold water. I was moved to
a cell. It was like the room I'd spent my evening in, except that
there was no table or chairs. There was a bed and a bucket.

The graffiti was cleverer than you might expect.

I lay on the bed. There was a peephole in the door made of
metal. Someone was watching me. I lay down, knowing that
I wouldn't sleep.

I went to sleep.

I'm not going to tell you what I dreamt.

Chapter Fifteen

I

I woke up on a filthy bed. I'd done that before. I didn't know where I was, and I'd woken up in that state plenty of times too. There was a light on. I didn't sleep with the light on. My father used to turn lights off wherever he went. As you went from room to room he'd follow you, turning lights off where you'd been. He thought that if you left lights on the house would catch fire or the electricity bill would increase exponentially.

These days we turn the lights off to save electricity to save the planet. The trouble with that is that the planet is too far gone. It's not the ice caps or the ozone layer. It's that the seasons have got out of whack, and the wind blows all year round. It's that we get sunsets that you only used to see on canvas. It's bees bumbling about in February and flowers dropping dead in June. It's never having a winter, just this period of colder rain and then back to the drizzle and wind.

Perhaps that's just Dudley. But I don't think so. I think saving the planet by putting less water in the kettle is like putting a sticking plaster on a leper. It's too late. The world is on its way somewhere. We're going with it.

Leave the lights on. At least we'll be able to see what happens.

I sat up. The bed was narrower than I was. It was hard and it had the smell of a dead dog in summer. The walls were painted that institutional shade. There was a metal door. Everything snapped into focus.

There was an eye watching me through the peephole. There were metallic sounds from the door and it opened. Moore stood outside, looking at me with no particular expression. Behind him stood PC Fields, his legs slightly apart. His bored expression looked as though he practised it in front of the bedroom mirror. Moore had the hang of it. Moore just looked bored.

'Mr Haines,' said Moore. He had the hang of speaking drily, too. 'Would you care to join us for a chat? A cup of tea perhaps? Most of our interviewees like a cigarette. I hope you have one, because we're not running a tobacconists here.'

He ushered me into a pale green corridor, and along it to the room I'd spent yesterday evening in.

'There. You take one side of the table and we'll have the other. I don't suppose there'll be much to say, to be honest. There you were with the evidence. Caught you with your finger in the till.'

'Someone else's finger,' said Fields, closing the door and helping me to sit by putting his hands on my shoulders and pushing me down into the chair.

'Fields,' said Moore, despairingly.

'Sorry,' said Fields. 'I always get a bit carried away when we finger a suspect.'

Moore gave him a pained look. The two of them sat

next to one another. The table was between us. Moore pressed a button on the cassette recorder and it began to play a tune.

'Ah,' he said. Fields stepped in and pressed another button. Moore leaned over the table and told the recorder what day it was and who was present. The red light on the video camera was still blinking. Perhaps it was a false camera. Perhaps it was a decoy.

They make them. You buy them and attach them to your house and they have a light that blinks and that's all they do. They aren't cameras. It's a bluff. It's a sign of something. I know about this. Everything is a sign of something. When you need a camera that isn't a camera to keep uninvited guests out of your house, that's a sign.

The world is on its way somewhere.

And wherever it's going, someone will be filming it.

It doesn't help, anyway. The more elaborate the security, the more equipped the people who will come through it. And – let's get this straight – someone will come through it. Whatever you have, infrared sensors, intemperate canines, gin traps, pungee sticks or landmines, one day it won't be enough. One day it'll be breached, and so will you.

And then they'll kill you, remove the odd finger or toe, and maybe (if they have time) burgle the house.

It must have been the room getting to me. I tried to think cheerful thoughts. I tried to think what I'd been told on those outward-bound management courses. We'd done imaginary interviews. Teams of managers would throw questions at you across a desk , and you'd fail to return them. It was like being in the British Olympic table tennis team. Everything that came at you caught you unawares.

This was the same thing. All I had to do was field their questions.

They were quiet. Moore was looking at me gloomily, as though I was a hole in his favourite slipper. Fields was cleaning nine of his fingernails with the remaining one. Moore looked at me. I waited. I had seen this in films. They were waiting for me to fall apart and tell them everything. Their problem was that I had nothing to tell them.

I thought that I probably had more problems than they did. I knew what they were up to. The cassette recorder ticked quietly, recording nothing.

After a while Moore stopped looking at me and looked at Fields.

'PC Fields,' he said, 'I was under the impression that you would be conducting this interview.'

'Oh,' said Fields. He gave up on his nails. 'Now. Last night you were found at the scene of what we suppose to be a crime.'

'We suppose that,' said Moore, 'because there were human remains there. They were in a poor condition. There were several of them. They're with Forensics. I don't suppose they'll find anything out from them. We've had people digging all night, and now everything is with the boffins.'

'I used to do that,' I said, meaning digging. I watched the two of them misunderstand.

'Is that thing recording?' asked Moore.

Fields nodded.

'That must be a first. Now, I think we've just had some sort of a confession. It isn't as lengthy or detailed as the one your friend Mr Ives gave us. That was more of a memoir than a confession. You say you used to bury people?'

'No,' I said. 'I meant I used to do digging.'

'So it was Mr Ives who buried the bodies?'

'Partial bodies,' noted Fields.

'Indeed. Partial bodies. So you were just there to do the digging? Well, I have to say that isn't the way Mr Ives tells it. He tells us that you made him do the digging.'

'And the murders.'

'So how did it happen?' Moore leaned forward, putting his hands on his knees. He looked mildly interested.

'It didn't happen,' I said. 'I know nothing about it.'

'And there we were getting somewhere,' said Fields. 'That's something we often hear. No one we talk to knows anything. I find that aggravating.'

'It would be nice to have some variety,' agreed Moore. 'Now. The thing I find interesting is this. I've done this job for a very long time. I can't say I've learned much from it. I haven't gained any special insights into human nature. I can't always spot the guilty ones. Sometimes younger people do it. Sometimes Forensics come up with something.'

'Not very often,' said Fields.

'No, not very often,' agreed Moore, putting his head on one side. 'But it does happen. It's always nice for them when it does. After all, they get most of the money, so it's only fair that they get to solve things now and then. I can't spot the innocent people either. I don't understand that. I've read about detectives. I ought to have evolved specialized senses. I should be able to smell guilty people.'

'Some of them smell,' said Fields, tilting his chair back onto two legs.

'Not of guilt. Now, by way of balance, from time to time I get hunches. I watched you dig up those bones. You looked as though you were surprised to find them. That doesn't suggest that you knew they were there. To me, it suggests the opposite. Then there was the way you slept. Guilty people behave strangely. They have moods. They become paranoid.'

'Until they're caught,' said Fields.

'Until they're caught,' agreed Moore. 'Once we catch them they stop all that. There's no point to it. They seem to be relieved. Obviously, they deny everything.'

'They weren't there,' said Fields.

'They didn't see anything,' said Moore. 'They can't remember anything and anyway, it wasn't them. But they're easy. The people who have a hard time of it in here are the innocent ones. That's partly because they do feel guilty. They feel guilty about all sorts of things. Little infidelities.'

'Family things,' said Fields. His chair was precariously balanced. I felt the same.

'Overdue library books,' said Moore. 'They don't know what they're going to be hit with.'

'That's an unfortunate turn of phrase,' said Fields. He had looked cheerful until then. His face tightened around a sharper expression.

'Possibly so,' said Moore. 'That may be the case. So innocent people have a hard time of it because they think about all sorts of terrible things, and guilty people know exactly what they're here for.'

'Innocent people also have a bad time of it,' said Fields, 'because it takes that much longer to get them to confess.'

'Most of them do, given the right stimulus,' said Moore. He sat back. 'Now, you are an interesting case. You behave as though you are innocent. You seem worried. You have things on your mind.'

'Family things,' said Fields for the second time. I wondered what he knew.

'And you seemed surprised to find those bones,' continued Moore. 'But then, on the other hand, we have the confession of your friend Mr Ives. He places you at the scenes of the crimes. And it's clear he's not making the whole thing up, because we have evidence. We have something to go on. Which gives me a little puzzle to consider. Because you can't be innocent and guilty. You have to be one or the other. So, what's the story?'

'I don't know,' I said. 'I know nothing about any of this. All I know is that Jack imagined all this.'

'He imagined it in some detail,' said Moore. 'He went to the trouble of imagining some body parts and doing such a good job of it that the rest of us can see them. Even Forensics can see them, assuming that they haven't lost them or eaten them or something. So we'll assume that he didn't imagine it, and that you do know something. You do know something, don't you?'

He leaned over the table and switched off the cassette recorder.

'Clumsy,' said Fields.

'That's the thing with old detectives,' said Moore, standing and removing his jacket. 'Too used to old methods. I do find that I switch things off accidentally.' He flexed his arms. He interlaced his fingers and cracked his knuckles.

'Now,' he said, walking around the end of the table. 'Let's do this the old-fashioned way.'

I looked at the camera.

'It's a dummy,' said Fields, standing up so sharply that his chair jumped back across the floor. He removed his own

jacket and walked around his end of the table. Moore put
a heavy hand on my shoulder.

'I think we could do with some refreshments. PC Fields,
would you be good enough to get us a cup of tea each? And
see if you can find someone to repair the recorder. It doesn't
appear to be working. I will make sure nothing unfortunate
happens to Mr Haines.'

'I'll be right back,' said Fields.

'Good,' said Moore. 'I wouldn't want to be left alone with
a prisoner without an escort or any means of recording the
conversation. Who knows what might happen?'

'I'll be a minute or two. I'm not sure where I last saw
the kettle.'

'Forensics,' said Moore. 'And wash it out before you use it.'

Fields nodded and left.

II

I was aware that the whole interview had been stage-managed.
It had been designed to leave me frightened and alone with
Moore. I was aware that it had worked. Moore let his hand
rest on my shoulder. He moved behind me, out of sight. I
wanted to turn around and watch him. I wanted to know
what he was up to.

'If I was in your place,' he said, 'I'd be a worried man. We'll
get to the bottom of this. You do know that? We'll find out
what we want to know.'

His voice seemed to be coming from all around me. His
hand left my shoulder. I felt myself hunching. I clenched all
over. I waited for him to hit me.

'You seem tense,' he said, with a hint of concern in his voice. 'You seem frightened. There's nothing to be frightened of. Tell me what you know and we'll be fine.'

I failed to relax.

'Well,' he said, moving back into view. He sat on the desk in front of me and put one foot on the seat of my chair. His shoes were enormous. They were very polished. I can never get my shoes to shine. Perhaps I should try polishing them. There was a smell of leather.

'Can I offer you a cigarette? If we're going to be at this for a while you'll be wanting a cigarette. You have a cigarette and a cup of tea and think about things. After that, if you want to talk to us, fair enough. Is that Fields with the kettle?'

He looked towards the door. I looked too. At once he straightened his leg. That enormous shoe slammed into my thigh. The chair flew back and fell. I fell with it. I landed badly, and discovered that solid cement floors are cold and hard. Something else hit me somewhere. Again. I didn't know what he was hitting me with. It might have been the floor. I hadn't been in a fight since I was at school, and in those days fights lasted until someone gave up or had a nosebleed. I didn't think I was going to be allowed to give up, and he was too efficient to make me bleed. I couldn't even tell what part of me he was hitting. The blows jerked my whole body. I was being mangled by a mild-mannered, middle-aged man.

It stopped. I waited for something else to hit me. When it became obvious that nothing was going to I raised my head.

Moore was back in his chair on the far side of the desk. He looked bored, as if this was all in a day's work.

'You appear to have taken a tumble,' he said. 'I hope you didn't land badly. This floor is a bit unforgiving. If you'd like to get back in your seat we can carry on chatting.'

My chair was back upright. I stood up and fell into it. I half expected pulverized kidneys to drop out of me, but they stayed where they were. Thinking about it, I'm not surprised. They were having a bad enough time on the inside.

I did an inventory of injuries. Nothing seemed to be broken. There were painful areas on the back of my head and my upper arms. My thigh hurt.

It wasn't the pain, anyway. It was an atmosphere. While he'd been attacking me I'd been helpless. All I could be was attacked. I was not in control of anything. I was only the thing being battered.

'I could report that,' I said. I knew it was a stupid thing to say. There was no one I could report it to.

'Report what?' he asked. 'You fell out of your chair. These things happen. Let's not try to make it into something it wasn't.'

'You put your foot on it,' I said, 'and you kicked it over. When I wasn't looking. The next time you try that I will be looking. I'll have my eyes on you. And I won't be the one on the floor.'

I don't know where the aggression came from. As a general rule I'm not at all aggressive. Perhaps it was simply that I'd had enough. I'd been falsely accused, falsely imprisoned, falsely beaten and I had no proof of any of it. I wasn't even bruised. Where were the Panorama team the one time in your life you needed them? By being aggressive I changed all that. I was in control after all. Moore was a middle-aged man. Suddenly, he looked it. Suddenly, the balance changed.

'Let's talk about things,' I said. 'Let's see where we are. You have no evidence. You have the word of someone certifiable. You have bones that don't belong to anyone. They could have come from a hospital incinerator. They could have come from a graveyard. You're the tail end of a dead breed. Why do you get this joke crime to investigate? Because you can't be trusted with anything else? How long until they shuffle you out of the job altogether? Where are you going to go then? Out there with the people who've been through this room.'

Moore linked his fingers. 'Perhaps so,' he said. 'But for the time being, you're the one in this room. And they won't be shuffling me anywhere until I've finished with you. And if you raise a hand to me three other officers will come in and use entirely unjustifiable force to subdue you. Then we'll sentence you for that and you'll spend a week in a soft prison and your employment prospects will look worse than mine.'

He leaned towards me. All of the control was back with him. My anger had been and gone. It had only been adrenaline, after all. All I had left of it was a taste like tin in my mouth.

The door opened.

'Here come the reinforcements,' smiled Moore, unbuckling his belt. 'Now let's see what we can get you to admit.'

Fields walked in.

'Hold on,' he said. 'There's a problem. It's Forensics.'

'What is?' asked Moore.

'They've done a quick test or two on the bones. They're too old.'

'In what way?'

'They can't be sure. But they're at least five hundred years old. They can tell that. Perhaps even eight hundred.'

'They did it bloody fast,' said Moore, his eagerness dissipating. 'Are they sure?'

'Very sure.'

'Such is life,' said Moore, buckling his belt. 'It appears that
the case against you is no longer tenable. You can go, Mr
Haines. Do be sure to pick up a complaints form from the
front desk.'

They let me go. There weren't any complaint forms on the
front desk. It didn't matter. I wasn't thinking about that. I
was thinking about Jack. He knew about the bodies. They
were eight hundred years old. That wizard, the one I'd read
about, the one at Dudley Castle; he'd be eight hundred years
old, if he wasn't dead.

Jack knew about the bodies.

Jack knew about the ritual.

I thought about his piercings and tattoos, his bizarre home
life. His damaged girlfriend.

I'd known him at school. I'd always thought we were the
same age. Now I wondered if he wasn't a little older.

Somewhere in the region of seven hundred and seventy
years, for example.

Chapter Sixteen

———◆———

I

When I got home I realized that I was late for work. I hadn't thought of that. I'd had other things on my mind – being arrested, having a friend who was centuries old, little things like that.

I was glad that Judy wasn't there. Sometimes, she would come and stay at my house and find things to complain about. I called work and spoke to Theresa. I told her that I had family problems, and that I'd be in as soon as I could.

She asked me to hold on. The telephone played tinny music to me. After a long wait Ted Wiggins said 'Hello?'

'Hello,' I said. 'Ted. I've got some problems at home.'

'Yes,' he said. 'Yes. You have some problems here, too. To be frank you're suspended on full pay. I don't suppose it'll come to anything. I suppose they'll bring you back in once it blows over. It's the police thing. It puts us in an awkward position.'

There was more of it, in the same vein. I didn't take any of it in. I had lost contact with my ears. They would sack me. That's what it meant when they suspended you. It meant they'd trawl through your personnel files and rifle your desk for anything incriminating.

If there wasn't anything they'd put something there.

That was the end of the job, then.

I mumbled something to Ted and put the telephone down. I hadn't had time to restock the alcohol department. I slumped onto the sofa.

Someone had stolen my cushions. The ones Judy had brought with her.

I noticed that other things had also gone missing. There was a blank space on the wall where she'd hung a small print of a pre-Raphaelite bint. There were gaps in the CD collection.

I checked it. It had improved. All of her top twenty things were gone. She'd also taken my Doves CD.

I knew what had happened. She'd gone.

The house seemed emptier.

I went from room to room. All of the female things had gone. All of the colours had been removed. I still had the gadgets and music. I still had the tasteless videos.

I called her but there was no answer. I let the telephone ring. She'd be at work, I realized. I called the work number.

A recorded voice told me to press one for timetable information, two for complaints, or three to talk to a human being. I pressed three and waited for twenty minutes.

'Yes?' said an angry female voice.

'I'm trying to get in touch with Judy,' I said. 'If she's there.'

'Is that Sam?' asked the voice. I recognized it. It was Lynn.

'Yes.'

'Then you're wasting your time. I'm sorry, Sam, but she doesn't want to talk to you. She's had enough.'

'It's a mistake. They've let me go.'

'It's not that. She hasn't been happy. She says that you look at other girls. All the time. She says you think she's a nuisance. If she tries to do anything for you, it's a joke. I don't think she'll talk to you. If you give her some time, that might do it. I'm sorry, Sam.'

There was a dead click. I set the phone down. It was obviously in a bad mood. Every time I used it, a part of my life was excised.

I knew what giving someone some time meant. It meant: go away – forever. Please. I wouldn't be seeing her again. I'd have to get my bus pass from somewhere else. I'd have to buy another copy of the Doves CD. I went to the bedroom and lay on the bed. There was plenty of room for me. The house didn't seem emptier. It was still cluttered with all of my junk.

I seemed emptier.

I watched the ceiling. I couldn't think of anything else to do. At least the ceiling was solid. Nothing else was. I couldn't rely on my friends, on the world, on anything.

If Jack had buried those bones, eight hundred years ago, what did that mean?

I'm no good with supernatural forces. I'm a modern guy. I have gadgets: DVDs, CDs, a PC. I have an MP3 player. The thirteenth century is a long way away.

Of course, you wouldn't know that walking down Dudley High Street, with its smelly market and its disconcerting townsfolk. Dudley never got past the visit of the warlock. I'd always thought that Dudley was awful for no particular reason.

Now I wondered.

Those bones meant that there must be some truth to the warlock's story. Before he went to Hollywood, surely James Whale had read about it. The castle on the hill, the strange noises and peculiar lights, the ignorant townsfolk burning it all down: he'd made a coded film about it. All of that was in Dudley's history, and in Dudley the history was close to the surface. All of those mineshafts cut into the foundations, and the wrecked castle still looking down at it all. The road system that had been designed for a light load of horse-drawn carriages, clogged now by traffic. The canals choked with shopping trolleys, the railway lines without rails.

Dudley had been sent strange in the thirteenth century, and it had stayed that way. Dudley was tainted.

So what about Jack? My childhood friend? At school he'd been the same age as me, to look at. He'd been a little boy. A strange one, granted, but not a grown man. Did he get older and younger cyclically as the centuries passed, so that he could pass for different people? Which one had he been, the warlock or one of the apprentices? Surely not the misshapen one?

I thought about the woodcut that had accompanied the tale of the warlock. There had been nothing obviously wrong with the misshapen one.

Perhaps it was something under his clothes. Jack had plenty of strange things under his clothes. All of his piercings and tattoos: didn't that seem ritualistic? Hadn't he told me that it was?

Someone knocked on the door.

I still trusted the door. It was the telephone that was doing all the bad news that day. The front door hadn't done anything to blot its copybook.

I rolled off the bed and went downstairs. I walked past my shelves. They were standing solid, packed with my junk.

That saucer of nails was still on the top shelf. I made a mental note to do something with them.

I opened the door and found Jack standing outside.

Perhaps we could do something with the nails after all, I thought. He was carrying a hammer.

II

He wandered in past me. I couldn't think of a way to stop him. If he had been alive eight hundred years he'd have picked up some survival tips. And he had a hammer. I closed the front door and followed him to the living room. He sat on the sofa. I stood by the door. If he turned nasty I'd be able to outrun him.

'They let me go,' he said. 'They had the evidence and they let me go. Did you tell them anything?'

I shook my head.

'No,' he said. 'You wouldn't have.'

'Jack,' I said, 'those bones were centuries old. Whatever happened to them didn't happen ten years ago. It couldn't have.'

'No,' he said. 'Fair play. The thing is, I remember it.'

He looked up. I'd been concentrating on the hammer, and I hadn't noticed his face. It was drawn in, closed. I knew what he was going through. He was shut in with his thoughts. I was in the same state.

He looked down again.

'I remember it,' he said. 'We were twenty. It was ten years

ago. I feel that. Ten years. I have these things in my head. I can't get rid of them. I was fucking delighted when they came to arrest me. I was over the fucking moon, and now they've given it up. Because they got the wrong bones.'

I'd been wrong about him. He wasn't eight hundred years old after all, and he had no more idea of what was going on than I did. We were both lost, in the same room but in completely different places.

'I got to thinking,' he said. 'You're there in the memories. It's the two of us, Sam and Jack. You're different, too. You're not you. There's something different but I can't see it properly. It's my piercings. It's them. Like I told you, they help me to see. They make me into a receiver.

'Your mate Spin told you that, too. You don't see him now, do you? He was on the news today. They showed me coming out of the police station. I thought it'd be a blanket over the head job, but they just shoved me out the front door. I saw Eddie. He's doing well out of this. He's got offers coming. Your man Spin came on the telly and showed this clip of me. He said I was confessing to stuff I hadn't done. Wasting police time.

'I don't remember how he sounded. I don't know if he spoke to tell you the truth. I got caught by a bunch of people on the way home. They told me what they thought of me. They didn't think much of me and they went into lots of detail.

'A lot of people round here don't like people who confess to things. Not if they haven't done anything. When the neighbours thought I was a killer I got some respect. Now they throw things through the windows. Broken glass all over the gaff.'

He considered that, and smiled.

'Been a treat for Lisa, though. The broken glass and that.'

I nodded as though he was making sense.

'So,' he said, 'there we are. Stuck with it. I remember what we did, you don't remember, the bones are too old. I can't make sense of that. You won't even try. I mean, for my sake. For our sake. If it's being pierced that makes me see it, then if you got yourself pierced . . .'

He let it hang. I shook my head. However he'd got to his state of mind, I wasn't about to follow him.

'Thought not,' he said. 'I know some clean places. Out on the bypass there's a studio opened, does body modifications. Fluorescent tattoos is the new thing. Done with bacteria. Bioluminescent. Have your name up in lights on your chest. We could go there, get you something small done. Nipple or something. No?'

I shook my head again.

'Thought not. So where does that leave me? I mean, I've got Lisa, she's not going to head for the hills just because of this. You, though. You're still cracking on that you're innocent. You aren't though, are you? I know you. I called round at your brother's and he told me you weren't there. You weren't going to be welcome there, not ever again. So, what does that mean? Your brother doesn't want you at his house. Does that make me think you're innocent? Not much, no. Not at all.'

'That has nothing to do with this,' I said. 'That's something else.'

'Oh yes? And what would that be?'

That would be family things. That would be private.

There are things I haven't told you. This is one of them:

III

Four or five years ago, when I was about twenty-five, I was doing nothing, going nowhere. I had no real job and I had no plans. I had no girlfriend and a rented flat in a block that's since been demolished. I would go to see my brother, good old Tony, and freeload off him. He didn't earn a lot himself, but not much is better than nothing, even split two ways.

He had a semi-detached house. It seemed wonderfully quiet. My flat was surrounded by three others on the same level, and by one on each of the adjacent floors. It was like watching a film in a multiplex cinema. Bits and pieces of other soundtracks rode into mine.

Tony's house was silent. It wasn't just the two of us, of course. There was his wife, Caroline, who was not my type. More to the point, I wasn't her type. She didn't know what type I was but she knew she didn't like it. She was rounder than the women I liked. She had one tooth that was larger than any of the others. It made her look like a rabbit.

We didn't get on, or not get on. We just ignored one another. From time to time she'd drop hints about finding work. I did some decorating for them.

They pretended to like it.

I tried not to go round too often. I knew I was intruding. I knew they didn't want me there every evening. I'd go to my flat and channel-hop using the unresponsive remote control on the unlicensed television. There were only three channels I could get. A man from a neighbouring flat had offered to get me satellite, cheap, ask no questions. I asked a question about money and found it was out of my reach. I was below cheap. This was before my days with the B&S Building Society. In those days I was merely flat broke. It wasn't until after I was a student that I entered the world of negative balances.

I would sit in my terrible armchair, wearing two coats because the heating was on the blink. I would press the buttons on the remote control with numb fingers, and nothing would happen. The remote control only worked when the light was right, and the light wasn't right very often. There were controls on the television but to get to them you had to leave the chair.

I didn't like to leave the chair. In any case, there would be nothing on any of the channels. Pressing the buttons was more a form of exercise than anything else. It was something to do.

I'd cook simple meals on the gassy stove. I'd wash the crockery once a week. I'd wait to go to bed and then I'd wait to go to sleep.

I'd go round to Tony's one night in two. I needed to see someone.

Caroline began to point out job vacancies.

'They're taking on people at Scratto,' she'd say. 'I hear they pay quite well.'

'You could go to college,' Tony would say. 'You got the grades, kiddo. You could get some qualifications and get a decent job. You're the one with the brains.'

Which didn't help to explain why I felt that I had failed. I was going nowhere. If I went to college, I'd be going nowhere somewhere else. I didn't want to be the brains. I wanted to be the one with the house and the wife. I wanted to be the one with the life.

The thing with depression is, you can't see it from the inside. From outside it's obvious. You see someone in this spiral down to their lowest place, and you tell them *things will look better next week* or *perhaps you should talk to someone* or *stop fucking sulking*, depending on how long it's been going on.

From the inside there is no outside. There's the room, and you alone in it, whoever else is there. There's no point going outside. There's no point in breathing, other than for the exercise. From the outside, depression is false. It's a skewed viewpoint.

From the inside, it's the other way round. Everyone else is wrong. They're the ones with the skewed viewpoints. The rest of the world has the wrong worldview.

I didn't even know I was depressed. It was something that happened to bored housewives or those madmen who take their satchels on bus rides. I was fine, apart from wanting to die. I was right. It wasn't until the depression vanished that I knew it had been there. Afterwards I was proud to have lived through it. It seemed to be something solid. It felt like an achievement.

At the time it felt like a sea, swamping me. I would go round and sit with Tony and Caroline and they'd ask me this and that and I would sit, silent. They'd go to other rooms and I'd hear them talking about me. Tony would tell me to pull myself together. Caroline would hug me.

That helped, that human contact. I felt as though I was part of a family.

The depression became cyclic, rising and falling. I became two people. I was the bright one who knew that the gloom was illusory. I was the dark one who could not see the point of breathing. We circled one another. Neither of them was complete.

When Tony was at work Caroline would come and talk to me. She tidied my flat and hid my gloomier records. I'm still missing a Joy Division bootleg, a live recording.

As if Joy Division could ever accurately have been described as live.

She would hug me and I would brighten. The depression left me, but didn't go far. I'd see it in corners, behind the television, waiting to engulf me again.

She would hug me, and I would pretend that I was still lost. Because I liked the feel of her, and I'd got used to that rabbit tooth she had. I wouldn't say I manipulated her, not as such.

It was a family thing, that was all. It was our business.

I got better, and she got worse. She said that she was bored. The bored housewife caught the depression. I consoled her.

I will not draw a diagram. I'm not proud of any of this. I slept with her, in the dead afternoons while Tony was at work. Not in their house. Only in my flat.

Because I was no longer depressed, life felt free to play a little joke on the two of us. She became pregnant. I impregnated her. She named the child Samantha, after me.

I went to university to avoid all that. I was away for the birth. Caroline would send me letters, photographs. I did not go to the christening. I fell away from the three of them, my brother, his wife, my daughter.

These family things; what can we do with them? How do we even survive?

She told him. She came out with it. That was why he told me not to go back to the house. I had no way to deal with that.

I could no longer hide inside the depression. You couldn't go there deliberately.

I did what he wanted. I stayed away.

IV

I didn't tell Jack any of that. It was none of his business. I told him that Tony had banished me for personal reasons, which was as close to the truth as Jack needed to go.

He seemed to take my word for it.

'That leaves us up the creek, doesn't it?' he asked, sitting on my sofa, swinging his hammer. 'That leaves stuff up in the air. Come on, mate. For my sake. Come with me and get yourself a small tattoo. See what that brings to mind.'

'There's nothing to bring,' I told him. 'There's nothing there. You read about it somewhere. You read about this wizard.'

'Wizard?' he asked, genuinely confused.

'It doesn't matter,' I told him. 'It's something I read. It's something you read, even if you can't remember it. That's all it is. You've got your wires crossed.'

'I thought that would be it,' he said sadly. 'I didn't think we'd get anywhere much. Tell you what though, if that's all true, how do you explain that?'

He pointed out of the window. I moved to see what was outside. The road was empty.

Something flew into me from behind. I hit the window and bounced back into the room.

I was getting sick of falling for the same trick. It had been bad enough the first time. The next time someone asks me what's over there, I'll tell them to look for themselves.

Jack was standing over me. He had a hammer in his hand. He reached to my top shelf and picked up a saucer. It rattled. It would do. It had nails in it.

'I think you need to be pierced,' he said. 'I think you're *this close* to understanding. And if the mountain won't come to Mohammed . . .'

He leaned over me. I blacked out.

PART EIGHT

Sam, aged twenty

Chapter Seventeen

I

I was sitting in my bedroom, listening to old CDs. The ritual was over. All we had to do now was wait, and we could do more of that than anyone else could. We didn't have all the time in the world – and neither did the world, according to the scientists – but we had more time than anyone else alive.

I hoped this wouldn't mean we'd be old for centuries. Hopefully, we'd age more slowly. Five hundred years of forgetting what your name was wouldn't be much fun. I was hoping for three hundred years of not quite being thirty. With any luck, civilization would cave in before my apparent age reached forty.

Apart from that, there was the question of finances. I didn't want to live for centuries on thirty quid a week. I wanted more than that. I wanted silly money. I wanted real money, not the seven-figure scrapings that keep minor celebs in champagne and cocaine. I wanted the sort of money that stopped being an amount any longer, the sort of money that became a thing in itself, giving birth to offshore funds and tax fiddles and accountants. I wanted football money. That sort of money would outlast the landslides and rising water tables. The gloomier scientists gave the world around a hundred years before it became untenable; the cheerier ones gave it three or four times as long. If the ritual had worked, if I lived that long, then I'd be around when London drowned. Land prices in higher places would go up.

Dudley was a long way above sea level. Land prices in Dudley were low, understandably. If I bought now, in three centuries I'd be able to sell it all on at a high profit.

The problem was that I didn't have enough money to buy anything. I wasn't working, and the country didn't seem inclined to pay me much for not working. I'd outlast the country, but still, it made things difficult.

The way to make money is to have something no one else has. If you could prove that you weren't getting any older, that would do the trick. You would tell the world you'd discovered an anti-ageing product. You could market any amount of placebos, at any price. In the low-end chemists you could place mid-price tablets and salves. You'd do a secretive trade to the extremely wealthy, getting them to pay millions – if *millions* still counts as a lot of money – for the same placebos in a different wrapping. You'd also sell the same stuff on the black market for even higher prices, putting the word out that a batch of experimental ultra-powerful age-preventative chemicals had been sneaked out of a laboratory.

The money would come in. Lawsuits would start, and you'd have your lawyers delay them, and the complainants would die of old age or sunburn or drowning, depending on how close to the coast they lived. The money would walk on in. At some point you become a celeb, and you're photographed with whichever celebs are still routinely photographed. Per-haps Tony Blair wants to be photographed with you. He seems to enjoy having his picture taken.

That would be where the money came from. And the prod-uct lifecycle outlasts, in this case only, the human life-cycle.

I have another idea. Get a chemistry set, do a bit of reading up, and build a psychoactive substance. Give it a trade name, put it in packets, and brand it. Sell it.

Hold on, you say. That'd be illegal.

Not yet, it wouldn't. It's new. And it's owned by a company. Better yet, a corporation. It's not a dirty street drug, cut with who-knows-what. It's a clean branded product, with an advertising budget like a telephone number and a stack of minor celebs eager to endorse it and get their names in the papers. Then you sell the brand name to a multinational and let them sort out the legal troubles.

The money comes in. It does. All you need is the will to start it moving. Once it starts coming, it keeps coming. There is a layer of people, out of our reach, and the money lives with them. We get enough for the mortgage or the four-by-four, and up there they write houses off against tax. There are layers above that, the millionaires and billionaires and the ones whose names don't get into the papers because they are beyond understanding.

You can move into those layers, you know. Look at the papers. Look at the charts. Look at the television. There are people there on six-figure wage packets and they have no abilities at all.

Money won't be a problem, then. Those comfortable layers aren't too far above us, it's just that most of us don't think of looking up.

So, we could sort out the finances, we wouldn't need to kill anyone else, and whatever strange fixations Jack was developing surely wouldn't last as long as we would.

It was time to celebrate.

I phoned Jack and asked if he wanted to go for a drink.

'What, just for a drink? No murdering people or anything?'

'Just a drink.'

'What, just the two of us?'

'Well yes, unless there's anyone else you want to invite along.'

'Nope. Where at?'

'Somewhere in town. The Dock?'

'Yeah, right then. I'll meet you there. Eightish.'

'This isn't a date,' I told him. 'We're celebrating.'

'Oh right,' he said. 'Like I'd want a date with you. Eight, yeah? And bring some money. I've got none on me.'

I had some. I'd robbed some of our victims. That wasn't strictly in the rules, but we needed pocket money. We needed drinks money. I needed money for new clothes. I couldn't say the same for Jack.

I hoped he wasn't going to turn the evening into something it wasn't. He wasn't my type. He wasn't anyone's type, really. I might have led him on now and then, but that was the best way to steer him. He wasn't in love with me, whatever he thought. He was mooning.

It was bound to happen. The two of us spending so much time together, going through adolescence. Everyone thought we were a couple at school. The other girls used to take the piss out of me. Fair enough, they'll die before I do. And I'll still be able to pull the blokes when they're all fat and forty.

I put a bra on. One of my steadier ones. One with wiring and pads, not that I need wiring. The pads don't hurt, though. I'm not what you'd call buxom. Sometimes I don't bother with a bra at all, but I didn't want to go through the evening with Jack staring at my breasts.

II

What do you mean, I didn't mention that before? I must have done. Or you were reading it wrong. Of course I mentioned it. It's not something I'd forget, my gender. It's not something that slips my mind.

It's not my fault if you're not paying attention.

III

The Dock was crowded. It was a Thursday night, and that's the night students go out in Dudley. Why students are in Dudley is a mystery. They can't all be studying urban deprivation. Why they go out on Thursdays isn't a mystery. On Thursdays the night club does an indie disco with free admission. Students will go to anything with free admission, other than bookshops, museums, or lectures.

So the Dock was packed with students, in the typical genotypes – male techies in clusters, talking about Star Trek and role-playing games; glum little goths sure that no one else had ever felt so miserable; bright couples that you wanted to punch; drama students making much ado about nothing; groups of lads out drinking. The quiz machine was taking their money by throwing in sneaky questions about baseball and jai-alai and other one-country games. The sound system was playing something by a boy band and the students were pretending not to like it.

I found a quiet place and stood in it. A gang of lads – rugby club, more than likely – gave me a few whistles. They must have been drunk. I imagined myself pissing on their graves and gave them a smile. I can cope with students. I'm old enough to worry them but young enough to be interesting. They hadn't been prepared for a smile.

'All of you,' I told them. 'And it still wouldn't be enough.'

I picked out the most frightened one and gave him a vicious kiss. They backed off. Men, honestly. I spotted Jack among the crowd, ogling girls. I'd thought he was another computer geek but it was just the way he dressed. He hadn't seen me. I was wearing trousers – the night was cold, and besides, I didn't want him looking at my legs. Not anymore.

I did tell you I was manipulative.

'All right,' he said, his little face lighting up.

'Got a drink?' I asked. He hadn't. He had no money. He was standing not far from a quartet of student girls. They looked about twelve. They looked like the poetry society. He had no idea, honestly. He wasn't anyone's idea of a romantic lead. There were any number of girls in Dudley who'd have fucked him senseless for a pint of lager and a bag of chips. Jack had romantic notions.

It was time to put a stop to all that.

I bought him a pint of Guinness, which he claimed to like. I had a vodka martini, James Bond style. I wasn't doing pints any more. I was after something higher. They didn't drink beer in the circles I was aspiring to.

'Cheers,' he said when I passed him the pint, downing a third of it. I sipped my drink. I didn't like it much. I'd get used to it. I had long enough.

'Jack,' I said.

He looked at me. He looked like a puppy. Fair enough. I could kick a puppy if I had to.

'It's about us.'

'Us?' he asked. 'We aren't anything.'

'We've been spending a lot of time together.'

'Yeah well, you needed someone. And I fancied living forever. What I think is, we need to get some money coming in. We can sit on investments no bother, but we need money to invest.'

I raised an eyebrow. He swallowed another third of a pint.

'What I reckon is, we can find something to sell. Come on, we've done things no one else has done. We can think of something to sell. Look at this lot.' He indicated the students with an expansive gesture. 'All you have to do is find something with a minority interest. Sell it to this lot first, let the word get into the magazines, let the name get around, and there you go. Bingo.'

'What's this amazing product?'

'That's a *detail*. I'm not doing *details*. I'm doing the big picture.'

I hadn't thought Jack knew of a big picture. As far as I knew, he was strictly a colour-by-numbers man. And without any of the high numbers.

'And where do I fit into this?' I asked.

'Up to you. You can drop the flirting, though. I only went along with that so you'd take me through the ritual. I know it now. I've been taking notes. I'll be holding onto a copy. I'll be giving copies to some people. Sealed and that. I wouldn't want anyone finding out what we've been up to. Neither would you. It was all your idea.'

Jack was turning out to have hidden depths, when all I wanted was shallows. I sipped my drink. It tasted awful.

'Have a drink you like,' he said, looking at my face. 'You aren't going to get anywhere drinking that stuff. There you are, dreaming. Good job one of us has their feet on the floor.'

I couldn't risk someone that close to me being clever. It wasn't what Jack was for. Jack was for donkey work and keeping people out of the way.

'I don't see myself staying here,' he said. 'I see myself somewhere better. Another drink?'

'I didn't think you had any money.'

'You cleared out Mrs Bolton's purse. You left her bank card. And she was a pensioner. Come on, pensioners can't remember what day it is. The number was on a piece of paper next to the card. She's overdrawn now. As well as dead. Not her year, is it?'

'They could trace that.'

'The card hasn't been stopped. It hasn't been reported missing. She's not going to report it missing. She's dead. Her cats will have eaten her by now. There won't be a smell. If there was, the neighbours wouldn't care. The rest of them will be the same. They're dead and no one cares. We know about it. We're going to keep it to ourselves. Two of them had their pin numbers in their purses. The men didn't. They had money under the mattress, though. In this day and age, can you credit it? I had to go back after we'd finished, obviously. There's not a lot of money. They were old and they thought a fiver was a fortune. But there's enough to start something.'

'You can't take something,' I said. 'The ritual won't work.'

'Obviously. None of that bollocks works. All you've done since I've known you is raise a woodlouse from the dead. And that came back all fucked up. One woodlouse. All of your books, and that's as far as you've been.'

'There were loads of them.'

'There was one of them. I've read a few books of my own. I've got a library ticket, you know. I know the people you know. I've always been with you when you've bought books. Those people don't care who they sell to, do they? I didn't fuck about with the major stuff. I don't want to piss Asteroth off. I learned illusions. I can do illusions. Here, check this one out.'

An insect crawled from his collar, chittering. He touched it and it wasn't there.

'I made you see them.'

'Why?'

'So I could make you think they were in your clothes. So you'd take your clothes off, really. And it worked. I got to see you mostly naked. Funny thing is, you looked the way I thought you would. I'd imagined you like that. I'd been thinking about it for years. But now I've seen it I don't think about it. You're not cover girl material.'

What was he talking about? I was wonderful naked. What else did he know?

'So. The ritual won't work, then? Because I blagged a few cash cards? You'd already swiped the money. So it doesn't work. What does that make us? Murderers, robbers, end of story. So we ought to do something with it. We should do something with the money. If we can't live longer, we can live better. Not if we spend it all on poncey drinks, though. I've got to get home, anyway. You think about it. We can be partners in the real world. That's not so bad.'

He downed the last of his pint and handed me the glass.

'Put that somewhere for me,' he said, and left.

IV

I couldn't do anything with him. I couldn't kill him. Perhaps he was bluffing about giving copies of our exploits to his friends. Perhaps he wasn't. It wasn't a worthwhile gamble.

You know in those old Frankenstein movies? The way everything is fucked over by the villagers at the last minute? I'd been forgetting. Long before the villagers turned up with their pitchforks and attitude, the assistant – Igor, usually – would have dropped the brain or spliced the wrong wires or done some other stupid thing. The villagers only got into the picture because the project had gone wrong.

And it went wrong – every time, without fail – because the good doctor put his trust in an untrustworthy assistant. I went home. I almost had a kebab. I didn't see how things could get any worse, and that's the time to have a kebab. It'll show you the error of your ways. With fish and chips you might get a bone; with a curry you might get a missing pet.

With a kebab you can get anything: hepatitis B, Ebola, leprosy, toenails, you name it.

I didn't have a kebab. I'd already pushed my luck far enough. I went home instead.

V

A few days later Uncle Mickey turned up. I used to like him when I was younger. He seemed dangerous and strange. He didn't work in an office. He didn't work at all. My father told me that Uncle Mickey used to work in an office but he got the sack and never got work anywhere else.

'He got work in the army,' I argued.

'Like they're fussy,' said my father. 'As if.'

The army might not have been fussy, but I was. I liked Mickey Payne. I didn't think he was an uncle in the real sense of the word. He was an uncle in the sense of, a friend of your parents. Except that neither of them seemed to like him. My father made it obvious, and my mother would go to another room when he visited. I used to like him. He had his scarred face and hands, and you wondered how far the scars went. He had stories of shooting Argies and being on the dole. He seemed happy to be doing nothing. He seemed happy to see me. Then I got older, and I went through puberty. I reached it a few years before Jack, because women do. Perhaps that's why men spend the rest of their lives trying to catch up with us.

Things changed. I went off my parents. They went off me, too, but they had more reason. I also began to feel that Uncle Mickey had other things on his mind. He seemed to be taking a personal interest in me.

'Growing up, aren't we?' he'd ask. He'd have his little tobacco tin – he couldn't afford to smoke cigarettes anymore, so he was on the Amber Leaf and Rizla diet – and he'd roll thin cigarettes and smoke them, eyeing me up 'Getting to be a young lady.'

It didn't feel lecherous. It felt worse than that. He seemed to be waiting for something. He seemed to think something would happen. He'd look at me, sizing me up.

He didn't come round as often. He'd come round and talk to me and then go. He'd say things that might have meant something. He'd say, 'Been keeping an eye on the papers, then?' or, 'seen that little mate of yours recently?' or, 'been up to anything?'

He knew something. He'd talked to me about magic, a long time ago.

I got into the habit of going out when he came round.

A few days after Jack had sprung his surprises, I was at home. My father had a day off, and he was doing something to the garden. I can't be a full adult yet, because I don't care about the garden. Perhaps the ritual did work. I try to spot myself getting older but I don't know what the symptoms are. I still look young, if you take away the shadows under the eyes. The doorbell rang. It used to play a little tune but the mechanism had a breakdown and now it just does odd notes. I opened the door and found Uncle Mickey standing there.

'Mind if I come in?' he asked, coming in. 'Thought we could have a chat. You're never in to chat to.'

'I've got to go out,' I said.

'Oh? Anywhere nice? Down by the old railway lines, say?'

I didn't say anything. I let him in and sat as far from him as the living room allowed. We sat and looked at each other.

'You still telling your little friend you've got a parchment, then? From the olden days?'

'I do have one,' I said. I thought about saying I didn't know what he was talking about, but it wasn't going to work. He knew what we were talking about. I wasn't going to be able to fool him.

'Have it your way,' he said. 'You want it to be a parchment, so be it. They'll catch you, you know.'

'They can't. No one knows.'

'I know. If I know, someone else knows. I can think of three people straight off. Four, if we include your apprentice.'

'Who?' –

'You don't know them. You've done five people, yes?'

I nodded.

'I could tell you the names and addresses. Stop me when I get one wrong.'

He went through them. He didn't make a mistake, and he went through them in the order in which we'd killed them. I couldn't imagine how he knew so much.

'I caught a live one, once,' he said. 'I might have told you the odd white lie about that. I told you the essence of it, though. I was going along, then bosh, in comes a live one and I end up like this.' He pointed at his scarred face with his scarred hands. 'Wasn't a hand grenade, though. It was a man, in a state. You have to watch out for a man in a state. You trust your friend? Little whatsisname?'

'Jack,' I said, shaking my head. I didn't trust him. I'd trusted a much dimmer version of Jack. The new bright one was somewhere far ahead of me. 'No. I don't. I thought I could.'

'Old story. Couples are like that. You can't trust them. Someone will turn up and change it all. Someone will walk out. That's how couples are.'

'We weren't a couple.'

'I know. But he didn't. And now he's calling the shots, isn't he?'

I nodded.

'Happens. Happened to me, as it happens. You trust someone, you get this.' He held out his scarred hands. 'Doesn't make any difference,' he said. 'The thing is, they'll catch you. Your friend there will go to one prison, you'll go to another. He'll come out all right. He'll turn in evidence. You'll go in for longer. There's a lot of talk about law and order these days. You'll do well, I think. You can be famous for what you've done. You'll get an agent. They'll do you book rights, film rights. You can get through it.'

The back door opened. I heard my father making his way through the house. He looked at Uncle Mickey.

'Mick,' he said.

'I was just saying,' said Mickey. 'I was just telling your firstborn here. You can't rely on trust. Not in a couple. People behave badly sometimes. People go astray.'

'They do,' said my father. 'Don't they just?'

'Family things,' said Uncle Mickey. 'Well, best be off. I need to be somewhere.'

'I hope they want you there,' said my father.

'I shouldn't fucking think so. And let's not be telling me not to swear in front of your daughter. She knows words I've never fucking heard of. And you wouldn't believe what she's been up to. I swear.'

He gave me a wink. My father walked him to the door. I watched him walk down our road, smoking another anorexic roll-up. That was the last time I saw him.

My father came back, trailing dirt from the garden through the house. I couldn't say what his expression meant. There were several emotions involved, and I couldn't identify a single one of them.

'Is he really my uncle?' I asked.

'Him? Hard to say,' said my father. 'He's really my brother. I'll give him that.'

'So he's my uncle?'

'Ask your mother,' said my father, and I spotted two of his emotions; anger and sadness.

VI

A week later I was sitting at home, watching the news. I had got into the habit of checking the news. If any bodies were found, I wanted to know about it. There was news on all day long, I'd discovered. Most of it wasn't interesting. I would watch it and drift. I didn't know where Mogadishu was, and I wasn't planning on going there. The new cure for AIDS would turn out not to be a cure. I was more interested in the ecological problems. This was selfish. I planned to live long enough to see what global warming would do and I wanted to know what I was in for. My best guess was that it would do nothing. In another decade or so there'd be evidence that the world was getting colder, and we'd all have to go out spraying CFCs into the air. And then they'd tell us that an asteroid could hit us any minute, which would wipe us all out just like the dinosaurs, give or take an inconvenient couple of hundred millennia.

That's the thing with scientists. They get a theory and they'll run with it for years. No amount of contrary evidence will worry them. Until one of them says, hold on, this is rubbish;

how about *this* for an idea? And off they all go again, proving nothing and getting nowhere.

I have a downer on scientists. I would do, being inclined to magic. We don't get on. Those urban myths that get put around, the ones about the Kremlin hiring psychic warriors? They're myths, false, full stop. Science and magic don't mix. They don't get on.

Neither side believes the other can be right. It's a left-brain/right-brain thing. It's a schism.

Take astrology and astronomy. Astrology is clearly bullshit. I'll believe in a lot, but that's nonsense. The only thing you can say in favour of astrology is that it keeps men who were raised by their mothers in jobs. Obviously it doesn't make a blind bit of difference whether Mars was in the ascendant when you were born. How could it? And why only bother with the stars that make nice patterns? Astrology is rubbish, one point to the scientists.

Except that astronomy is also rubbish. Astronomers have discovered that there isn't enough mass in the universe for the maths to work. There needs to be more mass, otherwise the universe would collapse. It's not just a little more mass, either. It's sixty per cent more than there is. So near enough two-thirds of creation is missing.

Astronomers explain this by saying that the missing sixty per cent is comprised of dark matter, which we can't see or measure, but which is there. Because if it wasn't there, the maths wouldn't work.

The obvious conclusion, to everyone else, is that the maths don't work. Get back to your drawing boards. Go back to the start and give it another go. You've forgotten to carry something. If you have a theory that says two plus three equals eight, all well and good. But when someone gives you two apples, and then another three, and you end up with five apples, you have to rethink. It's no good claiming that there are three mysterious dark apples, which are there although they can't be seen or measured. The thing to do is hold up your hands and admit that the theory was bullshit all along.

One all, then.

And that's before you even start on all the parallel universe crap.

So I was prepared to wait and see what happened with global warming. I thought it'd turn out to be another little scientific fad, like the global freezing that preceded it. If I was wrong, too bad. We could manage without the London Underground.

That day, while I was waiting for my deeds to make the news, my father sat next to me.

'I don't think your uncle will be round again.'

'You don't like him much,' I said. My father looked at the ceiling.

'No,' he said. 'I suppose I should. He is my brother. I suppose I should like him regardless. But I don't.'

'Is that because he doesn't work?'

'He used to. He tried. He's brighter than me, that's the thing. That's what makes it upsetting. I had to work like hell to get this.'

He looked around the room.

'There's worse than this,' I told him. He smiled.

'I know that,' he said. He let his gaze drop from the ceiling onto me. I felt it land.

'So what's wrong with him?'

'He got in with the wrong crowd. He got mixed up in something. Nothing was proved. In the end it turned out that he hadn't done anything. It was too late. He lost his job. He didn't apply for another one. He ran off. Changed his name and ran off.'

'Mickey Payne isn't his real name?'

'Of course it isn't. Does it *sound* like a real name? He's my brother. He'd be called Haines. He used to be. I told him to leave us alone, and he did for a while. For a few years.'

'Because of the job? Or the other stuff?'

'Because of something else,' he said. 'Because he did something unforgivable. Unforgivable to me, anyway. Your mother wasn't so sure. Looking at you now, I'm not so sure either. None of his genes seem to have got to you.'

'His genes?'

'Family things,' said my father. The words sounded like a code, like the public version of something that couldn't be made public.

He looked at the ceiling again.

'Family things,' he said again.

'So he joined the army?'

'No. That's another of his stories. The army didn't want him. They knew about his history. He made it to the national news, you know. Got his five minutes of fame. Lot of good it did him. He was never in the army. Anyway, he'd have been too young to go to the Falklands. Didn't you do history at school?'

'Not much. You saw my report cards.'

'I'd steer clear of history, if I were you. You think it's all gone away and it hasn't. It's there every day, all of the mistakes and lies. It's there every day.'

He seemed close to tears.

'What happened to him?' I asked, to turn the conversation somewhere more comfortable.

'His best friend did that to him. His hands and face. Parts of his body. I don't know the details. I don't want to know.'

I thought about that. I didn't think it made any difference. Mickey Payne hadn't been trustworthy. Even his name was false.

The news had ended, and the local news had come on. I had been too busy talking to notice what was on the screen.

There was a shot of a little sandy patch of ground in an entrenchment close to a tunnel. Yellow plastic tape marked off an area. Men in white plastic clothes were digging gently. Policemen surrounded them at a distance. A police spokesman spoke into a microphone.

'We were alerted by a member of the public,' said the policeman. 'His dog dug up a bone. He thought it was an animal bone, nothing out of the ordinary. Our tests show that it's a finger bone.'

There was a question I didn't hear.

'No, not in this case,' said the spokesman. 'We do have descriptions of the culprits. They're connected to five incidents.'

This time I heard the question, which was one word.

Murders?

'It would appear so. Our suspects are a male and a female, both in their twenties.'

He described Jack and I.

My father wasn't looking at the screen. He was looking at me. I couldn't control my expression. He looked at the identikit pictures that had replaced the coverage of the old railway lines.

'Is that?' he asked, and then left it at that. I knew what he was asking. Was that me? And it wasn't a question. He knew it was me. His daughter, the serial killer.

The reporter asked another question.

'No,' said the spokesman. 'That was a long time ago and no charges were brought. This area was examined then, as I'm sure you remember, and nothing was found. There's no connection.'

My father was standing. I imagine he was disappointed. He couldn't see all of the angles. He could only see the bad side of it.

'I thought you'd got away with it,' he said. 'I really did. But you've got his genes after all. And all of that. You did all of that?'

I didn't say anything. I didn't feel solid enough to speak.

'History,' said my father. 'Like I told you, history. You know where you got your name?'

'Samantha?'

'That's the one. It's for him. Your mother named you after him. As though she hadn't done enough. That's his real name, Sam Haines. You've seen it, of course.'

Of course I had.

It was written on the parchment that was folded in my pocket.

PART NINE

Sam, aged thirty

Chapter Eighteen

I

I've read about different methods that help you to remember things. There are books full of helpful information like this. You can buy books, there are shops that just sell books. I don't see the attraction of it myself, but then, that's just me. I'd go for the library. Once you've read something, why would you want it in the house? It'll be the same next time you read it. Books are like that. There's nothing new the second time. So get them from the library. That's my advice.

They have books about everything. I found out all of that stuff about Dudley from the library, and I didn't have to hand over any cash. They'll have books about improving your mind, too. Those books are everywhere.

It makes you wonder where all the idiots come from.

How to remember things, then.

You can associate a number with other numbers, break it down into smaller numbers, make it into a date. If you're a big fan of bingo you can turn long numbers into sentences or lists: two fat ladies, one little duck for 882. You can write things down. You can tie a knot in a handkerchief, if they still make handkerchiefs. If you live in Dudley, you can tie a knot in a tea towel.

You can turn lists into stories: two fat ladies cooked one little duck and left nothing, for 8820. You can create acronyms to remember sequences of letters: Studying Ones History Causes Ancient History To Occur Again for SOHCAHTOA, which is:

Sine = Opposite/Hypotenuse

Cosine = Adjacent/Hypotenuse

Tangent = Opposite/Adjacent.

Handy, that. I've never needed to use sines or their relatives, but I'd know which sides of a right-angled triangle I'd be dealing with. Triangles do crop up, in everyday life. They cropped up in mine. My brother, his wife, and I. There isn't a way to measure all of the angles in those triangles, though.

You can create mnemonics. You can relate unfamiliar words or concepts to familiar ones. You can break things down into smaller sections.

Alternatively, you can get your best friend to nail you to your shelves.

II

He only used two nails, one in each hand, straight through the middle of the palms. It seemed to take a lot of hammering. I made a lot of noise. I admit that. I see people at the bus stop with faces full of ironmongery. It must hurt like hell. Being crucified hurts more.

While my hands were out of the way he sorted through the remaining nails. I struggled but that made it worse. He'd given me a knock on the head to keep me quiet while he nailed me in place. That hurt, too. There was blood running down my face. I couldn't do anything with it. It ran down my shirt and dripped onto the carpet.

It was just as well Judy had left me. A mess on the carpet would have really pissed her off.

I still wasn't remembering anything. Jack looked at me. He was holding nails.

'Now do you see it?' he asked.

I shook my head.

That hurt.

He rattled his nails and looked at my face.

I looked at his face, the eyebrow rings and septum bolt and the rest of it and I knew what he was thinking.

'I remember it all,' I said. 'It's come back to me. I can see it all now.'

I forgot that my hands were nailed to the shelves and tried to hug him. I don't know if you've ever had a nail scraping against the small bones of your hands. I wouldn't recommend it. I had never really thought about crucifixion before. It hadn't looked so bad. Up on the cross, admiring the view. That seemed a fair way to go. I revised my thoughts. I imagined myself supported by the nails, all of those small bones pushed out of joint. The shoulders hauling themselves out of the sockets. Then hanging there until you died.

It's suffocation that does it, with crucifixions. The lungs can't work with the arms up there. The weight is in the wrong place. I didn't have the option of suffocating. My feet were on the floor.

Jack had hit me on the head with the hammer a few times, and while I was groggy he'd nailed my right hand to the shelves. After that, the other hand was a doddle. I didn't have any leverage and I was woozy. I couldn't push him away.

Now he was looking at my face, shaking a handful of nails. I bore in mind that this was a man who enjoyed having sharp objects in his face.

'Oh yes,' I said, 'it's all clear now.'

'I don't think so,' he said. 'I get things because I have all this metal. Close to the brain, is the thing. Needs to be in the face. Sorry about the hands. Bit of a waste, that.'

I was glad he was sorry. It made me feel better about the whole business.

He looked at my nose. He tweaked it.

'Fuck!' I said.

'Sorry,' he said. 'Wasn't sure if that would hurt.'

'Of course it fucking hurts! I'm crucified. Everything hurts. And you hit me with the hammer.'

'I didn't think you'd let me do the rest of it otherwise.'

'Too fucking right I wouldn't.'

He was looking at the hammer wounds. He looked concerned.

I thought about what he'd just said.

'What do you mean, the rest of it?' I asked. 'Haven't you *done* the rest of it? Isn't this enough? Jesus got away with less than this. No one hit Jesus with a hammer.'

'You can't see it yet. The two of us when we were twenty. When you can see that, I'll be happy. Maybe not happy, but I'll stop.'

'I can see it,' I tried.

'Sorry mate,' he said, genuinely regretful. 'Sorry and all. You'd say that about now. This won't hurt much. Comparatively.'

He tweaked my nose again. He tweaked my eyebrow and got less of a reaction. That was less sensitive.

'Right,' he said. 'Eyebrow for starters then.'

He pinched my right eyebrow, raising it from my head in a ridge. He held it in his left hand. His right hand manipulated a nail. It looked yards long. He put the point against the bunched flesh.

He pushed it. I screamed and jerked my head back. He held on and pushed harder.

I couldn't back away. The shelves were in the way. I wished I'd done a worse job on them. Why didn't they collapse? The rest of my life was collapsing.

Jack pushed the nail into my eyebrow. He'd been lying. It did hurt. I felt the skin stretch and then a pop as the point emerged. He let go of my eyebrow. I could feel the nail in it. He stood back.

'There,' he said. 'That's a start. You've gone white, mate. You feeling all right?'

I've heard some stupid questions in my time. I ignored that one. He looked at my face.

'Nasal septum,' he said. 'This one will sting.'

He gripped my forehead with his left hand and pushed my head against the shelves. I could see that map of Dudley he'd had tattooed on his arm. There were five red crosses on it. The murder sites, as he thought.

He took another nail and put it in my nostril. It tickled, and I sneezed.

'Fuck!' he said, jumping back. 'I've got snot all over my hand. You dirty bastard. Don't you have a handkerchief?'

'Well excuse me,' I said. 'I sneezed on you. That's a bit of a liberty. All you've done to me is nail me to my own fucking shelves and force a nail through my eyebrow. And hit me with the hammer.'

'Do you have to keep on about the hammer? That was just to keep you quiet. Didn't fucking work though, did it?'

'Couldn't you have drugged me?'

'I haven't got any drugs.'

'I'm sure you'll get some when they catch you.'

'They didn't catch me when I gave myself up. They've got no chance if I don't help them.'

'I wouldn't bet on it.'

'I'm not a gambling man,' he said, putting the nail back into my nose. It tickled again, and I sneezed again.

'Fuck!' he said, shaking ropes of snot from his hand. There was blood in it, I was interested to notice. 'Right,' he said, 'fair play then. If you won't behave for the septum it's going to have to go right through.'

He gripped my head again. He put the nail against the side of my nose.

I was in a good spot to watch this time. The point went into a dent in the side of my nose. He increased the pressure. I heard the skin give way. The point went inside my nose. He kept pushing. I felt the nail clear the first barrier and emerge into my left nostril.

He kept pushing.

It scraped the septum. It entered that. It scraped against cartilage.

'Carefully does it,' Jack said, looking thoughtful. He pushed again. The point emerged in my right nostril. He didn't stop. I felt the nail scrape again as it entered the last barrier. With my left eye I could see Jack's fingers, white around the joints, pushing the nail into me.

With my right eye I could see the flesh on that side of my nose tenting. It bulged out. I could see the nail inside the bulge. My nose stretched absurdly.

I heard the now familiar sound of my skin popping. The point of the nail came into view. Jack stood back.

'Nearly there,' he said.

'Nearly?' I shouted. 'Nearly?'

Jack laughed.

'Sorry mate, you sound like a duck. Didn't mean to laugh. One more will do it. Eyebrow, nose, what next? Ear's a bit too normal. Bit of a dead zone, the ear. Tell you what, I'll do you one in the lip. Goes here.'

He pointed at a small silver spine protruding from the front of his face, about half an inch below his lower lip. He pulled the lip out so that I could see it was just as horrible inside.

Then he got another nail. He put this one into my mouth without using the available opening. This one really hurt, and when I tried to complain about it the point of the nail scratched my gums and rattled against my teeth. I still tried to complain. I felt it was justified.

'Anything?' asked Jack. 'Any new insights?'

The only thing I knew then that I hadn't known before was that having nails in your face hurt. I'd already had an inkling about that. I wanted to put my hands on my face and feel the damage. I shook my head. I wasn't going to have delusions. Jack would carry on until he'd got it out of his system.

'Nothing?' he asked. 'Oh well. Sorry mate, the face isn't going to be enough.'

He unbuttoned my shirt.

'Time for a nipple,' he said.

III

That was the one. When he held the nail up for me to look at, I was solidly in the room with him. I didn't have much choice about that, being nailed to the furniture. The last nail went through my right nipple and I was somewhere else.

I was Sam Haines, aged twenty, helping Jack to hold a purring cat over a woman's face. I was Sam Haines but not myself, and Jack wasn't Jack. We were ten years younger, popping fingers from the hands of our victims. The dates were wrong. We buried the bones at the end of the railway line, where I'd found the bones. I saw all five victims. I was at the end of the railway lines, burying body parts. I was Sam Haines, aged twenty, doing all of the things Jack had said I'd done. Jack was going along with it all.

Only Jack wasn't Jack, and I wasn't me. There were some giveaway signs. For one thing I had breasts.

I would have noticed if I had breasts. I'd have stayed in more often.

They weren't large but they looked fine from where I was. They were pointed and unexpected. I was Sam Haines, aged twenty, female. And Jack wasn't Jack.

The time was wrong, the new bones weren't buried yet.

I arrived back in my body.

'I know,' I said. 'I see it.'

Jack looked up. He'd been unbuckling my belt. He looked at me and knew I'd seen it all.

'You thought it was us,' I said. 'You thought you were remembering it. You weren't remembering anything. Jesus jumping fuck. You were looking the wrong way. You were receiving signals, you said. And you never noticed. The Sam you murdered those people with. You never noticed she was female?'

He dropped a smattering of nails. They landed on my foot.

'What?' he asked.

'This memory of yours. Think about it. Look at Sam. In the memory.'

'I don't know,' he said. 'I can't sort it out. The face is like you. It's a lot like you. Who else would it be?'

'My daughter,' I said, seeing the whole thing, stretching on for decades yet. Going on for centuries, perhaps. 'She's my daughter. Samantha. In twenty years, she'll be doing everything you've seen. And your nephew will be going along with her. Picking up signals. You were right. You were just wrong about the direction. You're picking up the future.'

'Your daughter? What daughter?'

'Samantha. She's mine. That's why Caroline called her Sam. Because I'm her father.'

He seemed shocked by that. I was learning that he had a strange set of morals.

It became clearer as I told him. In twenty years, our relatives would carry out the ritual he'd confessed to. In twenty years they'd be murderers, and there was nothing we could do about it.

You can see an accident coming, sometimes. You sit in the passenger seat as the car approaches the pedestrian and you know that it's going to hit him. But if you tell the driver, they will tell you they've seen the man. There will be cross words. So you keep quiet and the car mounts the pavement and the pedestrian breaks against the front of the car. You can see an accident coming but you can't do anything about it. Voicing the prediction invalidates the prediction.

My daughter was going to murder five people. Jack's nephew was going to help her.

They were only children, now. I couldn't tell them anything. Tony would not let me in the house.

An old and familiar misery fell on me. It felt glad to be back. It had missed me.

I slumped, letting the nails take the weight. I thought I was going to faint, or become unconscious, or something else relatively painless. Everything went black. Then I found out why they used the wrists when they crucified people. Everything went red, I felt a new level of pain in my hands, and then I was on the floor with a faceful of ironmongery and holes the size of two-pound coins in the palms of my hands.

IV

Jack left soon after that. He helped me get the nails out and then went. I never saw him again. Some things can ruin a friendship.

The wounds became infected. Judy always said I should clean the house more often. Something got under my skin along with the piercings. I ended up losing a lot of skin. My hands were in bad shape as it was. I only have partial use of my fingers. The thumbs came through undamaged. I typed most of this with my thumbs.

The lost skin came from my face. It fell away from the

wounds in my nose and eyebrow. I looked like a guinea pig, half my face red, half of it white.

Jack had left, Judy had gone. My job had closed itself. I decided that I would go, too. I decided I would move away.

I gathered a few things that would be useful on the journey.

I prepared to leave. I had nothing to stay for. I could go somewhere a long way away. I could go to the coast. It had been a long time since I'd seen the sea. I could leave Dudley, as the warlock had eight centuries ago.

I'd thought that was all fiction. I'd thought it was storybook stuff.

I knew it wasn't.

What if magic has a half-life? What if it wears out? What if a warlock visited Dudley seven hundred and eighty years ago? If the half-life of magic was – say – eight hundred years, then he'd need to have the ritual renewed twenty years from now. He'd need to set things in motion.

He wouldn't want to do it himself. He wouldn't want to do his own ritual. He'd want someone else to do it for him.

He could get someone to do it for him, too. Plant an idea here and there, steer someone in the right direction, and that would be that. The events would be set in motion. He'd had eight centuries to learn manipulation. That would be long enough to get the hang of it.

If he found a couple of hapless pawns, he could use them. He could use their children. He'd be from the time when curses went like that: a curse on you, and on your children, and on their children after them, and so on.

Nearly eight centuries ago he'd left Dudley with his apprentices. Now he'd popped back to renew his magic, and with that sorted he'd be off again. I didn't know who he was. I didn't know why he'd chosen me. I didn't think any good fortune would be coming my way.

I didn't need my name any more. In twenty years, Sam Haines was going to be a bad name to have. It would be on the news, in the newspapers.

I wondered what Samantha would look like in her twenties. There will be pictures in the newspapers, if they still have newspapers. Perhaps by then Tony will have relented. You can only stay angry for so long. Perhaps by then I'll be able to go home.

I tried to think of another name. I looked at my scarred hands. I felt the itch of my healing face. I thought of all that pain, and got the name.

Mickey Payne.

I'm going to leave Dudley. I always said I would. I always said I wouldn't waste my whole life here.

I tried the new name out. Mickey Payne. It seemed to fit. It seemed apt.

I gathered my bags in the front room. I was ready to go. Whatever was going to happen could happen without me. My part was over.

I was wrong.

Someone knocked on the door.

PART TEN

Sam, aged twenty-five

Chapter Nineteen

I

It wasn't a parchment. I admit it. I lied about that. It looked like one, yellowed and crumbly, but it wasn't a parchment at all.

It was a cutting from the *Pensnett Herald*, and it was twenty years old. It was the confession of someone called Jack Ives. He claimed he'd killed five people, and buried parts of them at the end of the old railway lines. He claimed he'd been led to do it by another man, Sam Haines. My uncle. Mickey Payne, by another name. I'd often wondered whether the name had any significance. It was my name, after all. Samantha Haines; that was me.

Twenty years ago, there was a false confession. I knew what it meant. It meant that the magic was true. Someone else had tried to do it. I read about the ritual somewhere. I knew there had once been a wizard in the town. That wizard from the umpteenth century, he was the first. It was his ritual. We were only copying it.

In the next issue of the *Pensnett Herald* - the one after the issue my cutting was from – there was an apology in very small print, attributed to Eddie Finch, a reporter. I tried to track Eddie down, but he overdid the drinking and his liver gave out three years ago. They say that when he died, his liver accounted for half his body weight, and at the autopsy they dragged it out of him lobe by lobe, piling it onto the scales dish. Some versions claim a bell rang, others that it made the record books.

It made no difference. Eddie was dead. I couldn't trace the names. Sam Haines might have been a relative. My father told me he didn't know him. My mother went upstairs in tears.

She was forever going upstairs in tears. Everything turned into a little melodrama. I mean, I get emotional myself. I do. But not like that. Not to excess. Not in a mainland European way.

So, it wasn't a parchment. It was a newspaper cutting. And it was false, except that they found bones. That was in a later edition. They found bones that were eight hundred years old.

There you were, then. The proof. The ritual happened eight hundred years ago, in Dudley.

I'd guess that's the reason Dudley is the way it is. I mean, I can't see any other explanation. You can't blame everything on the recession. The recession ended years ago. All other towns are boomtowns.

Dudley is sinking into the mines.

The ground is honeycombed. Dudley never managed to get away from the past. It squatted in the dark ages and refused to budge, and now the old mine workings are giving way. Every day the local papers have pictures of houses leaning over chasms. Owners claim they won't move.

They will move. If they don't move in any other direction, they'll move downwards.

In ten more years, there will be the castle standing over a blasted landscape, all black holes and soot. The buildings will have been swallowed.

You don't get anything for free, in magic. I think I told you that. If you get to live for centuries, something else pays for it.

A whole town, perhaps. My town, I think. My town died for eight centuries.

Good riddance, I say.

II

Oh yes, and there's something else. I may have misled you. Unintentionally, of course. I was doing my best to run through the facts, but some of them wouldn't behave. Some of them didn't fit where they really should have done, and they got moved about.

My friend Jack Ives isn't called Jack, for example. That's not his name at all. When we were young, I used to call everyone Jack. I called my mother Jack, and my father Jack, and everyone else Jack. All because I had an Uncle Jack, who I don't remember. He was my favourite.

'Best sort of uncle,' my father once said. 'Not related to you at all. He was a friend of your real uncle.'

All of this is before my time, in any real sense. I don't remember it. It's become a family legend. It's become one of those things we talk about to avoid talking about anything.

It only had one lasting effect. I had a friend, whose name wasn't Jack. I started to call him Jack, and the name stuck. Names do. Jack was his nickname, not his real name.

His real name is Liam Ives. But come on, if you were called Liam, you wouldn't want it getting about either.

Almost everything else is true.

III

Bad times come from nowhere, and they don't always make a fuss when they arrive. It isn't always a hurricane that flattens the town, or the outbreak of a spectacular new plague. Sometimes bad times turn up in the form of a television broadcast.

After the police showed my picture to all of the viewers of the local news, the conclusion was foregone. They would catch me. They would track me down. They'd catch Jack too, thankfully, and that'd put paid to his get-rich-quick schemes. As a bonus, it would render his blackmail threats harmless. There's no point pulling the pin if the grenade has already gone off.

My father retreated upstairs as soon as the broadcast finished. I had the feeling he was not going to be approachable. I thought he might be after my mother, for solace.

Family things, as I've said.

The telephone rang. It was Jack. He was frantic.

I told him I'd already confessed. I told him I had no choice, what with his veiled threats and all. Kick them while they're down, I say.

I put the phone down before he'd stopped whining. There were possibilities in the situation. Things were bad, but there were possibilities.

I've learned this from magic; sometimes you need to suffer

to get somewhere. Sometimes suffering is the only way forward.

I dialled the number for the operator and asked the robot
for the number of the newspapers.

Which ones?

All of them.

IV

Being arrested is dull and procedural, in England. In America
SWAT teams swing in through windows, igniting flash bombs.
A fat sheriff makes you place your hands on top of the vehicle. A
bored cop with an Irish surname pops a bullet in your shoulder.

In England, you mainly fill in forms.

Some things won't help you. Here are some phrases that
will get you nowhere:

The right to remain silent.

Innocent until proven guilty.

Call my lawyer.

And here are some phrases that will do you the world
of good:

My exclusive story.

Percentage of the gross.

Call my agent.

V

The police turned up soon after. I was allowed to walk from
my house. The first of the camera jockeys were already there,

no more than ten minutes after I called them. I went to prison.

The court case isn't important. There was only one likely verdict. My brief played on the sympathies of the jury, pointed out inconsistencies in the police case, played with words. I pleaded guilty, and that shut him up.

Women's prisons, incidentally, aren't as cosy as men's. They can't afford to be. We're not like men. We have cycles, like history. In close proximity, our cycles coincide. In prison, there would be one week each month when the warders patrolled in groups of nine or ten, with hands full of tear gas canisters and polished batons. It wasn't necessary. Mostly we cried and thought that we looked too fat.

Jack – Liam, as they called him when he was sentenced – got it easy. That was down to me. I said that it was all my fault, and I'd forced him into it with my feminine wiles. I didn't want him getting any of the bad – i.e. good – press. Things are going well enough. In another five years I'll be out, home free.

Jack still writes to me. He sends unsolicited photographs of himself. He got a few prison tattoos while he was in his minimum-security, crying-to-the-warders holiday camp. After he got out he went in for body modifications. He also had a favourite uncle, apparently. Also called Jack. His favourite uncle was into body modifications. Jack got out and went back in time, as I understand it. He got out and turned into someone he used to know. He didn't know where to go, so he stayed where he was and turned into someone else.

I'm not sure who I'll be by the time I get out. I know how much I'll be worth. More than you're worth. You're in the wrong line of business. I'm on more than football money. I'm on prison money.

My story is everywhere now: tabloids, books, films. A miniseries.

I'm worth a fortune.

And I'll tell you something else. I won't be going back to Dudley.

PART ELEVEN

Sam, aged thirty

Chapter Twenty

I

I opened the door. A large white van was parked outside. It wasn't well parked. It was blocking the pavement, and the road. A familiar trio emerged from it.

'Put the kettle on,' said Darren. 'We're parched. Been a busy couple of years, I tell you that for nothing. Been a right pain. Come on in then.'

Mr Link and Spin followed him into my front room. The three of them occupied my sofa.

'You're still bloody lazy,' said Mr Link. 'And what have you done to your face? Is that the fashion these days? Bloody students.'

'Ex-students,' I said automatically.

'Do pardon me, ex-students. Now, are you going to put the kettle on?'

I went to the kitchen and put the kettle on. I hadn't bothered packing the kettle, or any groceries. I thought there'd be groceries wherever I was going to. I still had coffee and some milk that was partially liquid. I decanted the top part of it into four mugs, added coffee, and added water after the kettle huffily boiled. I took them through and handed three of them out.

Darren and Mr Link thanked me. Spin gestured.

I got it then. In the woodcut, the misshapen apprentice had not been obviously misshapen. In the thirteenth century, a black man in England would have been a strange thing. He'd have been a freak. He'd have seemed misshapen.

If he was also a mute, that would be enough. Political correctness was centuries away. They were there before it, and they'd be there after it had gone.

You couldn't depict muteness in a picture. In a woodcut, you couldn't show colours.

Spin was the misshapen apprentice. Darren was the other one, and Mr Link was the warlock; all three of them were eight hundred years old.

The three of them sat on my sofa as though they owned the place. Mind you, they'd been there eight hundred years ago. For all I knew they did own the place. For all I knew they owned Dudley.

'Finally got it, have you?' asked Mr Link, studying my face. 'Penny dropped? I tell you what, you're slow but you get there. I mean, we needed someone feeble-minded to work with. You and your friend Jack have done very well, considering your obvious disadvantages. Your young relatives will do our work for us, and then we'll be off.'

'It's got a half-life,' said Darren, running a hand through his black hair. 'In four hundred years we'll have to come back and do it all over again.'

'Not that that'll be bothering you,' said Mr Link. 'In four hundred years you'll be long gone. If there's still a headstone we'll pay our respects. As you've done so much for us.'

'Cheers,' said Darren. Spin gave me a thumbs-up. The three of them sipped coffee in unison. I tried to imagine how their lives had been, what they'd have seen in their lifetimes. I couldn't do it. I snipe at the narrow minds of the people around me, but compared to those three I'd been nowhere.

I imagined them in the future, with the ozone gone and the sea level rising. One day Dudley would be by the sea. Perhaps they'd come back and sail around it. They couldn't live forever. Darren had confirmed that for me. They had extended their lives, but not indefinitely. There were limits. There was a half-life. Four hundred years, the next time. Then two hundred, one hundred, shrinking intervals until they'd be carrying out the ritual twice daily. Perhaps by then they'd have had enough.

I doubt it. No matter how much life you get, you could do with more. There's never enough. That's what dragged me through my depressions; there was more life to be had. When my own life wasn't enough, I borrowed from other people, from Caroline and from Jack, from everyone else I knew.

'Been a laugh, hasn't it?' asked Mr Link. 'Of course, we'll be leaving the building trade now. We only started that so we could do some digging without arousing suspicion.'

'We couldn't remember where we buried them,' said Darren. 'We had to dig around a bit to get our bearings. See the lie of the land. Dudley's changed in the last couple of centuries.'

'Apart from the people,' said Mr Link. 'So we took on some local lads to help us, and lo and behold we get a joker in our midst,' said Mr Link. 'No place for jokes on the building site, I always thought. Jokes on the building site lead to weakened structures. There's a need for solidity in buildings.'

'He's never got over them wrecking our castle,' explained Darren. 'It's been a bit of a thing with him since then. He doesn't like doors or windows.'

'No,' I said. 'I remember that.'

'Not as bad as him,' said Mr Link, indicating Darren. 'Him and his hair. He went grey during the ritual. It was a bit of a nervy one, to tell the truth. So there he's been, grey hair for eight hundred years. It's a very sore point with him. So when you tried to play that prank on him, I had to intervene. And then I thought, fair enough, he's played a joke on us, we'll play one on him.'

'A joke?' I said.

'Oh yes. We own most of this town, you know. We were here a long time ago and we set things in motion, made sure things would be fine, kept the right families influential. It's nice to have somewhere to go back to.'

'Even when it's Dudley,' said Darren.

'So it was easy to get you a job with the council,' said Mr Link. 'Seeing as how we own them. And even easier to get Darren one with you, so that he could look after the rumours and make sure they got around. Then we got Spin a job on the television, so that we could get that documentary on and trigger off your friend. I put a few thoughts in his head, and there we were. It's been a laugh, hasn't it? I bloody hope it has, we put enough effort into it. I had to cast thoughts into your friend's head, not an easy thing to do. Magic doesn't get on properly these days. It feels out of place. It's not sure to work. Very much like yourself, back when you worked for us.

'Darren had to look into the future to make sure things would turn out the way we wanted them. That's all turned out well. Your daughter will be famous, you know. Not for very good reasons and not for very long, but still. Darren did that because I never got the hang of looking forward. I can cast thoughts into people, but looking forward is difficult. That's the way of it with magic. We only get one trick each. It's good the first time you see it, and then the effect fades each time.'

I thought of them destroying my life, Jack's life, the lives of our families. I thought of Judy, driven out of my life. She might still be upset.

'What did Spin do?' I asked. 'If your trick is filling people's heads with thoughts and his is seeing the future, what does Spin do?'

'He's got a good one,' said Darren admiringly. Mr Link nodded.

'Came in useful during this little campaign,' said Mr Link. 'Go on then, Spin old son. Show him what he's been missing.'

Spin began to gesture. He was still apart from his arms and hands. His wrists seemed liquid, the hands flopping around him. He twirled them around his face and his face ran, pouring down onto the blouse he was suddenly wearing. I looked at his sharp fringe, that black hair, those bright features.

It was a good trick, I have to say that. I'd seen the end result before. I'd been going out with it for months. I'd been going out with a warlock in disguise.

'Still haven't tidied this place up, I see,' said Judy; and then she darkened, grew, became Spin again.

'Good one, isn't it?' asked Mr Link. I nodded. They put their mugs on the floor and stood. 'Got to be going,' said Mr Link. 'Be nice to stay and have a chat about old times, but let's face it, your old times are a few minutes ago compared to ours. We'll be coming back, but you'll have gone by then. So long, then.'

He had walked to the front door while he was talking. Now he opened it and walked out.

'Cheers for the coffee,' said Darren, following him. Spin just gave me a wink.

The door closed behind them.

That's the end of it, then. That's the end of it for now. In ten or twenty years I'll come back here and see my daughter. It'll be hard, knowing what will happen to her. What she'll be doing. That's my daughter, after all, and she's going to be killing people and running off with their fingers. In four hundred and twenty years Mr Link will be back, along with Darren and Spin. I imagine they'll have different names. I know I will have. I've already chosen one.

I picked up my cases and left my house. The white van had gone. There was something wrong with the sky. At first I couldn't understand it, and then I realized that it was blue. There were no clouds.

You can never have enough life. There I was with a new one. This time I could be anything. I tried out my new name.

'I'm Mickey Payne,' I told the hedge. 'I'm Mickey Payne.'

It felt right. It felt like it had always been my name.

I walked to the edge of town and looked back. Dudley sat huddled on its hill. Sam Haines would never have left Dudley. He'd have complained about it all his life, but he wouldn't have left it. Sam Haines was all mouth.

I wasn't him. I was Mickey Payne. I turned away from Dudley and kept on walking.